PEN PALS

Pen Pals

DEBBIE O'BRIEN

Because sometimes,
It is what it is,
and we must accept it
as being so.

Chapter One

JJ

The airport seemed quiet but with so many thoughts racing through her head there was not enough room for outside noise. JJ's plane had landed an hour ago and the many sniffer dogs patrolling the corridors told her it may be a long wait as she seemed to have struck a targeted flight. She felt impatient, yet at the same time was glad of the delay. Reality was on the other side of the door, and it would take all her strength to deal with the days to come.

JJ had come, not out of sympathy, though of course it was there, it was something deeper, almost like the love of a mother to a child, a feeling so deep it could never be fully explained. Claire would be waiting for her. The gorgeous Claire, so unaware of her looks even now, would be fighting to keep her emotions under control as she waited. JJ's mind wandered as the line snaked forward one slow step at a time. People juggled their luggage and strained their necks hoping to see what was causing the delay, all anxious to be out and hugging their loved ones or taking the steps toward an exciting new adventure in this wide brown land.

JJ had been here many times, not only to see her friends, but as a young woman who had been bewitched by the landscape and a shy Australian boy. He still held her heart and even though they had eventually moved back to her home country, his failing health preventing him from joining her this time, JJ smiled at the thought of him and recalled the moment.

Looking up at him when she received the call, he, not even knowing what was said, had reached out his hand and said, tell her you will be there soon. He understood and yet he didn't. JJ wondered if he knew she loved him as much, or more than she loved them, he probably didn't think so.

The line shuffled slowly towards the desk where border force employees with tired faces counselled newcomers and disposed of their ridiculous food items which the incoming passengers thought they could not live without. JJ often wondered how they reacted when they stepped out into the busy cosmopolitan streets of Sydney to discover the rich blend of customs and cultures in this distant though modern city. Sometimes it did her head in wondering at the thinking of others. Did they not research before they came? Or did they really think everyone would walk on their heads because they were on the bottom side of the world. Sometimes JJ wondered if her straight forward thoughts had escaped her lips without her realising, or had they paused for a moment, before swirling back into the myriad of other ideas and notions inside her head. Her phone buzzed as she made it to the desk and the re-lieved officer recognised she knew the drill. JJ quickly pressed the power button to silence the call she knew would be Claire, JJ would see her face soon, and now would never have to listen to the message she knew, Claire was still relating to her machine. In any case if she did, it would be repeated over and over from the minute they saw each other's faces, so the least number of times she heard it the better.

'Enjoy your holiday.' The officer's voice broke her thoughts, and she moved swiftly toward the exit still clutching her passport.

Chapter Two

Claire

Claire clicked her phone off. She knew JJ would not be able to answer and would come through the doors soon. It was so hard to keep her emotions from spilling over. It was nearly twenty-four hours since they had last spoken, as JJ had been boarding her flight, and Claire knew she needed JJ's calm and solid influence to clear her anxiety and set her on a path where together, they would be able to support their pen-sister in her time of need.

Claire was a pacer, her husband had told her she would wear out the carpet one day as she paced back and forth across the room, lost in thought, worrying about the silliest things in his opinion. Claire was often in another world, dreamy was a term people used, though once her mind was set, there was no changing it and she would plunge into her final decisions with dedication and passion. It was the journey to those decisions which caused JJ the frustration. Claire was also kind, so kind she ended up being used by others which in turn, sent her back to worrying about why people acted the way they did or were so unfair and selfish. Whether it was to bring in the washing yet or what to make for dinner, or should she interfere when she heard the couple a few doors down arguing so loudly every word could be heard. Claire worried on the world's behalf before folding in a heap when it didn't give back. This is when Beth and JJ stepped in, and always had.

It had started so long ago, but they all knew the date as it had been firmly written in lead pencil on the top right-hand corner of the first letter. Beth had been the one, getting both their names out of a pool of nine-year old's from around the country and the world. Instigated by teachers they had all learnt the skill of letter writing and were encouraged to continue the friendships until the end of the school year.

Beth, both enthusiastic but lazy, had soon combined the letters and so the triangle began, one letter was passed to each of them to add on to before they sent it on to the next in line. To make it fair she had changed the direction of the letters each year on her birthday though somehow, she always remained the central figure in it all. JJ always said it was a day the gods had aligned as three little girls formed an alliance which would carry them through to the end of their lives.

Claire remembered the first letter clearly, and the second because it was the one which gave her this unexpected friendship. At first none of them had known what the others looked like, and for Claire asking for the money for a stamp was hard enough let alone to have a photo taken. Eventually her parents had agreed on a fixed sum for pocket money which just covered the international airmail, though her chore list became longer, and it was often with tired little eyes, hiding under her thin blanket when she found the time to reply. The year Beth swapped it about was easier as Claire could buy a cheaper local stamp, as she posted to Beth in Adelaide for the full twelve months. Claire remembered hoping she would save a little so she could send Beth a nice hanky or something for her birthday the following year, a thankyou of sorts. For Claire it was a big decision to make, and Claire had hoped she could decide well before the time came to post it. The decision never came.

Claire's neck was getting sore from straining it every time there seemed to be movement at the gates. She took off her glasses to rub her eyes, they were new, and JJ would be surprised to see her with them on. A deep sigh made her realise she had missed JJ's grand entrance and her friend was now right behind her struggling with her bags and trying to make herself seen. Claire thrust her glasses back on her face threw her arms in the air, then around her friend, tripped over the luggage and landed all legs and arms on top of JJ who was now spread eagle on the airport floor. People started to move towards them to help and Claire, horrified, her glasses askew, looked at JJ not quite knowing what to do.

'For god's sake Claire! What the frig are those glasses for if you can't see what's right in front of you?' JJ's voice boomed out, yet Claire could detect the laughter behind it and threw her arms as much around her neck as she could and squeezed with all her might.

'It will all be ok now you are here. I love you JJ.'

'Can you get off now Claire, it's kind of getting embarrassing.'

Claire rose both out of her fog, and off her friend. A kind man helped them both up as Claire apologised profusely, thanking him and half explaining her excitement at her friend's arrival. Glancing around she saw they had attracted quite a crowd and finally she glanced at JJ and watched as she dusted off her trousers while nodding thanks to her rescuer.

'Thanks everyone, but if I were you, I'd get out now, she drives like she greets people, it would be safer for you all to leave before us.' The crowd giggled and started to disperse as Claire tried to re-dust JJ down and repeated her apology.

'Geez Louise, what were you doing Claire, and what's with those glasses, you look like a geek. An attractive one, but seriously, could you not choose a better frame.'

Claire smiled, JJ's kindness was hidden inside, and her little joke made Claire know all was forgiven.

'We'll be on the six o'clock news tonight, I bet one of those young ones was videoing this little debacle. Were you off in one of your daydreams Claire? Really, it will say two fifty odd year-old women wrestling on the airport floor. What! Well, it is what it looked like, thank God I wore trousers otherwise it would go viral on YouTube or whatever it's called.'

Claire let JJ vent, it was her way and she hugged her again. Claire often wondered how she would have made it through life without them. The timid shy child she had been when she received the first letter was not much different to who she was now, but these women gave her strength and courage and dropped everything if she was in need, and Claire often was, or had been. Now it was Beth who was the one in need had thrown her. Beth was the strong one, the one who coped with everything life threw at her and came out even more confident than before. Beth was the one who listened and consoled before telling you firmly how to move forward, in her opinion, all the while holding you close as the tears turned to sobs and the grieving process began. As Claire pushed her friend's luggage, her heart filled to the brim once more and threatened to spill over, without hesitation JJ had said, I'm on my way, and here she was, without long explanations or any questions, knowing they needed her close and probably for an extended period of time. JJ would make it better, JJ would know what to do and with both her knowledge and strength of character together they would help Beth get through this, of this, Claire was sure, yes very, very sure.

Chapter Three

Beth

19th April 1969

Dear Pen Pal,

My name is Beth, and I am 9 years old. I got your name out of the tub at school. We are learning how to write letters and I think I would like to get a letter just for me so write back. I live in a place called South Australia which is a state. I have a new baby brother called Tom and a cat called Eric. I am writing to someone else too but maybe we can all be friends.

Yours sincerely, Beth.

PS, today is my birthday, please write back.

PSS: pretty please.

Beth was very satisfied with her attempt. She had decided to sneak two names out of the barrel in case one didn't work out and secretly hoped the girl in Canada answered. She didn't know anyone from another country and the thought suddenly occurred to her, the other girl may not speak the same language. Oh well, fingers crossed she could speak a bit of it and wanted to learn some more. It was a bit tiresome writing two letters but as she licked the envelopes and carefully copied the addresses on to each one, the thought popped in her head of next time simply writing one, and it could pass between the three of them, each one adding to the letter before passing it on. Brilliant! It would work out perfectly and be less writing for them all. The cat jumped on the table, sitting directly on top of the letters and curled his tail around his front paws. Pushing him aside Beth had another brilliant idea, (she was good at brilliant ideas, or at least she thought so), and grabbed the ink pad and pressed Eric's paw on it then gently moved it across and pressed it down on the seal of each envelope. Eric swished his tail not enjoying the moment and each envelope now had a tail print as well as it swished over the ink pad and across the mail leaving a speckled pattern.

'Good work Eric, it looks very artistic, they will be very impressed I'm sure and will want to write back now.' Beth used her hanky to try and rub the rest of the ink off his paws, but he became annoyed and jumped down leaving a faint ink trail on the lino as he strolled away to attend another important cat moment. Beth sighed and checking her mum was still out in the garden quickly spat on the hanky and rubbed furiously along the cat's path. There all done, now to wait for the postman so she could give them to him and then another wait, for the replies to come. Beth thought the girl in Sydney would be the first and had calculated on it being about ten days. Four days to get to her, one for her to read it and another for her to write a reply, and four days back. Yes, ten days should do it, though there were the weekends and mail didn't come on Sundays, I'll give her two weeks and if she doesn't write back it will give me time to get another name, she thought, before the Canada girl replies. JJ was a funny name, could her parents not spell or something, I'll guess I'll have to wait and find out.

'Beth, can you watch Tom for a bit while I duck next door.'

Beth sighed, this baby was becoming a chore and he cried, he cried a lot. Beth hated how everyone hovered over him and told her how lucky she was. There had been Beth and her mum before Jason came along, which was fine because she really liked him, and they'd let her have a pretty pink dress at their wedding. Jason's family were nice too and even though her dad had -gone to buggery- as Mum said sometimes, Beth wished he would come back so she could tell him all the things which had happened, even about Tom and maybe he would take her to see Granny and Pa, she had liked going there. Mum said they had moved far away whenever she asked, but Beth sort of thought it was a porky pie lie -which is what Jason liked to say. Beth pushed the pram out to the front porch and showed Tom the flowers and weeds in the garden. She picked a dandelion and held it up under his chin to tickle him and he rewarded her with a smile and yawned loudly. It made her laugh and Beth hoped he would stop the crying soon as it might be fun when he was a bit older and could sit up properly and walk around. The baby dozed and she pulled the pram towards her as she sat on the step listening for the postman's whistle when he came down the street. The letters looked a bit crumpled now and some of the ink had smudged back onto her hands. Beth tried to lick it off but worried her tongue might turn black and her mum would get cross.

The postman finally came in sight and Beth hurried to the gate to greet him.

'Well, hello young lady, to what do I owe the honour?'

Beth didn't know what he meant but burst into her carefully rehearsed speech.

'Could you take these letters for me please, I'm getting some pen pals and Mum said you could post them for me because I'm not allowed to go to the post office by myself.'

'Yes I can and if you like, when you are back at school, pop them in your letterbox and I'll look each time to see if they are there.'

'Thank you, one of them is going all the way to Canada, will it take a long time?'

'Maybe a few weeks but I have some special stickers in my bag so how about I give you some and if you stick them on up near the stamp, it might make it get there a bit quicker. In return do you think you could save the stamps when they come back, I like to collect them, and I don't have many from there.' He put out his hand and with a big smile on her face Beth shook it enthusiastically.

'It's a deal,' she said, and the postman laughed as he reached into his bag for the airmail stickers.

'It is a deal and I hope they write back, it is good to have a pen pal, someone you can confide in. I had one and we are still friends today, though we tend to telephone each other now instead of writing. I look forward to delivering your letters young lady, now I must be on my way, can't have the postman being late can we.'

He set off down the street, blowing his whistle loudly and giving Beth a wink goodbye.

'Thank you and goodbye,' she called climbing on the gate to hang over it and watch him as he rounded the corner. 'My name is Beth.' She sang out at the last minute, and he turned and waved one last time after slipping a letter into Mrs Long's box and calling back:

'Nice to meet you, Beth.'

Beth had hung there long after he was gone, her tippy toes pushing into the wire mesh and her hair hanging down as she tried to look at the world from upside-down. She heard her brother stir but didn't look up, didn't see the hot autumn sun shining on his face as he wriggled and squirmed to avoid it, rocking the stroller as he did. It wasn't until she heard the scream, and saw her mother running, did she realise it had rolled off the step, and her brother was now flat on the path, the quietest he had been since the day he was born.

Chapter Four

JJ

Dear Beth,

Thank you for your letter. I want to come to Australia one day to see a kangaroo. Do you have one as a pet? I live near the ocean, and I have a brother too. He is older than me and only has one leg. True! He had cancer and the doctor chopped it off to make the cancer go away. Now he puts on a fake leg every day and can run and jump the same like me. I like to jump, I don't know why, maybe it's why I'd like a pet kangaroo so we could jump places together. My real name is Janice Julia, but people call me JJ. What do you eat in Australia? Do you have real food and shops? They are going to land a man on the moon! I think it would be amazing. Do you think the moon is made of cheese, my brother says it is made of dirty old rocks. (I think he's wrong). What do they eat in space? I like to eat, my favourite food is fish and apples, I love apples especially when they are crispy and juicy. Does it snow in Australia? Well bye for now. I know we will be friends forever, I can feel it in my bones (I do that...feel stuff).

Love from JJ

JJ remembered the first letter from Beth. She thought she sounded nice and was excited to have a special friend no one else knew. JJ had shown her brother Will and asked him what to write back. Part of her wanted him to help her because she really wanted this girl to like her. JJ couldn't imagine living in Australia, it would be so wild and scary there.

Will told her to write whatever was in her head and quickly put it in the envelope and seal it before she changed her mind. He also said he would post it for her and once it was gone and a reply came, all her fears would drop away. 'This way she will know exactly who you are, write from your heart and you will always have a true friend.'

JJ loved her brother, nothing was ever a bother, she was never a bother, Will loved her and everyone who met him, loved him. JJ did as he said, and he took the letter straight away and even paid for the stamps. She understood what he meant, if she had read back over, it might not have been sent at all, but now Beth would know what a scatterbrain she could be, leaping with enthusiasm from one subject to another, wanting to learn so much yet moving on to the next crazy thought as each question was answered. JJ's dad said one day she would be excellent at trivia if she retained all the answers and JJ knew her dad was pleased by her enthusiasm.

The weeks passed and the letter was almost forgotten when another arrived. It had the same address on the back and her own address carefully written in rounded letters with lead pencil on the front. JJ had come in from school and it was sitting on the hall table where usually there was a pile of letters for her parents, full of bills to pay or a letter from an aunt. JJ's mum had put it right on the top so she would see it as she walked in.

JJ couldn't describe the feeling, it seemed to start in her belly and spread upwards across her chest. Beth had written back. The excitement mounted and her hand trembled as she picked it up. A letter, something just for her, a friend inside a little worn envelope with the paw print on the back. JJ didn't know whether to tear it open now, or could she wait until she had a snack and could sneak up to her room to sit in her tepee amongst the cushions with the oldest and dearest friends she had, her doll Belinda and her worn out teddy called Ted.

Will opened the door behind her.

'Whoa, another letter, I told you she would write back. Have you opened it?'

'No, I'm a bit scared too. What if she thought I was silly, like the girls at school?'

'Stop worrying, this girl will learn what you are like on the inside, before she ever sees you, and she has replied, there's your positive right there. Now come on, have you had your snack? Let's play a game about what we think she has written and after dinner you can tell me if I was right.' JJ smiled, he always made her feel good inside. Will wandered off into the kitchen describing how he was sure Beth went to school in a kangaroo's pouch and how they ate wombat stew for dinner. JJ skipped along behind adding to the tale until they were both laughing uncontrollably, and their mother shooed them out so she could start dinner.

JJ curled up inside her tepee and slid her finger under the flap of the envelope. The letter was quite thick which again, was exciting, and she soon realised the pages were written on both sides. Dear JJ, it began, and she was swept away at the frankness of the reply. Beth was indeed straight forward telling her of course the moon was made of cheese, and the astronauts would take some snacks and fruit as they would live on the cheese and bread until they returned. She said she liked how JJ wrote as it made her feel they were having a real conversation. Beth told her about her school and the weather, it was autumn there but still quite warm, she told her about her stepfather who was kind and her mother who was, well, not so much. It felt very personal, and JJ knew Beth would keep her secrets. Beth told her she'd had a brilliant idea and from now on JJ would be getting a letter from a girl named Claire. Beth would write first to Claire, Claire would add her bit and send it on to JJ, who in turn would write something and send it to Beth. Once a year on the anniversary of the first letter Beth would reverse the cycle and send it the other way. This way they could all look back and catch up on news in case they had forgotten anything. What did she think, was it a good plan? JJ thought it was and now she would have two friends. Two friends she could confide in and share her thoughts with. Beth was right, she was brilliant. JJ quickly pulled out her notepad and started scribbling her reply telling Beth, yes you are brilliant, and we will be friends forever I know it. Hopefully Beth and Claire could teach her all about Australia and she would tell them about Canada. One day JJ hoped they could visit her, and she would show them how pretty it was.

JJ carefully folded her reply and tucked it in behind Beth's letter. Part of her now wanted to keep it so she could read it over and over again, but with Beth's plan, each time she would be able to read them from the beginning. JJ felt like she was embarking on some great adventure, and it made her feel good inside, she also hoped Will was right and they would get to know her so well, when they finally met her, it wouldn't matter what she looked like. JJ was positive by then they would be like sisters, linked by letters of friendship.

Will helped her find a bigger envelope as she told him the plan. He had laughed and said he thought he would like this Beth, but wondered how much it would cost to post a big parcel to Australia when the girls had been writing to each other for years. JJ said she was sure Beth would have another plan.

This is where it began, three little girls each eager and each in need of a friend, the start of a friendship which unbeknown to them, would indeed last a lifetime.

Chapter Five

Claire

I'm Claire and I live near Sydney in Australia. I'm very excited to now have two friends and I hope you have Beth's letter telling her idea. I don't have much money so if my letters are a bit late it is because I am saving for the stamps. I'm pretty quiet and I don't have any other friends, there are mean girls at my school but now I have you and Beth and I want to be friends forever. Please tell me about Canada, do you have polar bears there? My brother and sister are nice, and I am the youngest. My dad works a lot in a factory and when he comes home, he is as black as coal with two shiny bright eyes. When he is not too tired, he chases us around pretending he is a monster, and it makes me laugh a lot. He hasn't done it for a while. I help my mum with sewing, it's my favourite thing. People bring their clothes and mum mends them, she is clever and teaches me the fancy stitches when she has time. If someone wants a dress made, she can make it for them as well and if there are scraps left over, I make dresses for my doll. One day I want to make dresses for people, I think it is a real job, I see them in shops, but I don't know how they get there. I've never had a dress from a shop. I wish I had a cat; Eric sounds nice, do you have a pet JJ? Why do you think the sky is blue, it's

a pretty colour but maybe it should be another colour, is the sky blue in Canada? This is so much fun please write back soon.
    Love Claire

Claire fussed as she led the way to the car. She was already worrying about getting out of the airport, would she take the wrong turn, she could easily be confused. Some days she wished everything would stay the same, it would be so much simpler. Why did they need new roads, and the motorways, goodness, the way they criss-crossed each other was only to confuse people Claire was sure. The quiet suburb Claire had lived in her entire life had, over the years, turned into a suburban sprawl with a constant traffic snarl to get to the local shops. Claire often wondered where all the people came from.

JJ let her fuss. Claire knew it annoyed her but was glad today she didn't comment. As they settled the luggage in the boot of the car, JJ held out her hand.

'If I drive you can talk, I still have my international licence.' Claire dropped the keys in her hand knowing JJ was trying to ease her stress more than take control. 'Come on I'm hungry, airline food never satisfies.'

Claire waited until they were on the toll road, relieved the toll thingy had beeped so she could check off in her head she had paid it after all. JJ glanced over and smiled, yes you did she said reading her mind, and Claire relaxed back in her seat to repeat the story again but with more detail, knowing whatever she said would be accepted and analysed from each angle until they could get to the truth of it and hopefully figure out what to do.

'So, when Beth called, how's Jim sorry, I should have asked about him first.'

'He's going ok, these last meds have turned things around a bit and if there was a perfect time to come this was probably it. The prognosis won't change, but how comfortable he can be, has, so it is good we live in an age with so much advancement in medicine. Will is there.'

Satisfied, Claire continued.

'As soon as I collected the letter, I knew something was wrong. It should have come from you still as it's not quite April yet, so I thought it strange before I opened it. The writing was different too, but it had Beth's address on the back.'

JJ had already heard all this but was hoping, now they were together, she would pick up on some minor detail which might not have filtered through over the phone.

'I of course rang her straight away, there was no answer and I let it ring out about four times before she finally picked up. I was shocked at her tone, I was checking the details in the letter weren't true, but I fear when we get there, they will be, the neighbour I think, has told the truth. Beth sounded so empty, and she was so rude JJ, not stern like she is with me when I carry on, but rude and lost and oh, JJ what if there is something else wrong, like big wrong, we knew this part was coming, I thought somehow she would be more prepared I don't know how I could live without her or you, my life would have been a proper mess wouldn't it.'

JJ always wondered how timid Claire always seemed to find a way back to talking about herself. Half of her agreed with her and wondered how Claire would have lived at times without direction from both her and Beth. The other half knew it was how Claire coped, by expressing every detail out aloud and examining each piece but often missing the answer right in front of her. Claire had always given them several scenarios she had reached, and if they could both guide her to one, she would snatch it and run with it, never looking back to worry if it was the other course she should have taken. It was as if Claire shut the door on each issue once, in her head, it was resolved, and moved on to a new worry or concern. JJ wondered if she would ever find peace inside or if this was the crutch which kept her living.

Claire could see JJ was shutting down so switched back to the subject at hand. Claire hated she was always seeking reassurance from them, after all she thought they have stood by me for nearly fifty years, you would think I would be more confident by now. Deep inside Claire knew she was, she did cope day to day, had managed a job and a mortgage, disappointment, and a divorce, she could be strong on the surface. With the girls she could let it all down, let the mask fall and allow them to catch her as she fell when it all became too much, and they had, every time. Together they had caught her, held her, and propped her up again, then waited until she was steady on her feet before sliding away gently, their arms outstretched towards her as if double checking she wouldn't fall again, before melting back into their own lives.

JJ pulled into Claire's driveway and sat quietly. Claire wasn't sure how long they sat as JJ allowed her to gather her thoughts. Claire loved this about JJ, she could be loud and brutal sometimes to get her point across, but she knew when stillness was needed and Claire envied her, to be still with an empty mind was something she couldn't imagine.

'It's our turn now isn't it, after all she has done, it's our turn to help, even if she doesn't want it, we have to be strong.'

JJ managed a nod and Claire could see the tears well, not quite ready to fall. She hoped she was strong enough for them all, it was her turn to step up, and as strong as JJ was, Claire knew this may be the time which would cripple her. Beth was their constant and always had been, the bright spark in their lives, the one who lifted them up and who in a heartbeat dropped everything to be with them in their time of need, just as JJ had when Claire rang. With no hesitation Beth would act, no matter what her deadline for some article or manuscript, she always seemed to squeeze it in and sort her own life in the background while holding their hands and giving them the faith to continue. Inside Claire made a hurried brunch so JJ would have time to rest, her journey was taking its toll. Later they would plan as much as they could and together do the last leg to Beth.

Claire sat on her back porch staring into the garden, her tea growing cold on the table beside her, she could hear a slight snore from the bedroom and was glad her friend could sleep. JJ would be tired from the journey and also her own life. JJ's husband's degenerative muscle wasting disease was gathering speed and Claire had thought Canada would be her next flight as it progressed into the last stages. She sighed without realising and her mind ran back over all these years and the journey they had each been on.

Claire had kept the house after the divorce, paying Johnno out and working hard to pay off her mortgage. Claire's little home business had grown over the years and, despite some setbacks and a zillion calls to the girls as to whether she was making the right choices, had been extremely successful and earned the reputation of being one of the top design studios in the metropolitan area. Claire was proud of herself and all she had achieved, her children were too, both now living abroad, they were confident and happy people, unafraid to take chances in life. Claire missed them but was proud of them, and for them. Paul and Charlotte were the highlight of her life, the bonus she had never expected, and for all her anxiety, they had grown and excelled beyond her expectations. Claire was glad they were not like her, a mix of herself and their overconfident father, arrogance some people may have said, but he too had shaped Claire's life pushing her out of her comfort zones. Both the children had the right amount, and she was proud of them.

Claire picked up the cup, the tea had cooled but the cup retained its warmth giving her comfort as she laced her fingers around it and slowed her thoughts searching for a solution. Sadly, she thought, time would be the slow healer and the way Beth had snapped at her and told Claire not to come and to definitely not tell JJ, had almost been too much. Claire for once had made the decision quickly before her head started to wind around looking at it from each angle, there were times Claire had discovered when you had to act first and consider the alternatives at a later time and this was one of them. They would go together, as much as Claire had wanted to be there now, she knew, together they would make Beth see into the future ahead, see she still had them, not the same, but for Claire, sometimes, these women had been the strength to pull her through, knowing they were there had been enough, and now it was Beth's turn. Beth would survive this, because she had to, without her, Claire would not be able to see the road ahead. Beth would see it was early days, they would get her through this and hold her up until she could see a future without him. So many years had passed but sitting here, staring out at the endless rows of houses which stretched out from her back fence as far as the eye could see, many of those years disappeared in her thoughts, and Claire felt like it was only yesterday this journey had begun.

....

Claire had written a reply to the first letter and then worried Beth would understand what she had written. Claire had struggled with her spelling and thought she had made a few mistakes. At least her Mum was encouraging her in this, to improve her writing, and hopefully her grades. Even at nine years old Claire understood the challenges her mother endured as she struggled trying to find enough money to put adequate food on the table, and regretted her lack of skills in a world which was changing at a pace Claire knew her parents would never comprehend, and her father would never try to.

Man landing on the moon was a sign to the young of the opportunities which lay ahead, to advancements in technology and to know, to have a dream was something which was no longer considered unattainable, if a man could reach the stars, the world could be their oyster. For her father, it seemed to crush him, hold him back, to dream outside his hardships would never be considered, lack of education and encouragement saw the curtain of survival hang heavy on his shoulders, always working hard yet never diverting from the path to nowhere. For him you lived and died in the job and hoped one day the boss would notice and hand you a bonus for loyalty. Claire's mother could see this would never happen so urged her children to study hard and seek a different path. As un-educated as she was, her mind was bright and her love for her husband was deep.

Claire could not complain, they had each taught her skills to move forward and cope with the rollercoaster of life. At school she had been teased for her second-hand uniforms and patched cardigan, though to tell her family was something she had not been able to do, as each day her mother straightened her collar and tied back her hair always with a pretty bow which she had burnt along the edges so it wouldn't fray. Study hard, mum would whisper as they traipsed out the door, and Claire had known to repeat only the good news from school when she returned and no more. The worrying from the bullying was tucked away each night to twist and turn inside her and to draw her in, hoping by hiding inside herself, they would retreat and pick on someone else. They never did.

Beth's letters, along with JJ's, had been a lifeline on to which she held and when Claire came in from school her mother would whisper, it's under your pillow, and her day would get brighter and her chores easier as she went about them with a lightness in her step. Once her father had handed it to her, a rare day when the weather brought him home early from work.

'I hope you're not wasting all your money and time on this, we can ill afford the money we give you now. Pocket money, ha! In my day you did it because it had to be done and you'd get a whack around the ears if you didn't, think yourself lucky girl and don't waste your money on foolishness.' Claire knew her dad was making an unwritten rule which she was expected to obey, his hard-earned money was to see her live a better life not wasted on trivial passions. Afterwards, and from then on her Mum would slip them under her pillow, and it became their little secret.

In the end Claire had not sent Beth a gift but had saved any left-over coins until she had enough to purchase her dad a new pipe. The look on his face had stayed with her to this day, her brother had bought a second-hand bicycle with his pocket-money and each afternoon delivered papers for the local news-agents, her sister did artwork and sold it at the front of their house. Together, to add to the gift, they had bought enough to-bacco for him to be content for quite some time. Their father's face had shown a pride he would never verbalise, he had done good, his kids had learnt the lessons he had urged them to see, but never had the time to teach. It was the day Claire saw love expressed with a gleam in his eye and a swelling of his chest as he held back emotions he had never been taught to express and she accepted it as being enough. Watching as her mother gently squeezed his shoulder and unconsciously parted her lips as she too held back words she knew would make him feel embarrassed and falter the moment. Seeing her dad lean toward her mum as he slowly raised his eyes and looked into hers showed Claire more about their relationship than she had ever been mature enough to acknowledge. It swelled her heart, and she knew her decision to put her family first had been the right one. Claire saw her sister turn away to dab her own eyes as her brother cracked a joke to release the tension and allow everyone to return to their comfortable place.

Claire had never forgotten the feeling, and yet, it was also another moment in which she saw how Beth's letters had changed her and brought about this moment. Because of Beth, pleasing her father had become a priority, and because of Beth, the secret she now shared with her mother had shown it was sometimes alright to, not lie as such, but evade, or not be forthcoming with the truth, unless it was completely necessary. Claire's mother never spoke of them again. Hiding the letters gave Claire a secret thrill of knowing something no one else knew, except of course Beth and JJ, and it made her love them even more.

With chores done Claire would slip into her room. Even her pillow looked soft and plump on these days and she would sit for a moment letting the anticipation fill her with happiness. The second letter was so wonderful. Claire was to post to a girl in far off Canada and she, JJ, in turn would write to Beth and so it would continue. It would take a bit of jiggling of her pocket money, but Claire was determined to not be the one to let them down. She would be honest and tell them sometimes her letter might be delayed, she was sure they would understand. Beth's letter had been long and jumped from one subject to another, her stepfather seemed a kind man and Claire was surprised at her words about her mother. Claire thought maybe Beth was like her mum and maybe it was why they clashed. Beth seemed to think it was because she blamed her for her father leaving yet couldn't make her see their life was so much better now. Claire was also surprised at how much Beth told her about her own thoughts and what Claire thought was private family business, yet on the other hand she realised she too, could do the same. Maybe these two new friends would be able to help her understand her own feelings, so she could recognise herself she was not alone in thinking differently to her parents. Claire put pencil to paper and was surprised in the end how many words she had scrawled across the page and how she had been so open about her biggest secret. Trust is what she had done, and what she wanted from them, even though she would now worry until she received a reply, at least if she did, she would know it was ok, and these girls really would be her friends forever.

Claire heard some rustling and realised she had been lost in her thoughts. She had bought a few provisions on the way to the airport so they could have a light snack before they headed off again. A pick-up was arranged, as the flight was late, but now JJ was refreshed from her nap and could have a shower, they wouldn't notice their weariness or the time difference as they changed states. Claire wished it was winter, somehow to her it seemed dreariness or unhappiness should happen on gloomy days, not on bright sunny ones like this. Maybe it would be raining in Adelaide? Should she take a proper raincoat or a jacket? Claire's mind drifted off as she visualised what was already in her packed bag. It is Beth who needs all my attention from now on, Claire thought, and knew she would have to keep her thoughts close so her words would not wander away from where her focus had to be. Gathering her cup, Claire made her way inside, JJ was still in the shower, so Claire went to her room and unzipped the suitcase for one last check in case she had forgotten something.

Chapter Six

JJ

Dear Beth,

Can you believe it's been seven years! When I looked at the calendar and realised you had already had your birthday, I felt bad. Happy Birthday!!! We have been away at the cabin and as usual Mum forgot to transfer the mail. She's now having a fit because of all the unpaid bills, as if anyone would worry about us not paying them. Honestly, I wonder where her head is at most of the time. So cool about the camera, I can't wait to see some photos. If you send some, I will keep them and not send them back. Please send me a photo of you and your family, I need to know you look exactly like I've pictured all these years. Dad nearly was going to come to Australia for work and I was so excited, but it has all been postponed for now. Imagine if I could come to and we could all meet. Maybe one day, but I promise by on our ten-year anniversary we will all be together, fingers crossed. Will is good, he has had a fever, but it is much better, and he is excited for his new prosthetic which is supposed to be a lighter weight and he hopes it will look more natural. He really is the best brother anyone could wish for and if I could give him my own leg, I would.

I finally got my period! You and Claire are so far in front of me. I felt a bit tired with it, and it is so ghastly we must put up with this until we are old! It doesn't seem fair does it?

The girls at school have a new prey and I am keeping my eye on them. She is a new girl and I think she is nice, but they pick on what she wears and stuff. I tried to let her know I understood but she doesn't seem to care, and they will probably tire of her indifference soon. At least she can change what she wears but this birthmark on my face is never going away. I'm enjoying the reprieve anyway as they will soon be back on my case. You would think they would be tired of it by now. My study is going well, I do enjoy it but some days I feel as if I do it to fill in time and use it as an excuse not to go outside, it gives me a reason to lock myself in my room and not have to speak to anyone. Dad has another business function here tonight and I can't stand the stares and whispers when they look at me. Will says to ignore it and makes a party trick by taking off his leg. I still think he does it to take the attention away from me even though he says he doesn't.

I'm going on a health kick! I want to learn how to be a jogger but if I do it now, I look plain ridiculous with every part of my body flopping about. God certainly wasn't kind when he handed out my looks. I started walking but do it after dark, imagine if the mean brigade saw me, I'd be the laughingstock! I thought if I start now, by prom I will waltz in, and they will be amazed at my transformation! What do you think? I know! Why do I still care what they think, but I can't help it, they seem to have stopped calling me Junkyard Jelly, and are probably using all of their small little brains to think up something else, ha! Have to go and survive this dinner party, Love to you both and thanks for the best seven years, I'm so grateful for you both. XXX JJ

JJ could hear Claire rummaging about in her room and knew she would be repacking her suitcase for the hundredth time. JJ shook her head and wondered, as she often did, how Claire had managed to make such a success of herself and yet still be so clumsy and disorganised in her private life. The warm water of the shower soothed her, and she lingered longer than necessary.

They had both wanted to go straight to Adelaide, but the flights had not worked in their favour, and they also knew they had to turn up together, Beth on a downward spiral would be hard to catch and without the neighbour taking the initiative to write, they might never have known until it was too late. Beth had always been the one to hold them together, she had started all this and never allowed them to let things slide. For all her worldly advice over the years, JJ had always known, Beth was the one who needed them most of all.

JJ's heart ached, one day, too soon, it would be her. To lose the man she loved would be the hardest thing she would ever have to endure, yet for Beth she knew it would be so much more. Jim's condition was similar to Beth's husband Marcus. Many would put them under the same banner, though the details were not the same. Jim's life would take its course and his last day would be decided by a higher being. JJ knew Marcus, with all his complications, had not intended to wait for whoever it was who made those choices. JJ turned the shower off and leaned back against the wall, trying to cleanse her mind as much as she had cleaned her body. Pushing away she stepped out and reached for the towel. Raising her eyes JJ watched the steam curl its way towards the vent in the ceiling and wished the following few days would drift away as smoothly.

Chapter Seven

Beth

Dear JJ and Claire,

I came top in English, I really think I want to be a writer, it all makes sense to me and unlike maths (brain explosion) I find it easy. Maybe all this letter writing has helped over the years. We don't have prom JJ we call it a formal, there is one at the end of year ten and one at year twelve which is the last year of high school here, mostly only smart or rich people go on to years eleven and twelve, so it counts me out. I didn't go to mine, couldn't see the point and Mum wasn't real keen on spending money on a dress for one night. Also, Tom had a school excursion, and you would think he was going on a big overseas trip not a simple bus ride to the local museum. Mum fussed like there was no tomorrow and I swear he had enough snacks in his bag to last a year. She does my head in the way she fusses, sometimes I'm glad I'm not the favourite as it would drive me mad. As if the teachers would not be prepared and he was going in the same bus he catches every day to his special needs class. I wish she would treat him a bit normal, after all he is just Tom and whoever he is, is how he will be and how people will treat him I seriously think all her fussing is holding him back and he is old enough now to play her against me. I didn't tell them about my award, she never bothered to come to the speech day so why bother letting her know. I've chosen more units of English for next year at technical college and am already searching out the courses for university, I can't see how I will be able to afford it even with a payment scheme. I'm pretty sure mum will want me out and earning money as soon as possible. I thought one day maybe I can study part time and work somewhere as well. Mum says more study is a waste of time though it's not like she has ever worked a day in her life, at least tech is now an accepted progression so I hope she will agree. It is all a bit scary isn't it, becoming grown-ups?

My stepdad is out a lot and I think maybe there is something going on as they are arguing more than usual, who knows? I am generally ignored so keep my head down when it starts, I must say it feels a bit déjà vu, and if he leaves I think I will have to as well as Mum would find some way of blaming me. I think I will have a talk with him, though she doesn't like it when I do. Study is my continuing way to hide away just as it has been for the both of you and one day I will make enough money to leave this place and live wherever I choose.

Much love, Beth xx

Beth was conflicted, she was excited her birthday this year seemed like it would be the best one ever. It meant she could get her licence, be more independent and eventually travel interstate. Her birthday meant freedom physically, and in turn hopefully would give it to her mentally. Claire had been working at her local supermarket and saving her money as well. Fingers crossed the pen pals would be able to meet somewhere and finally see each other face to face.

On the other side, Beth's mum's sudden passing had been tough, and she was still adjusting to being without her. Their fractured relationship did not mean Beth missed her less, yet it did mean the constant criticism and snide remarks were no longer present. Beth still heard them in her head and felt guilty some days as she was glad to not have to hear them spoken or hear the tone of her voice which had often been more offensive than the words.

Beth had received a lot of sympathy from everyone, and her stepdad had promised she was still his daughter, and nothing was going to change even though there had never been a formal adoption. Day to day errands still had to be run and as he disappeared in his grief it seemed it was up to Beth to take the reins and step up into her mother's role. Juggling school and running a household was hard enough but the guilt she carried was the hardest to bear, she was sure she should feel more upset and heartbroken than she really did. Beth loved her stepdad and his kindness over the years had shone though as he tried to protect her from her mother's sharp tongue. He had even asked if she would like to get in contact with her real dad, but Beth couldn't see the point, he had never returned once her mother remarried.

The letters had been her constant, as even though she did reveal some of her worries, Beth had taken on the role of mentor and constantly encouraged both Claire and JJ to be themselves, despite their bullying school mates. JJ had described her birth mark to them, and Beth had a picture in her head which she hoped didn't match reality. JJ said if you looked at her from one side you couldn't even see it but when she turned people would take a step back and gasp in shock to see the entire side of her face was covered. Beth envisioned something like Erik from the Phantom of the Opera. JJ was intending to go to university so was still at school until the end of her school year and she had made it quite plain to them money was not something she would have to worry about once she was there. Her parent's college fund would more than pay for her tuition and whatever lifestyle she wished to lead. Money was something which was not a daily battle for her.

Claire was the worrier of the three and had been shocked at JJ's description of people's reaction to her face. Claire thought she mothered them and if they voiced any problems she would mull over it and come up with a million solutions for them to choose from and be delighted if they took one of them up. Once she was certain of the solution she would move on to the next item on her personal agenda. Beth wondered how Claire made it to school each day and now, how she coped with the technical college and her new environment, every new thing worried Claire until she found her place, yet it was the worry which often held her back from finding it sooner. At least she had moved on from her bullying school bitches and seemed to be making new friends at tech. The part time job enabled her to buy the materials for her dress design course and Claire said she felt very fashionable wearing the outfits she made there.

Beth knew from Claire's school certificate scores all her studying had paid off and she really could have gone on to do whatever she pleased. Claire's parents weighed heavily on her decision to leave school to get a decent trade and even though her father wasn't entirely happy with her doing dressmaking, he could at least see it was her passion. To satisfy him Claire was doing a bookkeeping course as well and JJ had told her it would help her and keep her not so airy-fairy when she had a business to run. Claire's brother and sister were well on their way to long academic careers. Beth knew Claire relied on both her and JJ for advice and were the only ones who knew of her dream to design and sell wedding dresses. Beth also knew Claire hoped the first one she made would be her own.

Beth had sometimes wished she could write to them individually, to discuss the other one, but they had made a pact early on and no one had ever broken the code, or at least she didn't think they had. When they had something to say, they said it and there would be no going behind each other's backs, everyone's opinion was allowed. Beth smiled, there was never any problem with JJ telling you what she thought. Beth had never heard her voice but the amount of -Geez Louise- and worse expletives scrawled in her letters made her imagine JJ's voice to be loud and her manner to be direct. Claire had copped it a few times as JJ told her to pull her head in and stop worrying or to get off her backside and get on with it, and not to sweat the small stuff. Sometimes Beth had blushed and wondered if she should take out the offending page before sending it on to Claire, but she never had. Sweet and grateful Claire was always accepting and thankful for the feedback.

Beth couldn't wait until they met, it was as if they walked beside her each day and even though Beth was quite popular, she never let her guard down with anyone except JJ and Claire. About her mother they would understand her feelings, and she knew Claire would cry for her so much, the stain of her tears would be on the paper. JJ, the realist would tell her it was ok to feel like she did, it didn't mean she didn't love her mother, it was part of the grieving process to have regrets. Always grateful for their support Beth was glad she had now written the last letter and they would know her news. Beth had written she was managing it all and assured them she was coping. She had wanted to tell it straight but had also felt familiar walls building and knew she had to hold back a bit for herself, a tiny slice for her own self-protection. Beth was positive, deep down, if she ever told them the truth, she would lose them forever. For all her honesty to them, she had never told it all.

A car door slammed, and Beth looked out between the venetian blinds. Her brother was playing up, protesting to his dad about something he didn't like. Beth sighed and wondered what it would be like in a normal family. A family where everyone was kind and normal and cared. It seemed Claire's family was like it, as was JJ's. They all seemed to come together for special occasions and celebrated the highs and lows of life together. Beth wished she had a sibling she was close to, someone to share some of the increasing burden she felt, she sighed, it was how it was meant to be. Beth knew she could never erase what had happened in the past, yet knowing this truth, still didn't help.

Pushing back the chair, she slipped the half-finished letter into her desk drawer and made her way to the kitchen. They would be hungry now they were home.

In the cool darkness of the timber desk the letter lay for some days as Beth tossed and turned in her decision on what, and whether to write. The battle raged in her head, knowing she had to tell someone yet so afraid of what they would think if she let them know what a terrible person she really was, she wanted them to know, so she could begin the process to push them away too, when they rejected her, while the other side argued, and she secretly hoped, they would pull her up and out of the darkness in her head. To the world Beth was happy, brave and strong, to her pen pals she had shown a more fragile side, and in all the turmoil in her head Beth knew to which one she would turn, when she could hold it no more. She had one last letter to JJ before the turnaround and she wanted to get it right, to try to show the balance from both sides, to reach out before she drowned in the grief and guilt she felt. Finally, her decision was made, Beth was, just this once, going to betray the code and ask JJ a favour, she would ask JJ to listen and not judge or share, to think carefully about her reply and tell her it would be ok if their friendship stopped now, Beth would cope with whatever the outcome, she had to tell someone the whole truth before it ate her up inside, and to tell them both somehow seemed too much to bear, plus knowing sweet, sweet Claire would be tortured by the secret either way. Beth knew it would be a big ask and yet somehow she didn't think JJ would refuse.

Chapter Eight

JJ

Dear JJ and Claire,

I know this is late, but my Mum died. Sorry to shock you with this. It was so sudden, and we have all been trying to get through each day. She was hit by a bus, literally hit by a bus. When they told me I thought it was a joke, it's not a thing right, it's just something people say, something mum said, like, be nice you could get hit by a bus tomorrow. She had dropped Tom at school and went to cross the road in front of an empty bus and another one hit her, apparently she stepped straight out into it. Tom was inside luckily and didn't see, he still thinks she is coming back soon, it's been so hard. Jason walks around in a daze and people have been coming and going for weeks. I've snuck away to write to you. I feel bad, so bad. Mum and I were never great, but I miss her. Can I tell you something, I feel so bad, but all these people keep saying stuff about how nice she was and what a tragedy and all the bitchy mums she hated are bringing food and hanging over Jason as if, now he's available again they might be in with a chance. Ugh! It makes me sick, and they fuss over Tom and he's lapping up all the treats and when they leave he acts like a maniac, and I have to deal with it. I sort of hate Mum for leaving me, is it bad to say it? Why didn't she look? She would have screamed at me for not looking before crossing the road. It's all messed up now, what if Jason marries one of the other mothers? I'd bloody leave for sure, they are so fake. I don't know what to do, I feel angry, angry she didn't love me as much as she did Tom, in fact I don't think she ever loved me at all, and I'm angry she was so stupid she couldn't even cross a street. It sucks. I thought about running away, I don't want to live here anymore and I'm not Tom's mother, I should get a life too. You know what else, I think she did it now, so I can never make her proud.

I have to go, more people coming in the gate. Life is such a shit! I keep dreaming the last words she said were I love you Beth, but she never said it in real life so why would she say it at the end? I did ask ... her last word was Tom, of course it was. Jason said I can stay even though I'm not his daughter legally, it's nice of him, obviously mum didn't even think about something like this happening either, you think she could have, did she mean me to be left on the street? I'm lucky Jason is such a good bloke so at least I have a roof over my head for now.

Have to go, Love you both x Beth.

Ps: I'm ok, really I am.

JJ felt a tight ball in her belly. If she had known, she might have been able to wrangle a trip out of her dad to be with Beth. Beth had often mentioned different words her mother had said but JJ had not really believed her. Didn't every parent love their child as much as her parents loved her and Will? Poor Beth, she must be so sad. All of Beth's letters had always been positive and the few remarks or unhappiness Beth had expressed to them, JJ had dismissed as being from a normal, emotional, and hormonal teenage girl. JJ couldn't imagine it was any different in Australia than it was in Canada. Hormones were hormones! Between herself and Claire, JJ realised how much they both had unburdened themselves to Beth over the years. Whenever it was their turn to write to Beth directly they had taken it as their turn to unload their problems and she had never once complained. Beth was always there for them both. Their process of communication often saw a problem resolved by the time the answers came back yet for JJ, it had always mattered they had her back, and supported her in every way. For JJ their friendship was something she could not live without, it was the letters which kept her going no matter how bad things were. JJ still could not understand how the girls at her school had not accepted her for who she was and not for how she looked, it was not as if it was a surprise to them, they had been looking at her since they were little, yet none of them could let it go, none of them were brave enough to break away from the gang, in case they too, would be subject to the practical jokes and teasing JJ had to endure.

JJ pondered for a while as thoughts of Beth filled her head, she scribbled a quick note to Claire tucking Beth's letter in behind it. The sooner Claire knew, the better. JJ had explained she would write to her soon with her thoughts and then could they restart the letter trail again in its proper order. Licking the stamp, she pushed it on hard and headed out towards the post box calling out to whoever was in the house she would be back soon.

A cool breeze to remind everyone fall was almost here made her move quicker and a familiar warmth coursed through her as the jog became a run and her body now moved with ease at the momentum. JJ was happy with her progress, the weight was sliding off and the enjoyment of the exercise was now her drug of choice. For JJ each step took away the anxiety she normally felt and seemed to make her more relaxed and confident. She had picked out her dress for prom and knew some eyes in the room would pop when they saw her. It was going to be a masquerade ball, and little did the A-Team girls realise, they had picked the perfect theme for JJ. Her dad had been to Vietnam on business and returned with the most exquisite half-face mask which covered her eyes and draped down over her cheek and half her nose so it covered her birthmark entirely. Will was so excited for her and even though he had been asked to escort the most popular girl in her year, JJ was secretly proud when he told her he had turned her down saying he was already going with the most beautiful girl in town. Of course JJ had heard the snide remarks, of how she couldn't find a date, so her brother was taking her, but had brushed them aside knowing how much the top girl was hurt, and now scrambling to find a date because of Will's rejection. The girl thought the only way she could save face in her eyes, was to bully JJ, turning it around so she could blame someone other than herself. Will had laughed and told JJ he would have turned her down anyway as he was not blind to her past behaviour and selfish attitudes.

Slipping the letter in to the slot, JJ turned to retrace her steps, happy at least Claire would know soon and hopefully be able to organise herself to go to Adelaide to give Beth some support. It made her feel a bit jealous but one day soon they would all be together. Rounding the corner she pulled up short, almost tripping over a group of boys from school blocking her path as they huddled together. One reached out to grab her arm and steady her as the others straightened, almost circling her as she regained her feet.

'So looky here boys, the most talked about girl in school, I heard you couldn't find anyone to take you to prom even when your parents offered to pay them for it. Tell them I'll go for a thousand,' he leaned in close, 'but I'll want extras.' The others smirked and shuffled their feet, some looked at the ground and she could feel their shame, yet they were too cowardly to speak up against their leader. JJ tried to back away, but they stood firm.

'Sure Lindon Baker, I'll give you extras!' JJ kicked him hard in the groin and as he doubled over she leapfrogged over him and ran as hard as she could pausing at the corner to make sure they hadn't followed. JJ rested her hands on her knees as she caught her breath and looked back, they were all bent over as smart mouth Lindon rolled on the ground groaning in pain. JJ jumped as she heard a voice behind her.

'Are you ok, sounds like you've been training hard.' Will stood looking at her before glancing down the avenue to the scene at the bottom of the hill. 'Have they been bothering you Sis?' Will's face looked concerned, and his brow was furrowed as he tried to work out what was going on.

'No, I handled it, but I don't think Baker will be forgetting me anytime soon.'

Will went to go past her and she grabbed his arm.

'Leave it Will, I'm okay.'

'They never give up do they, can't they see what a great person you are, they are so shallow.'

JJ rubbed his arm.

'Thanks, it's ok I'm used to it, their time will come. Now do you think I can talk Dad into giving me a trip to Australia as a graduation present?' Will laughed.

'I think you could talk Dad into anything, Mother on the other hand, is a different matter. How cool is the mask he bought you, I can't wait to see their ugly faces when I escort the prettiest girl to the ball.' JJ hooked her arm through his.

'I hope I marry someone just like you one day, but I don't think I will because you are the best person in the whole wide world.' JJ smiled shyly as she saw the blush creep up her brother's face. 'Of course, they may not be as nice, but they will definitely be better looking because,' she paused as the laughter bubbled up inside, 'it wouldn't be hard.' Will turned to her as he realised her joke and she pushed him away gently before fleeing up the avenue, laughing loudly as Will chased her calling her names as he too laughed and pretended to be offended. The nasty boys disappeared from her head as she ran and JJ wished everyone could have a brother like Will, he really was the best.

Chapter Nine

Claire

Dear Beth,

I am so sad to hear about your Mum. I wish I could be there to give you a big hug. I know you had your struggles, but she was still your Mum and I'm sure she loved you very much. I don't know what I would do if I didn't have mine. Please try and remember all the good times and know I am hugging you from here.

Dad lost his job, it's the recession they say, but he doesn't know what to do, it is the only job he has ever had. I have been taking on extra sewing jobs with Mum, but it seems to irritate him more to see us working and him not. It's funny not seeing his face all black each night but he keeps busy and all the jobs we needed doing around the house are getting done and the garden looks amazing. He gets some money from the government, they call it the dole, but he is sort of embarrassed about taking it and swears he will pay it all back. A girl in our street has asked me to make her wedding dress and I am so excited. Mum will help but I have designed it all and asked my tech teacher to help me with some finer touches. I hope I make it good enough, imagine if I spoilt her big day. I'm so nervous about it some days I think I will be sick. The material is so luscious and it's like working with a cloud. Every time I touch it Mum says I look like I am dreaming. It makes me want to get married and have a beautiful dress of my own. Do you think we will all get married, how wonderful it would be to have you and JJ as my bridesmaids, I could make all the dresses and it would be such fun...I can't wait!

I did well in my exams and even though Dad would have liked me to go to university like the others, my tech teacher talked to him for me and has helped me apply for a scholarship/apprenticeship for a design course with one of the top designers in Sydney. Imagine, designing something and having a big show with a runway and models from all over the world ....is it too big a dream? Silly old me ..as if I could but Mum said if I don't try, I'll never know. I have an interview on Tuesday and I'm sure I'll get lost or forget my portfolio. Dad said he will go with me and wait outside and even though he doesn't say it, I know it means he is secretly proud. Oh Beth, so much ahead of us and it all feels so exciting and so scary. I have been doing like you said and writing down my goals and dreams and how I could get there, JJ was right too, it is sort of calming and I think it keeps me a bit on track. My sister is going to America as part of her externship and at night when I see Dad sit on the recliner smoking his pipe, staring at our photos on the wall I can see the amazement in his eyes of what she has achieved. I think he has told all the neighbours about his daughter going on a jumbo jet all the way to the United States. I don't think he understands why she's going but for him to fly in the sky was never a reality he thought he would have, and I wonder, Beth, JJ what will it be like when we are as old as our parents, will there be anything left to amaze us???

Gosh I've just looked back over this, I do ramble on, don't I. Oh Beth try not to be too sad and think of all the happy times. I am a bit sad I will be the last to hear about your graduation JJ, don't leave out any details will you, I want to know everything. Can you send a photo? Mum's calling so I must go. Cross your fingers for my interview and I'll hold my breath waiting to hear about the ball… no I won't, not really, it would be silly wouldn't it! Ha!

Much love to you both xxxxx Claire

about the ball… no I won't, not really, it would be silly wouldn't it! Ha!

Much love to you both xxxxx Claire

Claire remembered her letter so well and her sister flying off, intending to return to finish her degree before departing again into the academic world in Washington. Claire's parents had been killed a few months later in an horrific car accident and life had been turned upside down as the grief encompassed her and she tried to move forward without their support. Claire held a coat to her chest as her mind wandered.

There had been a knock at the door and a neighbour had opened it. Claire remembered hearing the accent and had risen from her chair as something in her brain had tried to connect amongst the grief.

I'm so sorry,' she heard, 'but I'm here to see Claire, can you point out who she is?' The neighbour's puzzled face appeared as she pointed in her direction. Another face had appeared, and Claire had instantly known who it was. As confused friends looked on, Claire had flown into her arms and JJ had rocked her as she sobbed and clutched her as if she would never let go. Claire's brother and sister had moved forward and wrapped their arms around them both, each realising the importance of the moment and the situation in which it was happening. Claire had heard her brother say: thankyou she needs you here. The arms had dropped, and Claire had stepped back to look at her friend, you're beautiful she had said, and their eyes had overflowed again.

'Beth's coming too, she's driving. We wanted to be here for you, I'm so sorry Claire, so very sorry.'

They had hugged so long and even as people moved forward to be introduced, JJ had never left her side. Her voice seemed to boom out across the room and Claire had wanted to squirrel her away to her room, to cry, laugh, and get to know each other in the real life. A lot of it was still a blur. Beth had arrived and Claire remembered feeling safe and more able to cope as they attached themselves to either side of her and held her up each time she felt herself begin to fall both emotionally and physically. It had felt almost surreal as each of them knew instinctively what to do or say, their letters bonding them together with a lifetime of memories even though they had only just met.

They had all now lost their parents, lost friends, gone grey and travelled a million miles whenever one or the other was in need, they had nearly lasted a lifetime and now with Beth losing the man she loved, Claire could see they were the top of the pile, no older generations, they were next in line. It was funny when she was married, she could not envision outlasting her own husband. As silly and lightheaded as she appeared to be, when she threw him out she had realised how strong she really was. Beth on the other hand, she now realised, had not been the strong one, but because of the man Marcus was, she had allowed him to share her load. Claire knew JJ and Beth still thought of her as they had when they were young, they kept an extra eye on her, and Claire had allowed them to do so. Now was her time to be there for her friend and she would not let her down. The letter wrote itself again in her mind, so much had changed and yet so little, they were all the same yet different, older, maybe not wiser but more and more aware of the important moments in life and to value every one of them. Each tear or laugh, kiss or embrace may be their last and Claire so desperately wanted to make her friend see the light again and vowed to be there for as long as it took, to show her the way.

Plates were rattling in the kitchen and picking up her bag Claire made her way to the front door to deposit it in such a way so she would trip over it, therefore not forgetting it. Not long now, a light meal and tidy up and they would be on their way. Claire paused for a moment to take a deep breath and made a vow to herself to stay strong as her friend's world crumbled around her.

As usual JJ was organising herself and found her way around Claire's kitchen with ease.

'Come on, let's get this down and be on our way. You know how waiting irritates me and we can fill in the time at the airport browsing for impulse items we don't need at the shops.'

JJ liked to be ahead of time and Claire wondered if it was because she had spent her youth always being on the lookout for trouble ahead. Once they were on their way she knew she would steady off and calm down, it was this in between time which always seemed to rattle her.

Claire allowed herself to be pushed along in the wave which was JJ. It seemed no time had passed before they were checked in and searching the shops for some little memento to lighten their day. The conversation had been sparse as each tossed their thoughts and ideas around in their own heads, occasionally throwing out pieces they couldn't connect, to lay in the air for consideration. Claire felt whole. It was as if every part of her fell into place when they were together. For her, they were not like sisters, Claire had a sister, and they were close, but the feelings weren't the same. With Beth and JJ, it was like they were part of her, conjoined triplets separated at birth and never whole again until they could see each other's faces. Beth had always made fun of this and often, when they were young had them join hands and made them swear not to let go as they battled busy pavements and dance floors. It had made them laugh and when they finally let go Beth would hug her tight, and she knew it was the same for them too. For Claire, luck had not brought them together, it was divine intervention, with Beth being the chosen one and her angels guiding her to both herself, and JJ.

Claire watched JJ's face as she browsed, her face moving as the different expressions attached to her thoughts furrowed her brow or raised her cheeks. JJ could say a lot without saying a word and Claire often marvelled at how so much could be expressed without JJ opening her mouth. Claire smiled to herself, you had to be careful when she did, as JJ never held back once she started. Added with her loud by Australian standards voice, JJ's opinions were never lost on anyone once they were out. Again, Claire could see how JJ had never lost her fierceness which had helped her through her teenage years and carried her through her adult life. JJ let all those who had tormented her know how well she had done, how much she had achieved, and how pathetic she now thought they were. Their boarding announcement echoed through the lounge and once settled in their seats JJ reached out and took her hand.

'I'm not sure about this one Claire, I'm glad you're here, I'm worried I might let you down, if she breaks I'm not sure I'll be strong enough.'

Tears came to Claire's eyes, there it was, the thread which joined them, the thread which knew one was weaker, frayed in the moment and needing the others to hold on and guide them through. Most times it had been JJ and Beth who remained strong, yet in this moment after all these years, Claire knew, for sure, they had always known her time would come, and she would be the one. The trust had always been there waiting, waiting for the time when they both would fall and she, Claire, would have to be the one to step up and guide them through. As much as Beth had always been their ringleader, their guide and influencer, and JJ had been second in command, Claire now knew they could never have flown so far without her as well. Her pen pal sisters were closer than family, thicker than blood. Claire squeezed JJ's hand too.

'To let go is not a sign of weakness JJ, I know it's my turn and I won't let you down. Beth needs us both, but I know, I truly do, how she is your one person. She has been mine too. I'll know when you need to turn away, and it's ok to do it because I haven't forgotten, not a single day, a single letter, a single moment and this may be the time when we need all of it, every ounce of it, to hold her up. I'm strong JJ, I can hold up two.'

JJ wiped her eyes and their hands remained clasped for the rest of the flight.

Chapter Ten

Beth

Dear Claire and JJ,

He's gone. I feel so angry, why him, after everything it took to find him and in a heartbeat he is gone. Who decides this, is this your god Claire, if it is I hate him, I hate him with all my being. Don't come, I don't want to see you, either of you. I mean it Claire! I want to do this alone, I did what he said, and I could have broken my promise, could have called someone he is the one person I cannot live without, and I could have saved him.

The tears fell thick and fast. Beth felt the pen slip out of her hand and watched it roll across the table. Every part of her had shut down and she wanted to close her eyes and disappear into the world which was now his. She had always known, they had a pact, he had looked deep into her eyes and made her promise, promise with all her heart, she would give him this. He knew he would take his own life, had always known. Marcus had spent half a lifetime thinking about it, planning the details and accepting, although his life would be shorter, he would live and die on his own terms and no one else's. Beth had agreed, looking in his eyes and repeating his words, yet secretly hoping the medical miracles which seemed to grace the news every other week would come their way. They were researching all the time and modern technology had made huge advancements across so many fields. Beth had been so sure. He had told her to walk away, if she found him, if it wasn't quite done, she was to walk away, not come back until she thought his last breath was gone, he did not want to incriminate her, this would be his doing and she was to respect his wish.

Marcus had been a man full of life, his body plagued by insidious diseases and infections from a young age. He had never given up or given in, cancer he chewed up and threw away, diabetes had restricted his timetable but not held him back, his muscles wasting and taking away his mobility had been the straw which would make his body take charge over his mind and the battle had been fierce. As much as he fought it, it had fought back, the scars of his youth created weaknesses for it to invade and she had seen the moment of defeat cross his face and he advanced his plans. As one by one the little things she set in place to make his life easier, were the things which made him bitter and withdrawn. Another man mowing his lawn, she had thought, would be a luxury, yet to him, with each lap of the garden it eroded him more, his licence was the last straw. The risk of heart failure thrown in as the medications and complications grew, had a doctor make the decision and no argument could bring it back. At each turn of the wheel, she began to feel his resentment, given to her but not aimed. Beth accepted his manner, understood his frustrations and still begged for him to stay. The light he had always held in his eyes for life was fading and she was not enough to draw it back. Maybe if they'd had a child, maybe it could have been the anchor to keep him here, she knew it wouldn't, but at least now she would have had someone to hold.

Beth had known it was close, his body had weakened, yet still the hope had been there. As he struggled to do daily tasks she watched with an eagle eye to ensure all his medications were swallowed so he could not hoard them for later. Marcus had never told her his exact plan and yet, on the day when she walked in, she had known and she had turned like a robot obeying a command, as he had asked her to, pleaded for her to, and walked away. Beth had been there, suffered with him and knew it would be for her own selfish self, if she made him stay. None of it made it easier.

The letter still sat unfinished. A neighbour came and went but Beth had shunned the rest, she locked the door and waited for them to tell her it was time. The coroner's report was delayed and her nonresponse to the telephone had hindered the procession of death proceeding. It would happen tomorrow, the funeral, and she had survived eighteen days without him. Clothes hung loose on her gaunt body and Beth could not remember the last time she had showered. The blinds were drawn and the noise of life continuing on the street annoyed her, she wanted to yell at them all to stop, to the children to stop playing, to the cars to stop moving, and the people to stop rejoicing. Most of all, for the sun to stop shining. The letter was something she felt she had to do, Beth had waited to write so they wouldn't come, so she could wallow alone in her own self-pity. To see Claire and JJ might be the card to break her, make her realise she had to keep living, they would make it real. Together they would make her live and all Beth wanted to do was die, fade away until she saw his face and took his hand for their next journey. The sobs racked her body as the light faded around the edge of the blinds, she so wanted someone to hold her, but the reality of it would be her undoing. Holding meant life and life meant moving forward, she was not ready and wanted to awake from this nightmare in which she was caught. The doorbell rang twice and Beth stiffened not wanting to let on she was here. One neighbour had a key and she heard it trying to find its home in the lock.

Muffled voices made their way toward her. The neighbour called her name and the Beth of old was deeply thankful for her persistence and kindness. Beth slipped the letter into the drawer and called out a reply, there was someone with her and Beth knew they would leave sooner if they saw some effort from her.

'We'll take it from here,' a voice whispered. 'We can't thank you enough for all you've done. Yes, yes we'll be in touch.'

Beth heard the door close, and a light went on in the hall making her blink as her eyes adjusted to its beam. JJ was first, she went to move forward but faltered in her step at the sight of Beth. Claire, the lovely Claire, stepped up and Beth felt any ounce of energy which had been in her body drain away as her shoulders sagged and Claire caught her in her arms.

'We're here Beth, for as long as you need, we're here.'

Beth sank in her steps and felt the two sets of arms guide her to the lounge where they laid her down and covered her with a blanket. Claire used soothing words and Beth allowed them to lull her senses and give in to the exhaustion she felt. JJ's distraught face faded, and Beth let the darkness enfold her.

Each time Beth stirred, she felt their presence. Sometimes she heard a whispered word and felt one of them squeeze her hand to reassure her. Marcus came to her in her dreams before fading away no matter how fast she ran, or how loudly she called, a pillow would be readjusted beneath her head and a hand would stroke her arm as her body tried to make her wake, and her mind resisted, wanting to stay and catch one more glimpse of his face.

Beth's eyes felt blurry and her body weak as she struggled to sit up. Claire was sitting on the floor, her head on her crossed arms resting against the end of the lounge and still dressed as she had been when Beth closed her eyes. JJ moved in behind to help her and sat so Beth could use her as support. Beth's eyes were heavy and the feeling of too much, yet too little sleep, made her feel drained.

'I didn't want you to come.'

'You knew we would.'

Beth looked across at Claire, her face aging as she slept, the tiny lines casting out across her face.

'Claire will cope better than you, she had no idea so she will manage, she doesn't know about before.'

'You didn't do this Beth, it could not be stopped, by you, by doctors, by anyone, he had planned too well.'

'I don't want her to know, I don't want her to know what I did, I should have tried, I didn't. Just you, no one else needs to know.' JJ squeezed her hand.

'Claire knows, she is part of us and even if you never told her she would know. We need her now, because for me to look at you is crushing, and we will both need her to pull us through.'

Claire sighed and stretched her shoulders as her eyes fluttered adapting to the light. She stretched her arms, smiling, her eyes conveying both the concern and the love she felt. 'How lovely you are Beth, let me make some tea and toast. We will talk soon, it is a big day, but after this we can hide in here and come together. JJ will hold you and I won't be far.'

....

'I forgot who I loved, 'Beth said.

Claire looked across at JJ as the tears filled their eyes.

'No, you didn't,' she said. 'It's because you remembered who you did.'

A car door slammed in the distance and Beth rose from the chair and made her way to the window to stare vacantly out at the overgrown backyard. She had so much more to say to him and would never hear the replies, now there would only be her own responses to what might have been said which would echo in her mind.

'It's time to go Beth, we're with you. Get through today and after this, in the days ahead, we can figure out what's next. Come on Honey, he needs you to do this too.'

JJ's voice was like a whisper which seemed to swirl around her mixing with the fog which wouldn't lift. It hung low and damp, so thick she felt each movement as she tried to push through it towards the daylight. A part of her wanted to get there, to reach the other side where the sun shone and the birds sang loudly and the other part wanted to swallow her up and take her to him, to a place she had no right to be yet, but to take her anyway, to where this pain might stop. Their voices combined so Beth could no longer tell which one of them was speaking. She knew Claire held her arm, her sweet perfume wound its way up her nostrils and her body followed the scent and the murmurs, as if it was a trail left to guide her through. They were all in the car and they both held her hands, one on each side of her These women did not let her down but Beth wondered if they were strong enough to catch her in this fall.

Beth was plummeting off a cliff at speed and she could almost feel the spray of the ocean below as it reached higher and higher with each wave trying to pull her down into its grip. She did not know if they could reach so far or hold on for long. The cliff grew higher yet still the water danced around her feet, and she looked straight out, not up nor down, silently asking the universe what she should do. This had been the plan, she had followed the plan, but it was what he had wanted, not her, she wanted him to fight some more, to not want to leave her, to cling to every moment fighting for them both. Yet she had agreed, thinking it would not come to this, and she could find another way, one where her guilt would not return, and she could accept the normal course of his life had come to an end. Had this been the time, or had she got it wrong? Beth knew the answer and had known in the moment, the one still moment as she surveyed the scene before her, and she had shut the door and walked away. Beth had walked, yet not cried, not at first. What would happen if she had red eyes, what would she say, they'd had a fight? Might it then look like suicide, not just a tragic mistake as he intended them to think. He had wanted her to be free, to grieve and live with a free conscience, they had talked about it, but now she knew, they had not talked enough.

The church was full, she had wondered at his choice. Familiar faces looked at her with sympathy in their eyes and genuine sorrow in their hearts. To know him was to love him, he had achieved so much, so much more than her and his struggles had been real, visible, and fierce. To look at him was to know his courage, and Beth had been there for them all. Love had blinded her, not to his needs but to the life choices she would have to make, she had taken it as a lifetime to change his mind, and could see now it had been her mistake, she had taken it as her lifetime, not his, which had stretched before her long into eternity. Youth and love, they had been her downfalls. To miss a moment she would have regretted, yet today, at this moment she would have sacrificed it all for him to live, even if it had been with someone else in another time, she needed to know he would take one more breath, though she had heard his last and knew another would never come.

It seemed it was over, and she wondered what had been said. People held her tight, consoling themselves, by being present here today had been the right thing to do, and in some way they were helping her to move forward, they would be there for her, she would only have to ask, they whispered. Beth knew, in reality, tomorrow they would go on with their lives, sometimes remembering they had asked her to call, their world would keep turning while hers was now changed forever. To wake tomorrow would never be the same as before, to set one lonely cup on the table would remind her each and every time. Amongst them now, as they mingled, unsure of when it would be appropriate to leave, Beth longed for solitude, yet felt only loneliness.

Chapter Eleven

JJ

Dear Claire and Beth,

You should have seen their faces. Dad took so many photos (getting some developed for you as I write). I thought we would never get there and in the end we were the last car to arrive. All the girls were showing off outside and they looked like flouncy bridesmaids not prom queens and were literally dripping with jewellery. Will said they looked like different flavours in an ice creamery which, when they came together, melted into a frothy mess with no individuality left to shine through. I was a bit nervous as the dress Mummy and I ended up choosing was so figure hugging (thanks for the suggestions Claire) and Will gave me a simple chain for my neck as a graduation gift. It is so beautiful, and I will wear it every day for the rest of my life. I have the best brother ever, so, so, lucky. Anyway, so we go to get out of the car, and they all are heading inside and, oh my god it was so perfect, they spread out on each side of the room and turned to watch the door as the teachers and special guests arrived and we were at the door. It was literally perfect timing. Will and I walked in, and a ray of sunshine lit up behind us (the official photographer said he caught it, can't wait to see). My hands were shaking but Will whispered – go get them Sis, and oh, I felt like a queen. I remembered all your advice and later someone said I looked like a movie star. You should have seen their faces, the girls were speechless they looked like fish gasping for air and Will took my arm and we walked the full length of the hall. The boy's eyes were popping out of their heads and Lindon Baker, well, I think he was wishing he hadn't picked on me as he now knew he had not a chance in hell of getting a dance. Oh girls, it was so wonderful, I really did feel like Cinderella at the ball. Nearly every boy asked me for a dance and even after I took the mask off they still kept saying how lovely I looked. I still feel like I'm dancing on a cloud. Everyone now wants to be my friend!!!! Don't worry though, the old JJ hasn't forgotten how shallow they are, all these years and they rejected me for the way I looked and now they all want to know me for the way I look??? I've friended a few of the girls and at least now the boys don't call me names as they all want to get into my pants and get a closer look at this gorgeous body I've worked so hard for the last few months. Ha! They don't fool me for a minute, but for a little bit, I want to hang on to the fact I was the most popular girl in school, even if it was only for one night. Will said it's always good to go out with a bang. He was so great, and we had fun. Mum cried when I told her, and I think she is happy people now accept me for who I am. I'll let her keep thinking it, but I know the truth. I actually think it has helped some of the others. The girls on the fringe who were afraid before, have now found the courage to move away from the A-team girls, and they aren't acting so high and mighty because their prom was ruined for them because the ugly duckling turned into the swan and outshone them all. It was the sweetest revenge after all these years. Is it mean? It is, but I don't care they deserved it and as Will said, they got their just desserts and I didn't have to say a word, it's true too. Enough about me, I'll send some photos when I can and I'm still working on Dad to give me a trip to Australia as a graduation gift, cross all your fingers for me.

How are you Beth, I feel there are things you are not saying, talking is the best way, believe me, I wouldn't have been able to withstand the bullies without talking to Will and my parents. Please talk to your stepdad. Is the other woman still hanging about? Yuk she sounds gross and it's not terribly long since your mum, I agree it's too soon. Don't give up on your dreams, hang on to them and they will be your ticket out. If you need money I can ask my dad, he will lend you some, I know he would. Please promise you will not give up, I know you will be the best journalist in the world.

Claire, wow I'm so proud and I bet secretly your dad is too. By the time I get to Australia the papers will be full of the story written by one of the top journalists in the country (Beth) about the 'Toast of Fashion Week' and designer for the stars (Claire). I can see it now, my two best friends I am so proud of you both and I pray we will all be together soon, what a party it will be. Love to you both times ten.

XX JJ

What a party, but instead, it had been a funeral which had first brought them together. Claire's parents taken too soon as JJ was about to jump on a plane to surprise them both. They had come together seamlessly, their letters over the years binding them with their secret thoughts and worries. Both Claire and Beth had been exactly as JJ had imagined and even within the tragedy the warmth of their embrace felt like coming home.

A neighbour had answered the door and JJ's accent had stilled the room. The puzzlement on the woman's face she could understand, as her question to see her friend, yet not knowing what she looked like, was unusual. JJ glimpsed Claire's sister in the background holding a tray of sandwiches, her body poised as her mind worked out who this could be, intruding at this time. They looked similar, yet JJ had known in a glance the girl was not Claire. This girl had an aura of strength around her, where JJ's image of Claire was one of fragility. They had never in the end exchanged photos, each holding back because of their own insecurities wanting to be liked for who they were, not judged by their looks, as their peers had done. They had written about hair colour as well as different styles and trends they had gone through. JJ had talked about her figure, her height and weight and the struggles she had felt to look and be like everyone else. JJ knew they would think her to be above average height and a muscley build. Her exercise program and the joy she now found in running had been shared on many occasions. Claire had shared her dress size, so JJ knew she was slender and petite. Beth had been more closed, yet the depth of her words made JJ envision an average sized person with mousy brown hair and freckles scattered across her skin, not big not little, more ... un-noticeable, JJ had thought. Someone who would blend in with the crowd, pleasant to look at, yet not someone who would make you stop and stare at their beauty. JJ thought Beth's beauty, like many, would be hidden inside, to show on special occasions when she smiled and gave you a piece of her heart, or held your hand knowing it was all you would need.

Claire was beautiful. As she had flung herself across the room into JJ's arms, the beauty of her almost made JJ breathless. They had clung to each other, and JJ knew it had been right to come. The perfect moment to share and support her friend, written words would never have been enough. Other arms had gathered around them and later as they were introduced, JJ realised the love in this family was the same as her own, and they understood, she too, was family as well.

At times JJ had wondered why she had felt no guilt at not being there physically for Beth when her mother died. Some of it was maturity, those last days of adolescence, where, if it wasn't happening to you it was not real, not yet being adult enough to understand someone else's pain. It was also Beth. From the second or third letter JJ had known Beth only gave them so much, keeping the hardest bits to herself. To Beth it was shielding them, somewhere for her to hide, to push people away, knowing in doing so she was hurting herself but not wanting to share the depth of her thoughts. JJ had drawn her out over the years, they'd had moments, the two of them, when Beth had leaked her soul. When Marcus came, he had drawn it out, eased the falls and caressed her in the darkness of her grief. It was grief JJ had realised, which held Beth back, made her aloof to some, but understanding of others. The day Beth had slipped an extra note in just for her, JJ knew Beth would need her more, more than funny, frivolous Claire, more than brave and courageous Will and more than JJ was sure she could give, but she had. JJ had held Beth's secrets, supported her excuses and denials, and in the quiet of a night or a whisper on the wind, she had held Beth's hand and let her know it would all be ok. They'd had each other, and Beth's time was to come, to fulfill her dreams, enrich her life with a person she loved and forgive herself for the crimes she had never really committed, yet blamed herself for.

All of it came back as JJ held Beth's hand and she realised the forgiveness had never come.

Dear JJ,

I have never betrayed the code before, but I really need some advice and somehow I don't want to hear all of Claire's alternatives. I'm feeling really trapped. I have to look after so much now, Jason is trying to pretend he has it all under control but as much as mum and I quarrelled she really did take care of everything. Tom is no help but I'm feeling really torn as even though we aren't close, he wouldn't understand if I left. There's a whole world out there waiting for me, and I feel like it is slipping away and I'm sinking into a deep mud hole. No matter how much I struggle it won't let me free. You know I want to be a freelance writer and I've been offered a scholarship and I want to take it, I want it so badly, but I will be letting them down, like I always do, fleeing from responsibility. I'm drowning and I don't know where to turn. I want to ask you something, I want to ask you to break the code, to not tell Claire. I can't bear her to know.

I know what I'm asking, and it's wrong but I choose you because you are strong, and I think you will understand. If you want to walk away I will stop the letters and you can be friends with Claire. I have to tell someone. I tried writing it down and burying it in the yard, but it haunts me not having a reply, something to set my mind at ease or send me down the correct track, so please, if it's the last thing you do for me, can you write back to me? Here goes ... and I hope I have the courage to post this ...if you are reading it, you will know.

I did it. I killed her! It was all my doing, and this is not the first time I have destroyed someone else's life, first Tom and now Mum. If I abandon them now, it would be exactly what my mother would expect of me, but don't I deserve a life too, she never let me forget it. Oh JJ, I hate her but what do I do I keep hearing her voice in my head about what a failure I am, my face looks calm, but I am dying inside ...

The letter had gone into the details and initially JJ had been horrified at Beth's words. JJ's first response had been to flee, to beg her father for some advice and to send her to Australia to save a life, and once saved, to walk away and leave her be. To cut Beth off, not for the depression she felt, but for the betrayal of not telling the whole truth from the very beginning and for deceiving them for the last eight years. JJ remembered how she had risen off her chair, how Will had poked his head into her room, his mouth open to speak now forgotten words as he saw her face.

'What's wrong, did those boys come back?' JJ had shaken her head.

'What is it?' Will had moved closer and knelt beside her, glancing at the piece of paper in her hands. 'What is it Sis, I'm happy to listen.'

JJ had hesitated, could she let it all out, her mum told her some secrets are too big for one person and when it is, it is alright to share. JJ began explaining how she had found the extra note, when she came back as she went to straighten the envelope.

'Beth's mother has died, and I wrote to tell Claire, but now I found this Will, and I think of everything I have told them and yet all along Beth did not trust us at all. You are my brother Will, but these girls, I thought they were my soul. How could she not tell me how she felt, I felt silly and embarrassed about being bullied but she was being bullied too, by her own mother? I feel betrayed, what else hasn't she said, I was always honest with her.'

Will had taken the note and JJ had waited for his look of shock and dismay. It had never come. Instead, he had taken her hand as he gently and quietly told her his thoughts, telling her to remember all they had shared, how Beth was barely eighteen, just old enough to drive but certainly not old enough to lose a mother he was sure, and for them both, this was too hard to imagine. Beth, he surmised was not old enough, or mature enough to examine her past from a distance. They had talked for a while in soft tones and JJ saw from her brother's eyes all the good Beth had brought into her life.

'You knew it was there underneath, though you are shocked someone could speak it out aloud. If Beth had told you how she felt about her mother in the beginning, would you have continued to write? Beth's family is different to ours and until we have lived in their house we cannot begin to understand, count our blessings as mum says and reach out to those who cannot have the same. I think the other part which is sitting wrongly with you is Beth is asking you to hide this from Claire for a lifetime.' Will paused so JJ could consider his thoughts. 'Think about this, if you are going to betray her, do it now and Claire can help you hold it together, tell her you did tell Claire and move on with whatever happens. Hold it and she will know her bank to add to, so be prepared for more to come and make sure you are strong enough to do so. Look at her words JJ, I don't think Beth has ever had anyone she could trust. I think she is showing you more friendship now than ever before as this is her deepest and darkest torment.'

JJ had wondered how strong a person she would become and how much worse the depths of Beth could be.

'You have one more choice and it is to trust in Claire and all you know of her, but it is to also break the trust the other way, to allow Claire to share your load without Beth knowing. Each one could strengthen or weaken your friendship, but each will hold the three of you together. It is a big choice to make but remember you have the last, what is it, seven or eight years of history to lead you on the path ahead. All these years you have thought you needed Beth, maybe now you will see it was Beth who needed you, and Claire. It may not have been a conscious thought at first, but her decision to choose two names in the beginning says to me she was already on her way, hedging her bets in case one failed and in her mind even back then, guaranteeing her at least one person who may care for her.'

JJ wondered how her brother had been so smart at such a young age, but cancer had made him mature beyond his years and he, in his own way, had shielded her from the highs and lows of life so she could have the childhood he had missed due to his insidious disease.

Before she had replied to Beth's letter, JJ had thought about all the words in between the lines which she had never seen before, Will was right, it had been her age, and immaturity, blinding her to the cries for help which had travelled across the sea. She could now see them and knew deep down she had seen them before yet brushed them aside in her selfishness to share her own life, but also because they were kids and a lot of it could have been discounted as the course of growing up. She was not going to hold on to any blame. It all seemed so long ago, and JJ still thought her decision had held the thread which bound them together for the years to come, each one of them holding untold secrets from another and none, willing to betray each other again.

JJ knew where Beth had been these last weeks as she shut herself away in the house and desperately tried to shut away her heart. JJ knew Beth had fallen farther than she had ever pulled her back from before, Marcus had probably been here at times, travelled with her to these depths to catch her and bring her home, but JJ wondered if he would ever have let her sink so low or let her fall this far. Claire was pulling them through slowly as she flittered and made tea, fussed and made meals, Claire allowed JJ to rest as she hauled Beth up the ladder towards the light.

All those years ago, Claire had healed, learned to live without her parents and though she had never moved out of their home, eventually buying it as her brother and sister had moved on, reached their academic heights around the world and they were happy for her to stay. JJ had admired Claire's strength of character, she retained her innocence but was her mother's child when it came to business. Her mother's determination for her children to succeed, live a better life than herself was deeply instilled and many learned not to push Claire once her mind was made up. At times, for all her success, JJ wondered how Claire could be so naive about the world and the people she lent her emotions to. JJ had never liked Claire's husband and had done a little dance the day Claire told her she had thrown him out.

When Beth had arrived the first time, it had been late, the neighbours had left, and relatives remained unsure of their place. The door had been open, and she had walked straight in, melted into them, her presence so calming, they had now known where to lean. Beth encompassed them and held them up, never wavering and building a support team in the background for the time she would have to leave. JJ had felt whole, a great sense of peace. When she was with Will he lifted her spirits, he had her back and always put her first. With Beth, it was the same but with the female version was a softness, and an understanding of the female mind Will would never know.

As JJ had watched Beth slide so seamlessly into their physical life, to lift Claire in her time of need and to not question in any way JJ's presence there, it had puzzled her knowing how much of Beth was hiding inside. JJ's dad had finally given in, with conditions, and as soon as the graduation was over the arrangements were made. She had kept it a secret and planned it so Claire would be on a tech term break, and she could scoop her up and whisk them both to Adelaide to surprise Beth. The days had ticked away as the plans were hampered by the distance she had to travel. Claire's sister's telegram changed her plans but not her destination and had arrived with almost perfect timing to align with her departure. JJ's plans became more important than ever, and she was so glad everything was in place. It had worried her the whole journey she would not be able to support them both. JJ had learned Beth was already a master at hiding within herself and showing the world the person she thought they expected her to be, not realising, by how much she gave, they all knew who she truly was deep inside. It was this person Beth could not see, and never would and it was this person JJ vowed to never let down.

Chapter Twelve

Claire

I'M GETTING MARRIED!!!!

Can you believe it! Beth and JJ you must be my bridesmaids, I won't take no for an answer, I'll make all the dresses, I've already started on mine. Now would you prefer a pale blue or apricot (the soft orangey-pink colour). I was thinking puffed sleeves, they are all the range at the moment, and falling straight from the bust from a satin ribbon which will be sewn in as a high waistline, I'll do a quick sketch on the back so you can see what I mean. Would you like hats? It will be summer so a wide floppy brim with matching ribbon might be nice. My family were quite shocked when I told them. I lashed out and called them on the telephone, I kept it short but am a bit afraid of the bill coming. Oh well, Johnno said it should be fine. We will live here of course and with his family being so close it will be nice and I'm sure a big help when the babies arrive. Oops, no I'm not pregnant, dreaming is all, I told him not until we are married, and he said ... I'm blushing as I write ... well it had better be a short engagement! I'm so happy to have found my one person, Johnno's not working right now but it is hard with the economy the way it is at the moment. If he doesn't find anything by the wedding, he is going to do some renovations and repairs on the house, and we are going to take some photos and I'll set him up in his own handyman/renovation business. People are getting so busy now and with the world changing they don't want to be doing all those kinds of odd jobs anymore, I told him it was a wonderful plan. I know he will be perfect at it and has so many great ideas, he is just a bit slow on the manual side of it, but once we are married and he has responsibilities, I'm sure he will find the enthusiasm. I must confess he is a bit of a mummy's boy, and she is trying to be kind and help me with the wedding. They want some huge affair with all their relatives, but I was thinking something more intimate, you two, my brother and his family and my sister would be enough people for me. Also I am paying for it all, they are going to pay for the beer which they said is what the groom's family does traditionally, I did think they might offer more, seeing as my parents are no longer here. It will be tight and at least I'll be getting the material at cost and doing the work on our dresses myself so it's a saving. I might have to ask you to buy your own shoes and if we carry a single flower instead of a bouquet, it will save a lot and I think it will look very elegant as well. I hope you agree. Oh girls, I'm so happy, now I will have someone to lean on and come home to. I wish we lived closer so we could go out together or grab a coffee (it's the cool thing to do now, to meet for coffee, my boss is always going out to meetings in café's, soon boardrooms will be a relic of the past and coffee shops and restaurants are popping up everywhere, maybe we should open a coffee house instead of renovation business?) Oh, I do ramble don't I, but I am so excited I wanted to tell you it all. We've set the date for March 10, so I hope it suits you both and I will keep you up to date on all the plans. A new year coming, a new decade and I feel so liberated. I'm not about to burn my bra but I can feel the change and see the shift in the way the world is thinking. Johnno's mum said she thinks I am very liberated to be going to work while my husband will stay at home. I feel like I'm leading the way in women's liberation in our street. I must go, I have so much to do. Johnno and I are going to the movies to see an Australian film, it's called Mad Max. I'm sure it will be a dud but at least we can snuggle and hold hands. Let me know what you think of the design.

Miss you both, love times a million,

Claire

PS: So glad the wedding is sooner because I will see you both.

PPS: Glad college is going well JJ.

PPSS: You've got this Beth, the job's temporary while you study, try and persevere at home, it must be awful to have another woman touching your mum's stuff and acting like she wants to be your best friend. Get the study done it's not long now and you can move out. We'll have a spare room if you want to change states, I'm sure Johnno wouldn't mind, and I would love it.

Xxxx (oh, PPSSSSS: A client requested me personally for a job, so excited, she is pretty famous so this might be my big break, finger's crossed X)

Beth was physically present, she shook hands, accepted condolences and managed to whisper enough of a reply for people to squeeze her arm and move on. Claire let her be and even though it was a struggle to not step in and cover for her, Claire knew it was Beth who had to reply. The light in Beth's eyes was dim yet each mention of his name held her here hovering in the present and it was this tiny dull light which held Claire back from hurrying them along so they could get Beth home. Her friend was an empty shell, and it would take all they could give to hold her here and bring her through. Claire was feeling the weight of JJ as well, she was happy to feel the strain and knew she had more to give.

JJ's face was ashen, Claire knew JJ thought this was more than she could bear. JJ would give them both her dying breath but seeing Beth not being able to lift herself at all was clawing at JJ's mind as she battled with her own demons and the realisation she could soon be in this same position. Claire knew it would not be the same. JJ had so much support in Will, and they had talked extensively about Jim's condition and lived through each stage always knowing the outcome of each. For Beth, it was different, the medical world had not decided his fate, Marcus had decided it for himself, on his terms. JJ did not live with hope, except maybe for a miracle, she lived with acceptance. Beth had lived with assuring herself she would change his mind, for him she would be enough, was what she longed for the most. Claire knew it was the final straw of feeling unworthy which was making Beth die inside, no matter how hard she had tried, how much she had loved, he had not been willing to stay. Losing Marcus would be with Beth forever and just as Claire had, after losing her parents, and even recovering from her divorce, Beth would struggle to see the light. Life had been there as Claire's strength returned, not the same, it had been hard to live without them, but life and love had shown her how to continue and move on, despite the loss of them. Claire knew it could be the same for Beth, the circle of life hit everyone at some time, the worry was, it was Beth, who may never recover from herself.

JJ caught her eye as they guided their friend into the car, Beth moved like a ghost seeming to drift from one side to another as her mind struggled to keep her balanced.

Doors were still closing as neighbours returned to their homes, some giving a final glance to acknowledge Beth was home, and in safe hands as they closed their doors and moved on with their lives. It was so hard, Claire knew, to see the world continuing while your own was shattered. They ushered Beth inside and all Claire could do was pray for Beth to break down, to kick and scream at the injustice of it all and to bury herself in their arms so they could start the process of lifting her up.

Claire turned on the oven and placed one of the many casseroles from well-meaning acquaintances in it to start to warm for their tea. When she returned to the lounge room, JJ had moved the lounge close to the armchair in which they had placed Beth, the other chair she had drawn in close as well so Claire would be able to squeeze through and their knees would have touched if Claire had not curled hers up underneath her.

'Beth,' JJ shook Beth's knee trying to make her respond. 'Beth, you have to talk, you managed to get through today but don't carry it into tomorrow, don't keep piling every day on to the next or we will never get you back.' Claire reached out.

'Yes Beth, start wherever you want to but at least talk to us, I simply can't bear it.'

Beth raised her tired eyes and Claire knew she had hit a chord, pinged it somewhere for Beth to come out and reach back to protect Claire from harm. It was almost instinctive now she had been doing it for so long.

'Please Beth, for me and for JJ, come back to us.'

'I never told you Claire, and I made JJ keep it a secret, I killed my mother, I pushed her into the bus, it was my fault, it was all my fault. We argued and I got out of the car and ran away, she called me, cried out for me to come back and I looked back to see her getting out of the car, so I ran back, and I pushed her, and told her to stay away, leave me alone. I hate you I said. It was the last time I saw her, she was falling, stumbling, and I ran away. I saw a bus and I wished her dead.'

Beth looked up as the silence encompassed the room.

'You knew, you knew all this time, I can tell. JJ told you didn't she? When did she tell you?' Beth turned to glare at JJ and Claire retracted her hand.

'I've always known, right from the beginning. You didn't kill her Beth, a bus did, bad timing killed her, not her daughter. Can't you see, your mum was always upset with you, it didn't matter what day it was or whether you were arguing or not, it was her day, she crossed the street, she stepped in front of the bus, for god's sake stop wishing it was you.' Claire knew her tone was angry, but she could also see the fire lighting in Beth's eyes, they had never argued, not once in all these years, and it had been JJ who had always been so direct about her opinions. Claire had been the pacifier, the soft hand who smoothed them over so as not to break the bond.

'You told her?'

'I did. I had to, we had to be honest.'

'So, what else have you said behind my back?'

'Nothing, as you and I have talked about Claire, sometimes we have talked about you. Not often, and nothing bad. We are a team Beth, you made us a team, but sometimes the players have to talk amongst themselves.'

'Beth.' Claire could see they were surprised by her tone. 'I'm glad I knew, and I think I would have figured it out anyway, how you felt, it has never let you go, the guilt of it all, of Tom losing his mother and your dad losing his wife, it wasn't your fault, sometimes shit happens, it is what it is, and no one can go back to change it, certainly not you. You were a kid, and you lost your mum. It's hard, and you know I know how hard it is. Tom was young and you were there for him or tried to be, what you must try to remember are the positives.'

'I almost killed him too, the day I posted the first letter, I almost killed my little brother.'

Claire gasped and couldn't hide it, Beth was hallucinating now, and Claire looked at JJ to try and judge her thoughts. Every letter ran through Claire's head as she tried to work out what Beth was saying or how she had come to this conclusion.

'Beth, come on now, where is this coming from? You must talk now.'

'I want to sleep and be by myself, I know you both want to help but I need some time to adjust, get used to it being a singular me.'

'Well, my dear, it won't be happening anytime soon, look at you Beth, would Marcus expect you to be like this, no he wouldn't. He would expect his Beth to be sad, yes very sad, but also for her to be looking around and making valid decisions.' Beth went to speak, and Claire put up her hand. 'No Beth, you know I am right, you have had nearly three weeks by yourself and when we arrived I did wonder if you had even showered at all,' Claire screwed up her nose. 'I know you are low, but you talked about this, with us a bit, and with Marcus, he must have thought you were ready Beth, and I'm sorry he is not coming back, I truly am, but his time was up, Marcus was done with this world, you know it, you know he would have hated wasting away in a hospital, full of painkillers with no quality of life. You knew the plan and you can't change it now, but eventually it was going to happen.' Claire's angry tone made Beth raise her voice.

'I wanted him to stay, how dare he not give me a clue the time was up, how dare he. When I walked in, it was such a shock, I had things to tell him about my day and now he will never know. I didn't think, I walked away, like he had told me to do. Walk away Beth, let me go, don't worry I won't involve you. Over and over, he would say it and even in the end he did not even have to use the words, because I could see the pleading in his eyes. Part of me hates him for leaving, I wish I had never heard his breath, I wish he had just been dead so there were no doubts and I had not had to choose. Shutting the door will haunt me for the rest of my life and he did this to me, so he could selfishly remove himself from my life, what if he made a mistake, what if it wasn't meant to be that day and he made a mistake, it's happened before, the medications, the injections become so routine, day in day out, so routine, maybe he didn't look, he left the flowers on the table, maybe he was distracted, maybe I'd put them in the wrong pile in the fridge or knocked them over and not looked as I straightened them up, what if I did it Claire, what if I did? If he had warned me I would know the truth, but now, now I don't know. I honestly don't know if it was the day he planned.'

As Claire leaned in to reassure her, Beth pushed her away angrily. It was like a drum roll as Beth's emotions spilled out, rumbling towards her, a steady beat gaining crescendo full of anger and regrets mixing with the pain she felt in her heart.

'Don't start Claire, you think I don't know, I do.'

Claire felt angry, Beth had worked out all the excuses, planning in these last weeks for every question they may ask so she could respond and push them away and retreat into the cocoon in which she wanted to hide. Over my dead body, Claire thought, it may be early days, but I will not let her sink or push me away, I will not fail, not now when they need me the most.

'You can sit there all high and mighty Claire, but you weren't there, I heard his breath and now I think I was wrong, he was trying to call for help, I know he was, he wanted to stay, stay with me and I walked away. It was me he loved, not you, it was me who wanted him to stay.'

Finally Beth broke, the anger dropped from her voice and the tears fell. Her sobs were loud, filling the room with their mournful sound. JJ leaned forward and rubbed her leg and Claire let a tear fall in relief, to reach the bottom was to start the long climb to the top and she would not let her slip back now. For all they had been through it was Beth who mattered the most, Claire had to save her, to pay her back for all the times Beth had been there for her, for giving her a connection at the age of nine and never letting it go.

Claire's phone buzzed and she clicked the power button to silence it. It vibrated and she could see her daughter had left a message. Quickly she texted back to reassure her Auntie Beth was ok and the funeral had gone well before turning it off. Claire wanted no distractions once Beth calmed, and the talking began.

Claire waited for the sobs to subside and the steadiness to return to Beth's breathing. The smell of the casserole made her stomach grumble and she looked to JJ who was stony faced and in a world of her own, her eyes almost as empty as Beth's. Claire had thought it would be hard, but JJ was like a statue, the shock of it all seeming to be too much for her to take. Claire had always known Beth and JJ had a special bond but had thought at least a part of JJ would be present enough to help Beth work her way through the grief, it seemed Claire had been wrong. Rising she set the table and laid out the meal. The quiet in the room was so alien to her, none of them had ever been short of a word and often had so much to say they talked over each other in a rush to fill the others in on their news.

The nourishment somehow lifted the mood, even though Beth still looked angry, and JJ's silence hung over them all. Memories clouded Claire's mind, both happy times and sad, so many memories which had brought them here, and as open as they had been, secrets still wove themselves around the three of them. Claire hoped some would stay hidden, because she knew the ones she had held back could tear them apart forever.

Chapter Thirteen

JJ

Dear god Claire what are you thinking???

Well of course I will be there but really, who is this guy, hope it's not the joker from down the street! What are you thinking? You know I will tell you straight. I know you miss your family, especially now your brother and sister are overseas, but this Johnno, is he the one? The man of your dreams? Don't jump in too quick is all I ask, wait a bit, your career is starting to take off, I'm so proud of you, I even saw it in the paper over here, I sent the clipping. I nearly jumped out of my skin, Mum wondered what I was shouting about and when I showed her she cried too. She is so famous and to say Dress designed by Claire, Sydney Australia. It's classy, to have your first name. I said to mum look at all the famous people who use one name, there is Cher and Marilyn, well we all know it's Monroe, but you have only to say her first name and everyone knows who you mean. Claire 'Designer to the stars.' Anyway, you are going so well, do you have to get married now? How hard is he looking for work, don't gloss over this Claire like you tend to do, and tell us all the shiny surface shit you want other people to hear, is it safety you need or security, is this what your mum and dad would love for you. Convince me this marriage is made in heaven because I know who the ones will be to pick you up if it fails!!! There, nothing I wouldn't say to your face but please take a step back and make sure this is what you want. If you are happy then I am too but please get a pre-nuptial agreement, I saw it on the news, all the celebrities do it now and I asked my dad and he said it sets out who gets what if they separate, and the house doesn't belong to you entirely. Are you willing to risk your inheritance and all the money you have paid back to the bank already? Think about it Claire, pleeeeeaaaasssse.

Now about the dress, if this all goes ahead my mum has a dressmaker so she is going to take me to get proper measurements and I will send them. I'm not sure about the hat but if it's ok with Beth, and you want it, I'll wear it. I've had my rant, I'm happy if you are happy Claire, I love you and I truly want the best for you. Now Beth, what if we come a bit early for the wedding so we can have some time before she flies off on a honeymoon... You've never had sex Claire??? God we all confessed, just do it, at least you will know if you want to do it again with him, after you sign the papers it will be a bit late, waiting until you are married is so old-fashioned Claire, get with the times.

Anyway, Beth, I was thinking after the wedding if you can work it, we might go on a trip as we've always talked about, Dad's a bit worried about us backpacking but said he will help with some accommodation and petrol costs if we take your car. I'd have about a month to spare, and do you think we can go and see that big rock of yours or even Darwin? Is it too far?. Thought I'd plant the seed, it would be good, and I've been camping before so happy to sleep in a tent and we can cook over a fire as well when we aren't staying in cabins. The outback seems so exotic, and I would love to see the red dirt, I don't believe it's true, I think they must gloss the photos to attract the tourists, but I think we could have so much fun. Please say yes Beth, I know you would hate all the dirt and dust Claire, so I don't feel bad at all about not asking you and anyway you will be away probably making babies somewhere.

Gosh I've said a lot today, I miss you both so much. All is good with me, I too have met a boy, not one I would marry but I'm going to have some fun with him anyway. He makes me laugh and it's fun to hang out with him and have someone to go to hockey games and concerts with. I haven't even told him about you two as he is not important emotionally to me which shows how popular and shallow I am now ha! Will is good, he is about to graduate and has a lovely new girlfriend, he is going to make the best physiotherapist, he has been through so much yet still wants to give back to others. Must go, Buck, yes his real name ((and he is very good at what it rhymes with) ha-ha Claire I can see you blushing from here). Hope the return letter tells me you have done the deed and are still committed to tying the knot.

Much love my besties xxx JJ

JJ felt like she was in a trance, the funeral had come and gone, and she felt like she was trying, although in reality it was her head which was running in circles, and her body in contrast, was moving in slow motion. JJ had been restless after they arrived, the shock of seeing Beth so crushed had been hard and as Beth had slept, both herself and Claire had nodded off at times or wandered the house like restless tigers in a cage. JJ had touched items in the house, lifting photo frames for a closer look, opening drawers for the want of something to do, stickybeaking yet with an absent mind as to what she saw. The desk drawer had been skewed so it wouldn't properly close. JJ had wriggled it open, to straighten it and push it back in. Beth's unfinished letter to them had caught and slid out with the drawer as she moved it. Now JJ wished she had not looked, yet it was the familiar paper Beth used which made her instinctively pick it up. Unthinking, her eyes had skimmed down the page and Beth's words did not really surprise her ... *He's gone. I feel so angry, why him, after everything it took to find him and in a heartbeat he is gone. Who decides this, is this your god Claire, if it is I hate him, I hate him with all my being. Don't come, I don't want to see you, either of you. I mean it Claire!*

This was why they had come, so Beth would push them away with all her might, knowing they would be there to catch her as she fell, and in her dark moments, be able to argue she had told them not to come. It was always her defence. When others stayed away Beth achieved her goal, put another brick in her wall to hide behind and protect herself from harm, emotional harm she was not prepared to confront or feel. JJ and Claire had never let her do it to them, each time they tore it down and made her confront her fears and move on knowing they were there to support, as she had done for them. JJ was lucky, her scars were literally skin deep, Claire was not far behind, her determination to succeed as her mother had wished had always allowed her to eventually propel forward and dismiss a past she could not change. Beth's scars reached down to her very soul, and she had held them there to rub and irritate so she would always have something to fight against or to hold up as an excuse.

Attempting to slide the letter back into place it had caught on another, its envelope was screwed, and the few pages folded together with it, had scrunched up at the back of the drawer. Pulling it out JJ unfolded them to straighten it out, she had nearly dropped them when heavily written words flew up at her from the page.

I know it will shatter you Beth, but I beg you, don't let it, a thousand times I tried to tell you, and if it wasn't for the child I might never have. I know this is the coward's way, to leave and then confess but I love you so, you have been the light of my life and I would never have traded a second of it, of what we had. You enriched my life in a way I never thought possible. I love you Beth and if I can reach out from the grave to find a way back to you I will. Please forgive me, you were the only one I ever wanted Darling, for me you were always enough. Forever yours Marcus

JJ had slumped into the chair. Part of her wanted to shove it back in as far as she could, yet to unsee it was something she could now never do. The pages had begun to separate, and she'd gathered them and laid them as flat as possible on the desktop, rubbing her hands up and down them in an attempt to iron them out. Claire's hand on her shoulder startled her and she had jumped at the touch.

'Sorry, I didn't mean to startle you. What are you doing?'

'Geez Louise, don't do that to me Claire, you frightened the living daylights out of me.'

'Sorry, sorry, sorry, I thought you would hear me coming.' JJ had snatched up the letter and folded it.

'What is it?' Claire looked puzzled.

'Nothing, it's personal, for Beth. It was stuck in the drawer so it wouldn't close, I was straightening it out so I could fold it better. How is she?'

JJ was happy to divert Claire's attention, she wanted some time to read the rest of the letter and hopefully find out more before having to share. Part of it was to protect Beth in case she overheard them talking about it, and the other part was a bit guilty she was going to pry into something she had no right to be doing. Back in the lounge room as Claire set the table for dinner, JJ's mind had whirled in confusion. He had a child, what was he thinking, is this why Beth was so tight inside, wound up so her grief could not be released as it was so encased in anger. JJ knew how much Beth had wanted a child, someone to love and raise with all the love she felt she had missed as a child. If Marcus had a child and hadn't told her, it would be the betrayal and the cover up all these years not the act of producing it which would hit her the hardest. JJ had sat like a stone, restraining herself from running back to grab the letter and read it out, show Beth she knew and tell her they could work it out, JJ wanted to so badly, yet held back, angry herself at Marcus.

They had been friends, it had been hard not to be, Marcus's acceptance of them all from the very start had won them over, somehow he had understood their need of each other and the role each of them played. JJ remembered the laughter when he had come to stay the first time, the love they both shared for Beth had bound them together, just as it had with Will and the girls when they met, they immediately were family. When Beth had been low he had known how to transmit his concerns to JJ with a single look, when he knew she needed more than himself he had stepped back and accepted both JJ and Claire's interference in his life, no questions asked. Marcus' betrayal of Beth was a betrayal to them all and JJ was feeling the hurt.

They had eaten the meal in silence, the glaze in Beth's eyes hiding her emotions from them. JJ knew Claire was trying her hardest to bring them out, her light chatter becoming irritating to JJ ears making her snap replies. Claire soon too, retreated into silence and JJ felt a huge weight hang over them, the cloud which hung over Beth spread its gloom into each of them. Pushing back her chair JJ excused herself and going via the office entered the bathroom locking the door firmly behind her. Sitting on the closed toilet seat she wondered why she was delaying, the weight of the knowledge the letter contained could change everything and the decision was harder than she would have ever imagined. The strong forthright JJ who had always faced adversity straight on even when the bullies had torn at her soul, was being crushed by the guilt she was feeling.

Letters had always brought JJ joy, from the very first with Beth's cat's paw prints on the envelope, each one over the years had brought her friendship and love no matter its contents. The paper made a crinkling sound, and she glanced up quickly double checking the door was locked, the sound echoing in the quiet room seemed louder than it really was. JJ realised her hands were shaking. Geez, she thought, do it, rip the band aid off and get on with it, you can't change the truth now she scolded herself, and better to know than not to know. One finger slid over the other, fingers crossed just in case, with a deep breath JJ put the pages in order and hoped what she would learn, would help her save her friend.

My Darling Beth,

I know how sad you are, please be strong my love, it is what I wanted, my life was rich because of you, and it is those mem- ories I never wanted tarnished by the wasting away of the body in which they're held. Please remember Beth, it is the greatest gift you gave by allowing me to live and die on my terms. I know Claire and JJ will be with you soon, and I feel comforted by the support they will be. They too were my family and if it is allowed wherever I am going, I will miss them, but you most of all. I am glad now we discussed this letter, I didn't know if I could, if someone found it, would it be evidence of what I have done, not just a terrible accident? What would it change for you if people knew it was my wish, I have thought long and hard and from as many angles to reach my decision and one burden has weighed upon me, a confession I never told, something I have kept from you when honesty was always what held us together. I have a child.

JJ almost felt sick, the contrast of the love he portrayed and these four small words, I have a child, which would tear Beth apart. JJ's mind filled with all the questions she wanted answers to, and the many more she knew Beth would have.

I know it will shatter you Beth, but I beg you, don't let it, a thousand times I tried to tell you, and if it wasn't for the child I might never have. I know this is the coward's way, to leave and then confess but I love you so, you have been the light of my life and I would never have traded a second of it, of what we had. You enriched my life in a way I never thought possible. I love you Beth and if I can reach out from the grave to find a way back to you I will. Please forgive me, you were the only one I ever wanted Darling, for me you were enough. Forever yours Marcus.

JJ sat stunned, Marcus of all people, it felt hard to believe and yet, somehow the truth settled quickly upon her, and she had no doubt about his words. JJ wanted to feel angry, to rage and storm at the way he had left this to be told, the coward's way, giving Beth no answers as to how or when this child came about. It puzzled her, there must be more, it was Marcus, and he would have to tell it all. For some reason he had told, and to tell would be to give at least Beth a clue to follow. Claire rattled the door.

'Are you nearly finished in there JJ?'

'Be right out,' JJ called back. JJ folded the letter and slipped it into her pocket. Flushing the toilet and making all the appropriate noises as if she was really using the facilities, JJ opened the door to Claire crossing her legs and bouncing up and down.

'Sorry, but I'm busting.'

'No worries, I seem to be doing everything in slow motion. Thanks Claire for all you are doing, I know I haven't been much help.'

'Can we talk later JJ, I'm well, you know, I have to go.'

JJ paused at the office door, glancing back in case Claire had been super quick. There had to be more, she thought, there must be an explanation of where this child was and most of all the reason why he had told. A noise from the other direction startled her and in the dimness of the hall Beth emerged, her hair ruffled, her eyes ablaze.

'Leave it JJ, I mean it, I can tell you found it but leave it, it's none of your business.'

'What else do you know Beth, there must be more, tell me, spit it out.'

'Leave it JJ, I'm warning you and while you are at it you can pack your bags and go. I don't want you here, or Claire, you can take her too. I want everyone to go and leave me alone.'

'Where's the rest Beth, Marcus would not have told half a story, why now, what does he want you to do?'

'You think I'm sad JJ, I'm sad, I'm so sad he is not here I can hardly function, and JJ if he was here, I'd be gone, long gone. A child JJ, he had a child and he never said, he knew, he knew how much I longed for one. You know how I did, how hard I tried and the heartache each time I failed. He said it didn't matter, he said, he was happy just with me.'

Beth's shoulders began to shake, and JJ saw her lean toward the wall seeking its support. Large tears balanced on her lashes resisting the fall, yet knowing they had to as the well of them behind was banking up, straining for release. It was both anger and grief, rolled so tight in a ball inside her twisting and turning so Beth could not distinguish one from the other. JJ stepped toward her.

'Beth, he loved you, there must be a reason he told you, tell me the rest Beth, I'll help you, you know I will, we all will.'

JJ reached out for her, hoping this was the moment when Beth would break, the moment she had reached the very bottom of her dark depths and the moment they could start to pull her free or at least towards the surface and back to them again. Claire stepped out of the bathroom and Beth turned into the wall the sobs shaking her body and her mouth filling with the falling tears.

'Get out, both of you. I don't want your help and I don't need your help.'

Beth fled into her room slamming the door so hard the pictures on the walls rattled. JJ heard the bed squeak as Beth flung herself upon it. Claire was looking at her with wide eyes, the venom in Beth's voice not lost on either of them.

'At least she looked a bit animated, as if she is starting to feel. I'll take this any day over the empty vessel I've been trying to reach out to.' Claire seemed to take what she had witnessed as a positive and JJ held her tongue, not yet ready to reveal the letter or its contents to Claire.

'Come on, let's have a cuppa as you call it Claire, I don't think she has any sharp objects in there so we should be safe for tonight.'

JJ sighed, Claire for all her fame and outward worldliness, was still the gullible nine-year-old she had first gotten to know by mail, and the look of astonishment on her face at this moment pealed back the years in the blink of an eye.

'I was joking Claire, dear god do you still not know when I'm being glib? Come on, maybe we should have something stronger than tea.'

Chapter Fourteen

Beth

Hi girls,

Wow, I can't believe you have been married for five years, the wedding seems like it was yesterday Claire, and now we are having another! All because of me of course, JJ and I's little jaunt to the outback after your wedding and me pushing her in the back to talk to the cute guy at the pub, who knew? I deserve to be MC as well as the bridesmaid at this one. I can't wait to be together again, sometimes I want to ditch the letter writing and call you, but I do love what we have. Do you think we should go to this new electronic mail as you would get my news straight away and I could send it to you both at the same time? I'm getting pretty skilled at computers and guess what.... drum roll please.... I landed the Sunday life column for the Adelaide tribune!!!! So excited! I have free range on topics so it can be political, though they will probably want to rein me in a bit there, or social events, current affairs, even fiction pieces. Don't worry JJ it won't stop me from coming over, as I can submit from wherever I am, you do have a modem I can use don't you? It seems our lives are all coming together at last my friends, Claire a mum, JJ with the man of her dreams and my dream job falling in my lap. Anyway, must go, can't wait to see your faces, don't be scared JJ but we have the best ever hen's night planned, so get your dancing shoes on.

Love, Love, Love to you both,

Beth.

PS How is little Paul going? It must be tough with the big show coming up, so I hope Johnno is helping for once. How do you feel honestly Claire, is this baby going to save your marriage? I can't wait to see you in Canada for JJ's wedding, are you still breast feeding? I hope so, you will fill out the dress nicely if you are. Ha, I can see you blushing from here. There done, bye.

PPSS:: JJ should I bring warm clothes as well? Can't wait to meet Will after all this time so good he is walking you down the aisle, with your dad gone it will feel like he is with you as well.

Beth knew she had been harsh, she felt crushed but raising her voice and slamming the door had given her a strength to start fighting back. What should she do though? Reveal all to JJ and Claire, air her dirty linen as they say, for them both to see? Why had Marcus told her, she wanted to march down to the cemetery and demand he come back to life to explain his actions. Beth needed to know why, she needed every detail, every moment so she could tear him apart, claw his eyes and weep until no tears remained. Beth wanted him to see how much he had hurt her, by his betrayal, and also by him running away, taking the easy way out, being a coward and killing himself so he would not have to tell this news to her face. Beth was angry, a stage of grief she knew would come, but the simmering of it, above all else from the start, had clouded anything good they'd had. In a few words he had destroyed her memories and raised doubts about every moment they had spent together.

Beth could see by the look on JJ's face, she didn't understand, how could she, she hadn't seen the final page, the page with the details of the child and his wishes for her, and for Beth to associate with her. It was almost cruel Beth thought, to tell her, she wanted to know, and yet didn't. Marcus would have known. If he had told her the news, and not the details, eventually she would have searched, deep down she knew she would have, yet by telling, he was also destroying everything she had, every relationship, every memory, every emotion. Beth wasn't sure she could live in this void. JJ was trying to pull her out of it, yet still she clung to the depression which had disguised itself as being a friend. Anger was fighting it, waking her up to move on, forgive and continue with life, but still she resisted, sadness was comforting, it held her, allowed her to resist the outside world to wallow in her pain and self-interest and make all her thoughts real, to be truth with no substance.

Beth could hear the girls talking, the low murmur of their voices drifting down the hall and winding under her door. She wanted them here, yet didn't, she feared JJ's honesty and as for Claire, her fragility was irritating, it crawled on Beth's skin like a rash. Claire's sadness, beauty and fame automatically made her the centre of attention, when it should have been Beth. Beth was the important one this time, and as each of the mourners had turned their eyes to glimpse the immaculately dressed woman they had seen on the news or in a magazine, more beautiful in real life than they had imagined, Beth had felt like slapping her, calling out to them all, this is about me, not her, I'm the one who lost, this is my day not hers.

The bedsheets felt crumpled and sticky, Beth realised they had not been changed since he left, at first she had wanted the smell of him to stay, so she could drift into sleep pretending he was coming back, would be home soon. After the letter she had fought him in her sleep, raged and kicked, tossed and turned, the souring smell of him allowing her to keep her anger directly focused on Marcus and his deceit. JJ's loud laugh echoed in the quiet house and the old Beth wanted to go and join in, forget these last weeks and be the same as before, share all the emotions she was feeling, she hated the war within herself, to give in to life or sit with darkness by her side. Each was hard work and every bone in her body longed for sleep to take her away from the choice. A tiny bit of her never wanted to wake.

Chapter Fifteen

Claire

Dear Beth and JJ,

The time seems to fly away and as much as I try to catch it and tell it to wait, it hurries by and disappears. Look at us three married ladies. I am a bit cross at you Beth, and Marcus too, sneaking away and not letting us come too. I am so glad you are happy Beth, it was written all over your face in the photo you sent, and it was your day after all and so romantic to elope on a tropical island. I wish you so much happiness, you deserve it and tell Marcus he always has a room here when he is in town on business. (He might motivate Johnno to do something!) What can I say, I am so busy at work, I love it but some days these brides do my head in, chopping and changing their minds and the emotion, goodness, there is way too much of it, do they think I would let them out on their wedding day in something less than stunning. I had a call from a tv show, they are going all out and having a week of episodes with the main character's wedding, and they want me to design it. They need two, one to almost destroy, and the main one which will be featured in their magazine deals and the newspapers. It is pretty exciting, and I get to go on set to do all the fitting on the day and go to the magazine shoots as well. Johnno said I shouldn't be fooling around with all the society stuff, he thinks it will go to my head, but it is such a great way to finally step into the international market. This show goes to fifty-four countries! I couldn't buy advertising like it! Johnno thinks I should be happy with the local scene and the occasional pop-princess, but I want to work with quality not quantity, you know I'd rather spend months on one dress than churning out a hundred in the same amount of time, I don't think he gets I am a designer not a manufacturer, sometimes I wonder if he understands what I do at all.

He has stopped going to the shows and gala events now and I can't say I'm sorry, is it wrong to say Johnno is a bit lower class to be there? I don't want to sound like a snob, but he thinks it is a place to drink at and then acts like a yobbo, it gets a bit embarrassing to be honest. I wish he would look after Paul more, but they seem to spend a lot of time with his mother and I'm not sure if she is the influence I want on my child. It is so hard being a working mother trying to weigh up what is for the best but at the moment I am the breadwinner, the one putting food on the table so at least my baby is nourished. To be honest I'm thinking of putting him into one of those new day-care places, at least he could play with other children and the caregivers are qualified to look after children, I'm not so sure his father is. Johnno's parents are retiring and moving to the Queensland, and I am actually glad! There, I've said it, I am feeling uneasy about the future because the one I see, doesn't seem to contain Johnno. You are probably dancing around the room by now JJ hearing this and I can see now I should never have married him but at least I have Paul and I would secretly (between us) like to give him a sibling. Johnno is never going to work in a real job, and I have given him plenty of room and money to make something of himself, but I can see he will never change and nothing I do will change him either, he is using me, and I think the time is coming where I won't take it anymore. Don't worry you don't have to rush over here I'm still in the realising stage and I will try to save my marriage ... there has never been a divorce in our family ... but I wanted to talk about it with you both and once again seek your advice, well Beth's advice because I think I know yours JJ. Other than wishing I wasn't married, all is good, I'll let you know when the tv show airs.

Much love xx Claire.

Claire knew JJ was hiding something. Beth was deep into the angry stage, and they had decided to leave her alone for a while. Claire desperately wanted to go in and sit with her, stroke her hand and reassure her it would all be ok, but JJ said to leave her, and Claire knew it was a command not a request. Beth would come out in her own time, whatever had fired her up tonight would wane and the exhaustion would break her down again. JJ produced some wine, and they gulped the first glass down in silence. As it mellowed their thoughts, Claire hoped JJ would fill her in on the discussion in the hall, she knew they hadn't always told her everything, but Claire was determined now to be included, she was a grown up after all and at their age it was time to say every truth they felt. A tiny snake of guilt slithered across her spine as she remembered the times she had held back, buried a secret hoping they would never find out or talk behind her back and know she was not the person they thought she was. Claire would not have survived without these girls, but there were times she had struggled with them. Beth and JJ had always seemed so self-assured, confident of who they were and their place in the world whilst all the time propping her up as Claire felt like she bumbled through life.

JJ started reminiscing, sharing the highs and lows of their lives, it was a time to share and remember the times they were together and those spent with Marcus, Jim and even rare moments with Johnno. Claire wished Beth would come out as they laughed and cried, it was a time to be shared, and for Beth to remember the good times. JJ refilled the glasses and Claire ignored each time she replaced the bottle with a fresh one. It felt good, right to be talking and letting tiny pieces of Marcus move on to where he had to be, remembered with love while still being missed terribly. As the wine loosened her tongue Claire felt the courage to ask JJ to include her in the conversations from here on end, whatever had upset Beth, Claire was here to be the strong one and she couldn't help if she did not know the problem. As she went to speak, JJ chuckled over the time herself, Jim and Beth had surprised Marcus on his business trip for his birthday, the look on his face as he had opened the door at Claire's home to be bombarded with balloons, gifts, hugs, kisses, cake and champagne, along with their three excited faces.

'We even surprised you, the look on your faces was priceless,' JJ giggled.

Claire's mind flew back. Marcus had been shocked, the excitement of the three of them at achieving the surprise had covered the terror Claire felt. She had been in her room straightening the bed when she heard the doorbell. Her first thought was she hoped Marcus was dressed, her second was relief she always made him put his clothes and toiletries in the spare room and the third was thank goodness they hadn't arrived ten minutes earlier or they may not have been able to answer the door or wanted to. Claire felt the heat rise up her neck and hoped it didn't reach her cheeks, tonight was not the night to confess her friendship with Marcus or their affair which had spanned for over a decade.

Claire zoned in again as the silence echoed around the room, JJ was looking at her with inquisitive eyes, squinting as if trying to reach into Claire's mind to read her thoughts.

'Are you still with us Claire, where did you go?' Claire wrung her hands and reached up to rub her neck.

'Nowhere, I was remembering too. Marcus was so surprised, what a great night it turned out to be. I remember I had been worrying it was his birthday and he was stuck in Sydney for work, I also remember being a bit cross you hadn't told me, I could have helped with the surprise.'

'No, you wouldn't have Claire, it's why we didn't, you would have worried so much you would have given the game away, Marcus would have guessed something was up. You two certainly did look surprised though.' Claire felt the heat rise and there was nothing she could do about it as the blush continued up her cheeks and her forehead burned red. JJ was staring at her now and Claire's mind tumbled around as she tried to find a reply.

'We, I, we were surprised, oh all this wine is going to my head, do you feel hot JJ?'

JJ was staring and Claire became more and more flustered, the words spilling from her mouth not even making sense to her as she tried to cover her deceit.

'It was you.'

'Me? What do you mean? Really JJ I think we had better call it a night, Beth will need us tomorrow and we have to try and get her to start looking towards living again, the two of us with a hangover will be no help.' Claire rose from the chair and attempted to tidy the table.

'You slept with Marcus didn't you, I can tell, whoa!' JJ put her elbows on the table and held her head up with both hands, a look of disbelief on her face. 'Geez, geez, geez Louise it seems so clear now, the look on your faces, it wasn't surprise, it was shock, no it was guilt! Oh my god Claire, Marcus? Of all the people, and how have you kept this a secret, you can never keep secrets Claire, how did I not know?'

'Shh! She'll hear you. It happened the one time, ... you all turned up and I ..., I knew it was wrong, but it was a weak moment, and he was so kind, and I was, well I knew it was over with Johnno and I would not be asking him back. JJ, I missed having a man around and it happened, and I felt so bad, and you can't tell Beth, no matter what. Promise me JJ, please promise not to tell.'

Claire was on her knees now, begging for JJ to stay true, to see by telling, would not benefit anyone, not now. Beth would not have Marcus to blame, and Claire could not lose her friends, not over this, not after all this time. Claire's heart was breaking inside as she pleaded for JJ to hold her secret. A noise behind made her turn, Beth was at the door, one hand clutching the jamb to steady herself, pale as a ghost was the term anyone would have used to describe her drawn and haggard face.

'Get out. How could you. How dare you, get out of my house now, I never want to see you again. Ever. Do you hear me Claire. Ever.' Beth's voice was low, her jaw clenched tight as the words escaped like a slow growl.

Claire stood up and stepped toward Beth, her mind was swirling, this was her worst nightmare, Beth was never meant to know, how could she have let this happen.

'No Beth please, let me explain, it was nothing, a mistake, we both knew it. Marcus, ... we never meant to hurt you, it just happened ...please Beth you're upset, we all are, and ...' Beth's palm hitting her face stunned her, Claire put her hand up to cover the sting as tears sprung to her eyes.

'No, Beth please, I'm sorry, so sorry, please forgive me, Beth.'

Beth stood firm, her hands now on her hips as the shock of hearing their conversation sank in and anger rose.

'Get out.' Beth's clenched teeth barely moved as the words snapped the air. JJ stood, not knowing which one to comfort first.

'Go to your room Claire, let me talk with her, go, give her some space and I'll come get you when we are ready to talk.' Claire felt JJ's arm across her back as she nudged her gently towards the door. Stumbling she made it to the hall and used the walls to guide her as the emotions overwhelmed her and the tears began to fall. It was not meant to be like this, you are so stupid Claire, she thought, all these years and tonight of all nights is the night you make a mistake, what a fool you are. The few seconds, which had now turned her world upside down, swirled in her head. Claire flung herself on the bed as the sobs came thick and fast. As Claire's body racked itself with grief and torment, all she could think clearly was, thank goodness she had not told the whole truth.

Chapter Sixteen

JJ

Dear lovelies,

I never knew my life could be so full, being with Jim makes me so happy, and I even think Will is a little jealous all my affections are no longer for him. My mother always told me I would fall in love one day with the perfect man, I wish she was here to meet him. Yes Claire I am counting my blessings, all your yoga, mystic stuff is rubbing off on me. We are enjoying Darwin, bloody hot but it has such a relaxed feel it is hard not to enjoy. As a Canadian the temperature change is certainly extreme! I am so happy for you Beth, I wondered if you were keeping a secret, too many sunny letters gave you away. I think Marcus is super and the perfect man for you. Jim's contract here has been extended to three years and so there is plenty of time for us to organise an outback trip for you all. Now we will have to juggle the men's schedules as well, but I think the dry season (it's what they call winter here) is probably the best. I realise you probably knew all this, but I love learning about the diverseness of your country. I miss Will terribly, but his wife Jen is so terrific, and I couldn't ask for a better sister-in-law, they are perfect for each other.

Beth, remember the barmaid the night we rolled into the pub in Bourke, where we met Jim? I ran into her, yes quite literally, and she remembered me, and you as well. She had seen the article you did about our trip and really enjoyed it. I'm meeting her for a coffee later, it would be good to have a girlfriend up here to connect with. This girl, Lisa, said you should write a book. I think it's a great idea, you have such a way with words across so many subjects and it could be something you could do on all those boring plane trips you have to go on, I swear I don't know when you and Marcus will see each other, though I suppose it will be like a honeymoon every time you do.

Claire, I can almost read your mind, yes all this love is making me soft, but if you must we will support you no matter what decision you make. I want you to make the right decision for you and if divorcing from Johnno is the answer, so be it. At least he gave us little Paul and as I say, people can be in your life for a short time, a long time or a reason and the blessing of Paul is the only reason I have ever seen in your union. (See, I am hiding in here still and will always be honest with you.) I do have one request; remember I asked you to think about getting married and you didn't listen? Well, please think about this, is another baby for Paul? Or for you? Feeling the way you are, could you do it? I don't know I could, and Claire, it could take months to fall pregnant. Eww, just saying.

Must go, love, love, love xx JJ.

JJ's mind was all over the place. When she turned back Beth hadn't moved, and her body was tense.

'Sit Beth,' she urged placing her arms around Beth's shoulders. 'Sit so we can talk, come on.' Beth's face was rigid, but she was grinding her teeth unconsciously from side to side. JJ was relieved when she moved forward and sat down at the table. Grabbing a fresh glass JJ filled it to the top with the ridiculous thought if she got Beth drunk enough, she may not take to Claire with one of the kitchen knives. Her second thought was ... it might make her grab two!

'Beth, think this out,' she urged while thrusting the glass into her hand and raising it towards Beth's mouth. 'Wait to hear the whole story, Claire has had a lot to drink, it has been a big day, don't make decisions now which can't be undone. Beth, Beth are you listening.'

Beth nodded weakly and took a sip as she closed her eyes. JJ could see the fight draining out of her, and her mind raced with words which would clutch onto Beth, and not let her drain completely away to be an empty shell. Leaning forward she rubbed Beth's forearm.

'Beth, Beth, let's talk it out, it's like a double blow isn't it? First the letter and now this. Please don't blame Claire, be angry, be as angry as you like, but please hear her out. I know you feel like you have been betrayed from both sides, but please, let's mourn Marcus first and work out the rest later. Yes, he has betrayed you, and now we know it was more than once, the child, we can sort later, maybe he left another letter? Wait, please Beth, let's cry and grieve for the man we knew and leave the rest until we are sober. We love you Beth, Claire needs you, I need you. Don't leave us now, not over this.'

JJ bit her lip, halting herself from rambling, making it too complicated for Beth to comprehend. Beth raised weary eyes.

'How could they JJ, how could he do this, how could she, and they hid it, all this time.' A lone tear broke free and she let it fall. Crossing her arms in front of her on the table, JJ watched as Beth's head fell and the sobs wracked her body. Beth flinched as JJ rubbed her back, each circling movement giving comfort to JJ as her friend's anger finally broke into despair. Despair JJ could handle, it left a thread and JJ knew the strong Beth, the tough little nine-year-old would be there, hiding inside, waiting to push through back to the surface to find a purpose to hang on to. JJ's one wish was she hoped it was not to harm Claire.

Finally Beth raised her head. JJ thought if she wasn't sitting there, she would not have recognised her. Beth's face looked devoid of life, deep wrinkles, not visible earlier lined her face dragging it down to look long and haggard. JJ now knew what the bottom looked like, yet deep in Beth's eyes she could see her old self there. The Beth who knew the truth, knew she had to fight, knew she had to continue on with whatever else this life threw at her until her days were done, and JJ, with relief, knew they had turned the corner.

As sad as Beth was, JJ saw her eyes begin to clear and said a silent prayer of thanks to whichever God may be listening.

'JJ, I don't know what to do, everything I thought I knew, now seems wrong. I thought he loved me, he was my one, the only one, how could he, and how many more women did he have?' Even as the tears continued to roll, JJ could see the old Beth returning.

'I don't know Beth, we will probably never know, but remember, he always came home to you. You were his rock as much as he was yours, he always came back. Remember when you met?'

'Yes,' a small smile played across Beth's face. 'I thought he was way too handsome for me, the way he played around touching people on the arm, circling the room, he never took his eyes off me once he caught it, and I remember feeling like a silly teenager inside. Oh JJ, he was so good looking, and I was sure every girl there had more chance than me, when he slid in beside me I could have melted into the floor.'

Beth's eyes became dreamy as she remembered. Marcus always had an air about him, charming enough to make even JJ's heart skip a beat, yet genuine and kind, someone you always thought you could trust. From the moment he had captured Beth's heart they had all loved him, right away they had felt her settle, finding comfort with who she was and the course her life had taken. From her first letter about him JJ and Claire had loved him for giving their friend everything she had emotionally ever desired. JJ played through her mind every moment from the start, Marcus had said this, was it true? Beth said Marcus was spending a lot of time in Brisbane or Melbourne, Perth or Darwin, was it all business? Questions and conflicts raged as JJ tried to set them aside and keep Beth on the upward journey.

'I remember the time there was the plane strike, and I was trying to get to Claire, Charlotte had arrived early, and I was beside myself as I had promised to be there. Marcus hired a car and drove from Melbourne to be with her, and when I arrived I went straight to the hospital. Johnno came barging out the front doors, and he glared at me and started ranting and raving, throwing his arms about, security started to come closer, so he left. It was the last time he saw his daughter wasn't it, the first and last time?'

'Yes Beth, I remember. It was the best decision Claire ever made, to turf him out, he was a loser, a tosser is what Jim would say? Pregnant and brave was what she was, though he was gone before she found out Charlotte was on her way, I always thought it was lucky really, and once he found out she was not going to give him any more money he showed his true colours. You know, I have never wondered what happened to him because I never cared. Do you remember how he used to snarl at us behind Claire's back, he hated the influence he thought we had over her.' Beth's brows were drawn as the memory played out.

'He said something at the hospital, Johnno, he said, don't know why I bothered she isn't mine anyway.'

Beth raised her eyes and JJ could clearly see the question which now hung between them. In front of her JJ saw Beth shrink, her blouse seemed to have become two sizes larger with Beth the hanger holding it up. With sunken eyes, yet what, to JJ felt like acceptance of a past she could not change, Beth spoke the words JJ was not yet able to believe.

'He's Charlotte's father isn't he?'

Beth paused and JJ stared at her with wide eyes, not willing as yet to confirm, she too, had come to the same conclusion. The moments kept adding up in her head and the obvious lay between them.

'We don't know.'

'We do.'

'How could it be, how could they cover something like this up? All these years, how did they not give it away? Don't jump to conclusions Beth, Marcus we now know had something to hide but Claire! Claire would have broken, I'm sure she would have told me at least, Claire would never have coped if this is the truth, it would have eaten her up inside.'

'It's true, I see it now, maybe I always did and didn't want to recognise it, she is like him, I can't believe we didn't see it before. Think about it JJ, all the times we were together, and people would mistake him as her father, never Paul. No one ever said it about Paul looking like him, no one ever said to Jim about his daughter, or Will or any man for that matter, but they said it to Marcus all the time. Once when she was here a woman asked if she was his daughter by a first marriage as she looked nothing like me! The whole world could see it JJ, even stupid Johnno could see it in her face when she was a baby, how did we not? What a fool I've been.' Beth's eyes welled again, and she hung her head. 'A stupid gullible fool. Well, they got me, the biggest prank ever pulled, and they pulled the wool way down over my eyes.'

JJ was still stunned by the whole revelation and her own inability to see what had been going on right in front of them for so long. Why, why, why the one solitary question swirling in her head. Beth continued.

'It's not the act so much JJ, it's the betrayal, two of the people I love most in the world have lied to me for all these years, why didn't they say, we made a mistake, Charlotte is the result, and we could have all moved on, why JJ, dear god it's like a knife is twisting inside and it's unfair JJ, it's not fair. This is my time to grieve, not hers, this is mine.' Beth's voice disappeared in the sobs and all JJ could do was rub her back and murmur consoling words which had no chance of fixing the situation.

JJ wished Jim was here, it was almost too much, Claire had said it was her time to step up, be the strong one. JJ felt a wisp of anger begin to rise and she fought internally to contain it, this was no time to be angry, Beth would have enough for them all and yet all JJ could think was how could they, and conflictingly, how could they not tell her.

JJ felt stung, there were so many questions and so many answers they would never know or simply hear only Claire's version of. Claire, their Claire whom they had held so close at times, laughed with, shared with and all the while she was the sneak, the one they couldn't trust, how could JJ not have known, and how could Claire of all people not tell her. JJ felt so betrayed by them both, Marcus, her friend, her confidante when Beth was down and together they held her up, and all the while he had at best, been half in the game. Together they had been a force Beth couldn't refuse and he was like a brother to her, a friend so close JJ had even asked him once if he was adopted as well, as she secretly thought they might have been separated at birth, so tight was their bond, she called him her Australian brother, the one she needed when Will couldn't be around. Just once Claire had said, JJ didn't believe it, though Claire had looked so innocent, the lie sliding out like a well-rehearsed habit. The glances, the odd words now popped out of old conversations, tiny moments now exploding into a world bigger than the two people it had held. JJ felt the anger rise, it was too late for it, the time had passed, how old was Charlotte now, late twenties? It had all happened so long ago, was it worth the anger? Part of her thought it was.

JJ rubbed her eyes, this trip was too long, and she was too far away from the man she loved, she needed to talk with him while he held her so she could sort the confusion in her head.

'We need to sleep Beth, talk with Claire tomorrow, until we know for sure it is no use making it up, we have to wait.'

Beth looked at her and JJ could see how they had aged, their lives together reaching back so she could now not remember the time before they both were in her life. Before the first letter no longer existed as they became her lifeblood twisting and turning throughout her life, catching her up and carrying her until today. 'No matter what happens, nothing is going to change it and I think we must try to remember all we can do now is move forward from today.' Beth's eyes were dry.

'You know JJ, this morning I loved him, and I thought it was something you could never lose, but now, now I feel empty, like a vacant block, an empty stretch of land where nobody wants to live, not even me.'

JJ rose and put her arms out to Beth, together they stood feeling a comfort of sorts as JJ realised she too, felt drained of all emotion.

'Come on, maybe sleep might help, and if not, at least we might have some energy for what is to come.'

Together they shuffled down the hall and JJ laid with Beth until her breathing steadied and a faint snore escaped her lips.

The ceiling seemed to be closing in and JJ felt its invisible crushing weight. God damn you Claire, she thought, nearly fifty years and I still don't know who you really are, what else have you been hiding? JJ's eyes closed and she never heard Claire as she entered the room nor felt her tuck a blanket around them both.

Chapter Seventeen

Claire

Dear JJ and Beth,

Well, it's done, I am now officially a divorcee! Johnno has moved north to be near his parents, I told him he couldn't take the children out of the state, but he wasn't particularly interested in them anyway so unless they do well in life they will probably never see him again. When I told Paul his dad was moving away he didn't even look up from his toys and Johnno hasn't bothered to visit him since. I'm still not regretting the baby, it will be good for Paul to have a sibling and I know I'll be busy but it all somehow feels easier without him, I was always looking for his support and it never came so I no longer have to waste my energy there and can put it to better use. Also, his mother won't be butting in every ten minutes this time, so I am feeling quite relaxed about the whole deal. I can't wait to see you Beth, thank you so much for coming to look after Paul while I'm in hospital, Marcus is so great when he is here, doing little jobs for me and helping get the baby's room ready, I secretly hope his business trips to Sydney never end. I am so blessed to have you all in my life, my life would have been so very different without you.

My neighbour tells me there have been rumours around, what with Johnno leaving (well he was vocal about it, and me throwing the last of his belongings in the street did bring the sticky beaks out), and with my pregnancy now visible for all to see I suppose I can't expect people not to talk. She even asked me if Johnno was the father! Sounds like his mother talking, I said, well if you would like to see the video of the last wham, bam thankyou Mam, come right in and I'll show you. You should have seen her face, you would have been proud JJ, though I feel like everyone is looking at me every time I walk outside.

I'm sure this baby is a girl, and I am trying to give her all the courage she will need to get through life, if I start banking it for her now she will never have to worry, as you both know I have enough worry genes for ten people. Of course, she will have both of you to teach her and be strong for her. Paul is growing like a weed, and I must say Beth it was nice to have Marcus here for a few days, he is so kind and takes the time to play with him no matter how big a day he has had. The season has wound down and I will take on fewer jobs for the next one, I have enough money put aside (thanks for the offer JJ) and have interviewed a girl for an apprenticeship, now Maggie has stepped up into the manager's role for me, she will need a hand. I feel quite excited about everything in my life, getting Johnno out of my life, and my house, has been the best for me. I feel freer and more in control, though I think he has made me stronger, more able to speak my mind, which I could always do with my work mask on, yet never at home. I can see now how I was always searching for security, Johnno gave it to me while my confidence grew but, it is about all he did. I know, I know, groan, groan JJ, but it is true, and it is nice to be relaxing in these last weeks and making peace with my past so I can move on and give these children the best possible life.

So enough about me, fill me in. Beth, Marcus told me about the last IVF attempt, I am so sad for you. Each time I hear I want to fly over there and wrap my arms around you, It's not fair. When I see neglected kids in the city with drug addict parents screaming at them I feel like stealing them away and sending them to you. Imagine the life they could lead. Marcus didn't seem keen on adoption when I broached the subject but Beth how much more disappointment can you take, I worry about you so much. Please, please tell us how you feel xxx

I was thinking, once I'm settled with the bub in a routine, maybe we can have a meetup in Hawaii or Fiji? I read in the paper they have these kid's clubs now at resorts and they take the children for activities so the parents can relax, it's a great idea and I will so want you and Jim to meet Charlotte JJ, (what do you think of the name?) I was actually thinking Charlotte Elizabeth Janice. It sounded so grand when I added your names so I hope you don't mind, I want her always to know how important you were in my life and will be in hers. I will be at a loss if it is a boy I really don't mind either way, but I can't seem to settle on a perfect boy's name, maybe he is making me wait until I meet him to decide. Time to go, I miss you both so much and hang on to each minute until I see you again. Much Love and can't wait to see you Beth.

xxxxx Claire.

Claire heard Beth rustling around and closed her eyes pretending she was still asleep. Whether she was ready for today was something she did not want to think about yet. Today it could all end, and she would be the one who destroyed it. Part of her had known it was always coming, and to be honest, after each time they met, she had breathed a sigh of relief she still had more time with them.

Last night as silence stole its way around the house, Claire had checked in on Beth only to find JJ fast asleep beside her. Quietly she had tucked a blanket around them, a part of her wanting to climb in too and wake together in the morning to face the world as a united team. As she watched their faces soften in sleep, it seemed with each settling breath the years had peeled back to reveal the fresh young faces she had first seen so long ago in their teens. It had been with sadness she had turned away and padded softly to Beth's office to read the letter JJ had flattened, straightened and returned to its hiding place. If I had seen this earlier, if JJ had showed me, I could have been more prepared she had thought, again a moment in time, was about to change everything.

It had become easier over time, Johnno's noninterest in the children had helped her avoid having conversations about fathers as the girls had dismissed him from their lives the minute she had. Beth had been with her after the birth and Claire never knew how she couldn't see Charlotte was the living image of her father. Over the years it faded a bit, as Claire's features softened her tiny face, yet her height and stature were all him. With each letter she ever posted Claire had hesitated before dropping it in the slot, saying a silent prayer they would not, this time, read between the lines and see her guilt laying there. With each reply she breathed out with relief they hadn't. The guilt had been there, Marcus had held it too, yet somehow each time they had apologised for what they were about to do and after, for having done it. He had made her world and Claire would never be sorry for the gift he had given her in Charlotte, nor the time he had spent in her life.

Part of Claire had reasoned if Marcus was going to cheat on Beth, at least he had done it with someone who had Beth's best interests at heart, they had both agreed, once they thought it was affecting the girl's friendship or Marcus's marriage they would end it. It had seemed so simple.

After the first time had been when Claire felt the most guilt, she had even cried, cried for Beth, cried for Marcus and cried for herself. The guilt had overwhelmed her until she broke down and he held her in his arms once more. She could still remember the look and the way the world around them disappeared to be dealt with in another time, all in a single moment. As the children grew older they'd had to be more discreet, meeting in the city to share dinners and a motel in some high part of town. Claire always paid so no trace of the transactions could be found on him and as the years progressed their clandestine dates had added an extra element of excitement to their affair. Sometimes a social page would snap them together at a gala somewhere and Claire had become skilled at letting the girls know, always joking it was about time she borrowed JJ's husband for her some of her plus one society-dos, so as to give poor Marcus a break from their friend who could not find a date. Months had slipped by turning into years, Marcus had become a bit relaxed about it, but Claire always checked and double checked every detail and searched for every piece of evidence which may be screaming out for all to see and connect the dots.

At times when the steely core of Beth showed through, Claire had wondered if she knew. More and more she had met the others on their own, arranging girls' weekends in one state or another. It had been easier to hide it from JJ once her and Jim had moved back to Canada, get- togethers were scheduled and planned well in advance and surprise visits moved further apart. Marcus had the advantage of hearing secret plans and so after the first near miss, they felt quite safe as, if Beth was surprising him, Claire was in on the preparations and visa-versa for Marcus.

Claire remembered the day she missed her period. She had waited, half of her willing it to come, pleading with it until the test proved her fate, and still it had been the biggest shock. Not once had the thought crossed her mind not to go ahead with the pregnancy and at first she had kept it to herself trying to decide the best lie to tell. Should she tell Marcus it was Johnno's? Deep down she had always known she would let Johnno believe the baby was his, or should she tell him, throw caution to the wind and confess to them all and let Marcus decide his fate? In the end Marcus had guessed and together they decided to lie together, in every sense of the word.

Claire had slept with Johnno one last time to cover her tracks, before Marcus guessed. As Marcus ran his hands over the fulness of her breasts and the broadening shape of her hips, his eyes widening as the idea sunk in and he had looked at her incredulously for confirmation of his thoughts. She had already confessed to the girls of her last-ditch attempt to save her marriage to Johnno and the repulsion she had felt too late before the deed was complete. JJ's expletives at her foolish-ness had been like manna from heaven as they both believed it would be something silly old Claire would do. It also fired them up even more to protect her once she revealed the result of her liaison. Marcus had been harder to soothe, he had under-stood and, as his hands circled her body, she had confessed her attempt to cover their affair and told him her plans to raise his daughter on her own while the world acknowledged her as another man's child.

Claire remembered the moment, she had felt so strong, so confident of her future with or without him. Claire had felt every mother's power of a lioness to protect this child, even if it was from their own father. Marcus had agreed in the end, she had seen he was torn, it had been Beth who had wanted a child, yet now the child was his, she had seen he was thrilled, excited at the prospect of becoming a father. This baby had not brought endless injections and millions of tears, she had appeared, no drama, no anxious waiting for a tiny line to appear on endless tests, the twinkle in their eye had become a human being, growing strong inside Claire and she would defend her against all. To be honest Claire had never considered Marcus would leave Beth and had been shocked when he suggested it, a baby had been her focus, a sibling for Paul, the rest she had thought would run its course and fade away in time. Naïve it seemed now, but at the time Claire had been the strongest and most confident she had ever felt in her life, her business was thriving, her child healthy, her support network was strong and Johnno for all he didn't give her, had made her step up and she was determined never to go back to the person she had been when she married him. JJ and Beth had given her the encouragement to push forward with her career, while her skills and dedication for perfection learnt from her mother, had guaranteed her success.

The letters had masked her newfound confidence, the lies and silliness of the old Claire had been the perfect cover. She was still the worrier of the unimportant, but not as much as she let on. The mask she pulled on for work now had a twin, though this one was of her old self, and fitted comfortably whenever either of the girls were around. To be honest some-times it felt safe there, but the new Claire was always wary in case she slipped back into her old ways, once the plan was set there was no going back, and no mistakes could be made. As Claire lay listening to the others shuffle to the bathroom and back again, she let a few tears slide onto the pillow. She had loved Marcus, not the way Beth had, for her, he had been her everything. Claire had loved the excitement, after the initial horror of what they had done it somehow gave her power, a confidence she secretly enjoyed, it made her feel sexy, wanted and admired. After Marcus she could see what others already knew, she was a beautiful woman, stunning at times, and Marcus had given her the confidence to open her eyes to see herself as the rest of the world did. To the girls, she could still show all her vulnerabilities and still savoured the feeling of safety it gave her, a family she could rely on no matter what happened. Of course some of it changed after Charlotte, and Claire had surprised herself how easily she had deceived them all. As her career took her to levels of society she had never known existed and she witnessed the falsehoods, bitchiness and power played out there, Claire had been glad for her sub-urban house, with an ordinary garden, in an ordinary street, a place where she could hide from the world and allow her children to grow. A full bladder niggled her to rise and relieve it, yet still she lay, knowing what could be lost today. Claire had lied again last night, told them it had only been the one time, they would work it out, JJ probably quicker than Beth. All those times when Claire could not cover her lie would now stand out, JJ was no fool, and never had been, she had often seen emotions beneath Claire's surface, a worry hovering not wanting to appear foolish if she spoke it out aloud. JJ would see it and draw it out, but this, Charlotte, she had never, nor would ever have thought to look for it. The adoration and affection they had all given to Claire's children had been genuine, they all loved them for who they were and because they were part of Claire, the Claire who now was the one about to tear it all apart.

Pulling the covers up a bit more Claire knew it was time to face the music, there was no going back, she knew the lies now had to stop. It was a shame it had to come out now, now when Beth and losing Marcus should be the only focus, it had been taken out of her hands, Marcus had knowingly done this, she was not angry, she knew why, but the timing made it so much harder. Oh Marcus, I wish you had told her yourself as maybe then, I wouldn't be about to lose it all.

Claire heard the phone ringing and pushed herself up, no mask today she warned herself, tell it all or there will never be any chance they will forgive you.

Chapter Eighteen

Beth

Dear JJ and Claire,

I have decided to give up on the IVF. I have rung myself ragged and I can't do it anymore, so many ups and downs, highs and lows and each time the lows have sunk deeper. I can't do it to myself anymore and Marcus has pleaded with me to stop trying. As he is older adoption is out of the question and fostering, after this I'm not sure if I could keep handing them back without it destroying me. I'm done. I feel like I have let him down, he is so great with kids and would be the best father. I am so lucky, and I am trying to stay positive, I miss you both and think we should have a girl's trip so we can all break down, get it out and rebuild again. It seems my life is a constant roller coaster and I want to get off it for a while. I have wept enough for all the tiny embryos my body has rejected, sunk to blaming the Beth curse on all I do and truly am seeing how lucky I am. I have a good job, which I love, wonderful husband and the best pen pals who have stuck by me all these years. We will have to borrow Charlotte and Paul more and spoil them rotten, Claire. Marcus does love his time with them, and I know we shouldn't have favourites but I'm sure Charlotte has only to blink her eyes at him, and he would give her whatever she wants. It is so cute she is sending him drawings and calling him her pen pal, he loves it. So, although in a way it makes me sad, as I really did want to give him a child of his own we really are blessed Claire jumped in early and had her two beautiful babies for us all to share.

I've left today to stretch away in front of me, my decision is made, but I wanted to tell you both, and it is all I intend to do for the day. I will probably grieve some more but Marcus deserves to now have my full attention after supporting me in this for so long. Last night when I told him he said he had wanted it for me but for him, I was enough. I love him for saying it. Fingers crossed I can finally pull myself away from the fog of depression which has always seemed to reach out and tap me on the shoulder and my letters to you both will be brighter and full of all the good times ahead. Thank you, thank you for all the support, I love you both so much.

xxx Beth

Beth couldn't seem to find anything in the kitchen, each cupboard she opened seemed full of gadgets she would never need. Her face felt stiff as if the salt from the endless tears had seeped in leaving it feeling like parchment drawn tight across her cheeks. Beth knew she had lost weight, her clothes hung from her shoulders and her body felt weak and small inside of them. The phone was ringing and she ignored it, there was too much here to face today without letting the outside world in. Although she was angry, Beth felt resigned to what she was about to hear, deep down she knew the truth. It would shock JJ, for all her worldliness and straightforwardness, JJ had not seen this coming. In the night all the tiny scenes had come together. Beth had suspected there had been a moment with Claire, yet the realisation of Charlotte's parentage had held itself back unwilling to let her see it or had it? Had she closed the door on it, unwilling to lose the person she loved most in the world. Beth longed for Marcus, part wanting to feel his warmth around her, and part wanting to rant and rave, to call him out on his behaviour, his lies and betrayal of her.

In the early hours she had risen and foraged in the office under the light of the small desk lamp for the box. In it were all their letters from the start. When they were young and the envelopes became too thick or expensive to post, Beth had started afresh leaving the last full one which they had all seen at the front, filing the others away, too precious to destroy. As they had grown older and started to meet, each in turn would bring a small pile they had collected for the same reasons to give back to Beth. Each time she had laid them out and put them in order, it had soothed her to see how her life had moved ahead away from her unhappiness as a child. Beth had never reread them except occasionally going back a bit to catch up on a date or a comment made she had not noted on the calendar or such like.

The box was large and though often used, had been pushed to the back. Beth had seen how some letters had been re-arranged and knew by instinct it would not have been JJ or Claire, so it had to have been Marcus. Had he been looking for clues, clues of his betrayal penned by Claire to both her and JJ? Beth would never know yet knew it would always be what she would believe. Thumbing the sheets Beth had realised the love they contained, she too had held back details of her life, they all had, yet still, they had all known the pain or joy hiding inside between the round childish writing. As the hall clock ticked over another hour Beth felt no need to read them, she knew them all in her heart, each one had been read quickly at first for the news, set aside and re-examined later at a slower pace, each time picking up the clues and the words between the lines. It was all there, every moment, maybe she had just not wanted to see it. Resignation of what could not be changed had sent her back to bed, and restlessness had made her rise early to try to find the courage for what lay ahead.

As she dragged herself around the kitchen, half wanting them to wake and get it over with, the tiny ball of Beth inside rumbled and turned making her feel the pain, for without it she would not exist another day. The pain and anger it seemed was all which was holding her together. Beth wondered if it would ever leave, as the person who it was directed at the most, was no longer here to face her charges.

A noise made her turn, it was not the hasty worrying step of a Claire anxious to make sure the day was bright and the world not about to end, but one of certainty, one also wishing to finish it, cop whatever was to come on the chin and move on. Beth knew the outcome, after all the final result of this was up to her, to carry on the pain and blame or to move on, never quite forgiving yet still with one of the few other people she loved almost as much as she had Marcus. Hurt caused her to sway one way and a lifetime of support the other. Beth had decided to hear her out, as long as it was the full truth. As it was all laid bare on the table she would pick and choose the memories she wanted to keep and stow the others away locked in a box somewhere without a key so she could no longer return there. Beth knew she would forgive Claire, but the hurt side still wanted her to suffer a bit more and to hear her rage as she released it to the world. Then and only then would they cry, cry together and mourn the man they had both loved and lost.

'Beth.'

Beth raised her hand.

'Not yet, wait for JJ. I want her here, she is the one person we can trust to keep us on track. I love you Claire but today has to be done.'

Claire looked shocked, she had probably been expecting the worst, for Beth to be throwing her clothes out the door and telling her to never return. The fight was leaving Beth, she was too worn out to hold it there and the sunshine moving its soft fingers across the table were the hope she wanted to hold on to.

'Sit, I made coffee.'

'Beth ...'

'No, wait, let's sip our coffee and sit quietly as the world wakes up around us.'

Claire accepted the cup, sipping the hot liquid tentatively, Beth knew she wanted to fuss, tidy the sink and put some order into the day. Part of her enjoyed the extra struggle she knew it caused for Claire to be patient and still. They heard JJ rise and listened as she shuffled from bed to shower and back again. Beth was happy for her to take her time and rose, going through the motions of making toast for them all. Claire too went to assist but sat down again almost at once as Beth's look said the words she did not have to verbalise.

JJ halted at the door, Beth could see her surprise, there was a mellowness in the room not even she had expected.

'So, is it done?'

''No, we were waiting for you.'

'Geez, geez Louise, I would have been happy if you had started without me.'

A smile played across Beth's face which she could not contain, and she saw Claire's shoulders relax slightly. This is why they needed JJ, at the best and the worst times she always made them see through themselves with new eyes, reminded them of what was important and with never saying a word could chastise you when you were wrong even while consoling you. JJ hated liars, the truth could always be worked through she said, yet for each of them at times she had hidden a truth for them from the other. They had let Beth think she was the centre of their sisterhood, after all she had brought them together, but Beth knew it was JJ who had held them true and strong.

'So do I get coffee first or are we doing this on an empty stomach?' Beth pushed the button for the bread to toast.

'We were enjoying the calm before the storm, sit and I will make you coffee and the toast won't be long.'

Beth turned away and heard JJ scrap back the chair, she did not have to look to see JJ's eyebrows raise or Claire's shoulders shrug in resignation. The toaster flung its contents out across the bench and Beth even giggled at her antics as she made to catch it.

'Beth.'

'No Claire, I will be the one to start.'

'But I ...'

'I said no, and you know how JJ gets if she is hungry, at least let us eat or she will be unbearable.'

They all obeyed and ate, even licking their fingers to get the last crumbs from the plate and delay what could no longer be avoided.

'How long?'

'Ten years.'

'Fuck!'

Beth was silent, as JJ repeated the F word and Claire's name over and over.

'Why?'

'Because I was weak, and stupid and oh Beth we never meant to hurt you, it happened, an impulsive moment and after Charlotte, it continued, became a habit we finally woke up enough to break.'

Beth raised her hand to give herself time to digest every answer.

'Ten years, wow. Why did you not tell me? Has my life been such a lie? You know how hard I tried to give him a child and you watched me cry. YOU WATCHED ME CRY CLAIRE ALL THE TIME KNOWING HE ALREADY HAD ONE!' Beth had raised both herself and her voice. 'How could you?'

'I wanted to Beth, I did. I wanted to share Charlotte more but Marcus, he said you would not cope, it would be too much, Beth please, we never meant to hurt you, I promise, I really do. I can't lose you Beth, it's why I did what he said, I couldn't lose you. My life would be over if I didn't have you and JJ.'

'Did you love him?'

Beth saw JJ hold her breath as they waited for Claire's reply, she had blurted out the question and was not really sure she wanted to know the answer.

'No.'

Beth's head sunk to her chest.

'Did he love you?'

'I don't think so, he never said. All he talked about was you, and Charlotte, but no I don't think he did.'

'Why did you stop?'

'Beth, once the joy of Charlotte arriving was done, I don't think we thought about it. He thought he had to be there for her, and it became a habit really, a convenient habit which I finally saw through and put a stop to as, well ..., what you had with Marcus is what I wanted, and continuing would mean I would never go out and find it for myself.'

'... and it took you ten years to decide!'

JJ's head which had been back and forth like she was watching a tennis match, paused to wait while Claire considered her reply.

'Don't think about it Claire, I want the truth, don't play around with the words.'

'I'm not Beth. The speech to tell you has been in my head so long and now it seems so meaningless and shallow. I will say this, I will never regret getting Charlotte, no matter who her father was, and if he was a man who knew how to love, not me but someone, as much as Marcus loved you it meant she had a chance of having a good heart, not like Paul who struggles because his father doesn't love him, and he is always seeking it, whereas Charlotte is happy to be loved by whoever is willing to give it. It makes her content, happy within. It is a subtle difference yet one which, as their mother, I can see guides their lives.'

'We never loved Paul any less, he is an exceptional boy even though he was more like Johnno in looks, Charlotte won everybody's heart by being who she was, even Pauls.' JJ spoke the truth, both Claire's children had been their world.

'I know JJ, and I am grateful, you didn't know anyway, you probably thought Charlotte was more like me. I will always love Marcus because he gave her to me, but I was never in love with him and he loved you Beth, he would never have been anyone else's, he was only ever yours.'

Beth put her hands to her face, soulmates they had said to each other so many times, yet did soulmates betray each other? Is Claire's heaven when you sorted it out, where soulmates met each other and made the promise for a lifetime, and did one of you, on the way back to a mortal life change your mind and feel locked into a promise made in another world and were forced to keep it? Beth wanted to hug Claire, hold her tight and squeeze every ounce of Marcus out of her and back into her own body, to take back and hold everything he had given to another without her permission.

The silence let JJ speak her peace.

'You've shocked me Claire, I don't know how I didn't see it, and Marcus, I thought we were close. I love you but I must admit I feel a betrayed. You lied to us all these years, both of you.'

'Not all, but yes for some, most of the time it wasn't an issue, once Charlotte was her own little self it became easier and Johnno not wanting to be involved helped as well. I think he suspected, but he never said. I'll give it to him, if he knew, he kept his mouth shut so his son would not be hurt. After Charlotte was born Johnno stayed away so the conversation was never had, at least not with me.'

'He told me.'

Claire looked shocked.

'When I was walking into the hospital, Marcus was already there with you. Johnno went past and said something about he didn't know why he had bothered because the kid was not even his, he was his usual rude self, so I kept walking. In the lift, I remember wondering, if it were true, who it could be, or if Johnno was drunk which could definitely have been true. I walked in your room and Marcus,' Beth released a sob, 'Marcus was leaning over the crib and the look on his face,' the tears trickled down her cheeks, 'he was already smitten and all I could think was how a baby was the only gift I could not give him and how much I had let him down. I never thought about Johnno's comment again until last night, I read the letter again and I remembered.'

'Oh Beth.' Claire rose and came to gently place her arms around her shoulders, tentative at first Beth felt herself relax as she accepted the embrace.

'Who else knew? Do Charlotte and Paul know?'

'Charlotte does.'

Now was Beth's turn to be shocked.

'When did you tell her? Why did she never say? If you told her, why not Paul?' The questions tumbled out, each wanting its own answer, yet also not wanting to be lost in another.

'She told me.' Claire moved back to her chair and placed her head in her hands, elbows resting on the table. JJ rose to fill the kettle.

'Wait Claire, I need more coffee and I'm looking towards a liquid lunch.' JJ still seemed the most shocked and it was taking her a lot longer to digest each piece of information. She muttered under her breath. Geez Louise, seriously Marcus and F-me were repeated often as the other words slipped away not making any sense at all. Placing the fresh hot brew in front of each of them she said.

'Maybe we should all get pissed, look it's nine-thirty, we could be roaring drunk by twelve and you two can say whatever you like and tomorrow we will go on as before except for knowing where Charlotte did inherit those extra-long legs and her nose. What do you say girls, shall I pour something stronger?'

Beth actually wanted to agree with her, the thread which ran through them all knew it would not break, it may fray a bit for a while, before hopefully gaining more strength than before. Each of them believed they could not live without the other, their individual strengths over the years combined to make them feel whole, and wanted, when they were together.

Beth wondered if it was how it felt for Claire with her children. JJ had resigned herself to the fact they were not going to take up her offer of alcohol, well at least not yet, though when Beth tasted her coffee she had a strong suspicion JJ had added a drop of something stronger to start them on their way.

Claire waited for their acknowledgement before she began again.

Chapter Nineteen

Claire

Dear Beth and JJ,

Oh my, I am so proud of me! Designer of the year again!!! I look back at my childhood and I think how proud dad would have been, I can almost see his eyes shining, brimming with the tears he would never allow me to see fall. We have all done so well and I wish I could give mum one more hug to thank her for all the sacrifices and encouragement she gave. I wish you could be here Beth, but Marcus told me your schedule and this overseas trip is such an opportunity you must take it. I swore him to secrecy so I could tell you the news myself, I still don't think he gets how much we enjoy getting news by snail mail as they call it now. He argued you would get it last as it has to go via Canada first and I told him it made no difference, and didn't he know his wife started all this and the rule is never to be broken. Men! So what if we even hand each other notes when we are together, it is how we are and how we were meant to be from the moment Beth reached in the box to draw our names out, even before her when the teacher chose our names from them all to put in the box, it was meant to be. Anyway, thanks again for lending me your husband for the big night, I still turn into a bowl of jelly be-forehand and can't ever seem to pull my security/society mask on until the last moment. I do know if I didn't have Marcus or one of you to accompany me to these functions I would never make it out of the house. It still annoys me how all these in-securities from our youth never leave us.

On the family front the kids are growing like weeds. Johnno stuck his head in the door again but when I asked him why he hadn't sent Paul a birthday gift he slunk away again, Slunk is it even a word? Anyway, it suits him, and it suits me not to have him in my life. In all honesty I think the kids are better for it too. Charlotte can't wait for the school holidays, all she talks about is going to see Auntie Beth. Some days I think she loves you more than me Beth! Charlotte so loves writing with you and all the activities you always have planned. She certainly loves organisation and structure. Paul is disappointed but he does love his tennis and this camp is a great opportunity for him. (I think Charlotte is secretly pleased it is just her for once - double spoiling is what she is expecting). Don't worry JJ they still have loads of love left for you and keep nagging me for a trip to see my family in the US and apparently on to you for an 'extended stay' They are so funny, it's their new word of the week – extended! Apparently it should apply to bedtime as well. Once this season is over I am going to slow down a bit, I can almost name my price on designs now and Jim's sound investment advice has really paid off, so while the kids are still wanting to hang out with me I want to take the time to spend with them, it won't be long, before they will be teenagers and the time will fly. I must fly myself now, talk soon and a million kisses to you both for all the support. XX Claire.

'I was getting ready for a fashion award event and was stalling a bit, probably reluctant to be going on my own. Charlotte was about nine at the time, actually it was not long before we all went to Cairns, remember the three of us and Charlotte? I remember it was after she came to you for the holidays Beth.'

'Claire!' JJ made her jump and for once she was grateful to be reminded to stay on track. With a smile of thanks, she continued.

'Charlotte had been playing with my makeup as she watched me get ready. Paul was on his new PlayStation, I remember,' she looked at JJ to indicate she was staying focused, 'because later I was glad of the background noise, so I knew he had not heard our conversation. I turned to look at myself in the mirror and I could see her reflection as well, she so loved the dresses I made, as I had loved my mothers. As I did the last-minute touches she piped up and said, I think Daddy would be sad he is not going with you. I was taken aback a bit and said but darling Daddy never liked these events at all and I'm sure he prefers to be busy doing other things rather than going to one of these silly functions.' Claire paused as she remembered. 'I honestly was imaging Johnno and was shocked she mentioned him as he never, as you both know, bothered with the children much once he left. Anyway, I said, Daddy's in Queensland so he wouldn't be popping in for another silly old fashion show. No Mummy, she said, not Paul's daddy, Uncle Marcus. I had to sit down on the bed and all I could think of was, not of denying it, but who had told her.'

Claire gulped her coffee loudly to cover the memory as it played across her face.

'It was probably the shock which luckily halted my words until they were thought through. Uncle Marcus I said, and tried to sound surprised, we had been so careful Beth, two bedrooms when he came to stay, we always waited until the children were fast asleep, or at school. We weren't affectionate outside of ...' Claire glanced up and wondered if this was too much information for Beth to handle, she looked resigned to hearing it all and Claire was determined to stick to her vow to tell the truth.

'I was staring at her reflection, she looked so innocent and positive it was true I knew I couldn't lie to her, but Beth, I also knew I would have to tell her to keep this secret to herself, to ask my daughter to sometimes tell a lie. It was a big ask of a little girl.' Claire paused again to let Beth's mind settle on each slice of information.

'Who told her? Was it Marcus?' JJ looked as if she was sure she was right.

'No. I had actually started to churn inside with anger at him, well who else knew? I thought it must have been him, I could not believe he would go behind my back, at least not with this. It all ran through my head. Charlotte never blinked as she waited, it was like she was staring me down and it took all my control to keep my face clear of my thoughts.' Claire caught herself before her head wandered too far away.

'In a way she worked it out for herself. Apparently there had been a few comments over the years at shows and events, people mistakenly, though they were actually right, ... sorry JJ, I can't help myself ... people had said to her over the years go over to daddy or you really are your father all over or be it her legs or her smile were him, it sank in, and she started to notice how alike they were and added it up herself. I couldn't lie to her, what if one day she was sick or needed medical history? I told her it was true, and I had to soften it, she was only nine. I told her we cared for each other but because her daddy loved Auntie Beth so much it had been impossible for us to tell anyone.'

'What did she say?' Beth was curious and Claire felt awkward finally telling it all. It was like a piece of her had broken away and she was reaching out to catch it, but it kept slipping out of reach. Each time the rest of her body seemed to settle knowing it would be ok without it.

'She said,' Claire looked directly into Beth's eyes, 'she said, I love Auntie Beth, it would hurt her, but I wish she knew so I could tell her how I feel.'

Claire felt a tear run down her face.

'Charlotte loves you so Beth, sometimes I think more than me, from the beginning you were always her favourite.'

'Probably feels sorry for me, she's a smart kid.'

'No, not true Beth, I love her too, but it was always you, I was a touch jealous at first I must admit.' JJ looked sad even though she smiled.

Claire wondered how Beth felt hearing those words, would it help heal her for what could not be changed? Without Charlotte in their lives, everything would have been so different. Charlotte loved every one of them unconditionally, and even as a baby shared her time, never once leaving out her brother whose nature was so unlike her own. Charlotte had enriched Beth's life, yet Claire knew Beth had never quite forgiven herself for being unable to have a baby of her own. Beth not forgiving herself, had held her down and Charlotte had always given a tiny bit extra to her as if to compensate.

They all sat quietly as the minutes ticked by softly in the background. Tick, tick, the sound of the clock, regular, routine, an everyday sound to soothe and heal. Each moment seemed to stretch out as if to give them more time to settle inside, to choose their words and be ready to accept the outcome.

Claire recovered first. It was as if she had woken from a long sleep where tiredness hung on, making her limbs feel heavy and slow, a heaviness which had no weight just an emptiness now the story was told. Claire found she now felt relieved, there was no yelling or accusations as she had expected. Beth seemed resigned to knowing it could not be changed, this chain of events could never be undone, and acceptance was the road forward. Claire longed for Beth's forgiveness, yet she knew it was a lot to ask for, a lot to expect.

JJ stirred, Claire wondered if she had been hurt the most, betrayed by her friend for so long. right up until last night. Until the letter, JJ had trusted her, looked after her, loved her children and would have done whatever she could to protect them all. All this time, Claire thought, she did not know I was the one they needed the protecting from. As guilt tried to edge its way back into her soul, Claire watched Beth carefully wanting to catch every emotion as they flickered across her face, each one would give a warning of her fate.

A tiny sigh escaped Beth's lips and Claire hoped it was one of resignation. As Beth raised her eyes to meet hers, Claire could feel the same heaviness she had felt, the effort it took for such a small task. Claire leaned in, praying to everyone she had ever known to ask Beth to forgive her, I am strong, I will survive, but dear God I want to survive with them for my life will never be the same without them. JJ coughed awkwardly, not quite enough to clear her throat and again Claire wondered what JJ would do, how torn she would be. To sit on the fence between them would irritate Beth, and JJ too, though Claire knew she would not be able to cut either one of them away, yet pushed, and they both knew it would be Beth they would protect. If it all were switched around Claire knew she too, would make the same choice. Beth was their centre, the nine-year-old had bound them up and they each would be loyal until the end. Claire clutched her hands over her heart as a large teardrop rolled over Beth's eyelid and slid slowly down her cheek. Claire stretched her hands across the table towards her.

'Beth, I'm so sorry, I love you. Beth I ...'

JJ too reached out, the need to touch each other, remind each other of everything they had been through, the need to transmit the memories, both good and bad made this moment halt itself, pause before the clock pushed it to carry on, wait it cried, and when it could hold no longer, Beth spoke.

'You asked me JJ,' her words were slow, as if she had to consider each one carefully before she spoke. 'You asked me where the rest of the letter was, the part with the details, the part Marcus would have left, organised as he was, with the details.'

Claire realised she had not taken a breath, holding it in until the verdict was given.

'He left one, it has all the details on it, her birthdate, her address, even the colour of her eyes, they're blue you know, he was very thorough.'

'No they're not Beth, you know Charlotte's eyes are brown.'

Beth continued to speak in a monotone way, as she looked directly at Claire and waited for the penny to drop.

'Charlotte's eyes are brown Claire, but Willow's eyes are blue like her mother's I presume, she is fourteen years old and lives in Brisbane.'

Claire's mouth was open, she was stunned, JJ had not moved, and Claire was afraid to look at her.

'Thing is, it seems Marcus failed to tell her or her mother about me, so he would like me to let her know.'

All Claire could think was, I didn't have to tell.

Chapter Twenty

JJ

Girls, I know we said we would never email but I've decided it makes it easier this once to get to you quicker. Jim and I are booked mid-May to see the family in Young and he will stay on, and I will fly up and meet you both in Cairns. Claire, your preps for spring shows should be well under way, and I thought, probably in the lull period when you are waiting for details to fall into place before the countdown begins and Beth, you said Marcus has a conference in Brisbane so maybe you two could have a wild night there, and you can leave him wanting for more and continue the journey. It is a bit of short notice, but I rang, and they have a vacancy, so I booked it in. They have a kids club Claire, and it won't hurt them missing a bit of school. It has been way too long, and I said to Jim if I don't do it now on impulse, we will all over think it and another year will go past. Lock it in!!!!! Promise I will rewrite in a proper letter for the record but email straight back if you cannot fit the dates below. I'm excited!

REPLY ALL:

JJ It must be a while, you have forgotten how old they are now, lock me in but Paul with his sporting commitments is not keen to be away so is going to stay with a friend, should have seen his face when I said about kid's club Ha! I'm not a kid he said. I think you have slightly offended a teenager. Charlotte is so excited to think it will be all girls, and missing a bit of school comes into it as well. Timing is perfect for my schedule Thankyou will lock in our flights today! Claire xxx

REPLY ALL:

JJ See you in Cairns! xx B.

JJ recalled the trip. Charlotte had been so excited and had run across the terminal wrapping her arms around Beth as if she would disappear if she let go. JJ remembered feeling a bit miffed, after all it had been herself, who had arranged it. She remembered pushing the thoughts aside as the ever-generous Charlotte unwound herself and proceeded to give JJ a hug which wiped away any doubts of her affection for her.

JJ didn't know how she felt, Claire's confession seemed to have been almost dismissed by Beth, yet she hadn't had any knowledge of it, or so she said. Beth seemed too calm, JJ supposed she'd had some time to digest the letter and come to terms with its contents which may have helped as Beth knew she had held the trump card to play in the end. Claire's face for once was blank, no rivets of emotion running across her brow or skipping across a chewed lip. Even without them JJ knew what Claire would be thinking, it had crossed her own mind the first instant as well. Claire didn't need to tell. Another hour or day and it all would have been different, though not really her brain argued, Charlotte would still be his daughter, nothing would have changed except the knowledge of it, you would simply not have known about it. A thought popped in her head, and she wondered how many more there were. What a cad! The ball of anger started to rewind inside, it was confused as to who to be mad at, Marcus, yes of course, he had deceived them all, betrayed Beth and used Claire. Marcus had used Charlotte too, used her to fulfil his dream of a child perhaps and left her to a life of lies. JJ's anger surged, what a mongrel as Jim would say. Another child, she couldn't quite understand, he had always shown so much affection to Beth, held her every moment it had seemed to JJ in his thoughts. Too many thoughts rattled and shook, gluing together in a format JJ could not comprehend, she shook her head as if trying to straighten out the thoughts, make them confirm they belonged in each allotted moment of time as she remembered, but they didn't, they tossed and turned moving to parts un-known to her as the puzzle of Marcus's life came together. JJ rubbed her eyes and sighed, she wished she could remember how much she had loved him, because in this moment she wondered if she ever had.

JJ pushed back her chair and stood up.

'I need a moment or two. I might order in some lunch as I will definitely need something to soak up the alcohol I feel I am going to consume. Beth, why don't you have a shower and get dressed like a normal person, and Claire ...' JJ covered her face with her hands, 'I don't know, do whatever it is Claire would do.' JJ retreated to her room and grabbing her phone off the charger had speed dialled Jim before she even realised. The ringing irritated her more than it should. JJ felt explosive, every nerve seemed to be tingling at the same time as it felt a thousand tears were about to fall, she was pacing impatiently and was about to hang up in annoyance when he answered.

'What's up?'

Two words and he released all her tension, she missed him more in that microsecond than ever before, all the times he had stood by her, heard her out and held her up came crashing in, he had never once let her down.

'I want to come home.'

'Whoa, hang on. Beth needs you, how did it all go?' A pause, 'she needs you my love. I want you, but for now, she needs you, I know you can do it, where are you?'

'I'm in the bedroom, it's madness here. Marcus ...' JJ took a deep breath. 'Marcus was not who we thought he was, he cheated on Beth, Jim, he cheated on Beth with Claire!' The silence was telling, and it literally knocked the wind out of JJ.

'You knew.' It was almost a whisper as her breathing re-turned and grew louder as anger crept in. 'How did you know, and more important, why didn't you tell me?'

'Hang on JJ, I didn't know, I suspected. You only have to look at Charlotte to see she is Marcus all over. The few times I saw them together it struck me, and I did say once about how their mannerisms were the same, remember, you were all so thrilled as if a bit of each of us was rubbing off on her. Poor old Paul, I always tried to give him extra time as Charlotte was so clearly everyone's favourite.'

'What else?'

'It was a few different things. As you know Marcus wasn't always my favourite person, too smooth and the few times he and I had a drink, there were comments he made, and I wondered if he was really the person behind the front he was presenting. It was the three of you we had in common and not much else. I put it down to how different we were in every way, he was the educated high-flyer, and I was the average bloke, we never did find common ground. Take a breath, ... better? Now tell me what's happened and who spilled the beans? How did Beth find out? Is Claire still there?'

JJ rattled off the events of the day, it still didn't make it clearer to her, a lifetime of memories now jumbled and messed with would take time to sort out. Jim's calm voice and his solid way of putting aside the unimportant calmed her.

'Do you want me to come?'

'Yes, no, yes. I miss you. I love you.'

'I know and ditto back my love. I would be there as soon as I could but Will's not great, he'll be fine, another down time, and I think you would be more settled if I were here. Beth needs you and I understand, I do, and Claire does too, you would never forgive yourself if you left them now. Stay with her, go and meet these people for her and get Beth started on her life ahead. Look out when you return though, as there is some serious loving to be done so you may not see the light of day for a week.'

JJ blushed, he still made her feel like a girl. Although she longed to feel his arms around her, she knew he was right, she would not forgive herself and could not abandon Beth until this whole business was done and Beth was on the path to recovery or at least acceptance. As for Claire, somehow she felt it would all be ok, Beth had acted strangely JJ thought and somehow she thought there was more she wasn't telling. If JJ could get Beth to leave the house for a while she would have a good old snoop around. Snoop first, apologise later would be her policy, and while she was at it she might rummage around Claire's luggage, somehow Claire being Claire there would be something she had in there which might hold a clue to the truth of it all. Marcus, being Marcus would have left something, somewhere which would reveal it all, he would not have been able to help himself, and Claire seemed the easiest target JJ thought. Jim was still waiting for her to answer.

'I love you more you know.'

'More than what?

'More than them, more than Will, you do know, don't you? No matter how high or fast I jump for them, it is you I love the most.'

The silence was full of emotion and JJ could picture him rubbing his eyes with the thumb and forefinger of one hand as he held the phone in the other and let her words seep deep inside his body.

'I know,' he whispered, 'though there are times I wished I didn't have to share.'

JJ let the tears roll, she knew what he meant. His family and her family had kept them travelling across the globe, each of them too nice to say no. Their decision to not have children came into it as well, the family they had, and this extra family they had made was their all and without saying it, they had both tried to be everything to everyone, mother, father, aunt, uncle, cousin and friend.

'I'd better go, I told them I would order lunch in as I will need it to soak up the alcohol.' JJ laughed as did he and it felt like she could feel Jim through the phone.

'Good idea my love, get outrageously drunk, do mud wrestling if you have to, sort them out and come home to me safe and sound.'

They murmured a few words of endearment as husbands and wives do, before saying goodbye. JJ held the phone to her chest, trying to keep him with her for a moment more. In this moment too, she felt grateful for the man who gave her so much yet took so little. The shower was still running, and JJ hoped Beth would emerge as refreshed inside as she would be on the outside. Memories nagged at her brain, but there were too many for her aging brain to take in or were they finally trying to sort themselves into a new order? An order where JJ could see the clues, recognise she had seen them at the time and start the road to acceptance. Claire would be a step further, she had known the truth all this time yet now there was another child, would this news spin her out of control as well. JJ sank to the bed, her shoulders slumped in a way she had not felt since she was in her teens. When the bullies at school had teased her all the way home, she had gone to her room and drawn her shoulders in the same way, protection mode she called it, huddling in to protect her feelings and rounding her back as if to ward off the ugly stings and barbs. Words had been JJ's enemy, yet so too, they had been her saviour. The letters from Claire and Beth had held her up and helped her move forward, they had been her rock on which to cling and mast to strap herself too as her high school years tried to batter her down. In return she had tried to give back as much as she could, Claire had been poor, but she'd had her parents support, Beth had been troubled and losing her mother had not helped to ease her insecurities as she could never now, get the answers she needed. JJ realised how much baggage they had all carried from their youth. Three strong, independent women who had each taken on their worlds, yet crumbled beneath at times, as history and their own expectations let them down. This is where the love thrived, deep inside each of them as they learned the depths each other could reach and held out their arms, and letters, to haul themselves back up. JJ knew she would have survived without them, though could not imagine her life would have been as full or as fun. JJ had other friends, but Claire and Beth were closer than sisters, the invisible thread could never be broken.

The Cairns holiday memories seemed to have settled in their place. Beth had been quiet, though Charlotte's chatter and excitement had filled the gaps. Beth had done every activity with her, even taking Charlotte for a day-spa treatment. JJ had protested no child of her age would need one, but Claire had seemed welcome of the break and enjoyed watching her child looking so happy as she sipped cocktails by the pool. Their talk had been general, always waiting until there were three to discuss any deeper issues they may have about life in general. One night at dinner, after a fantastic day trip on a train up the escarpment to the village of Kuranda, and a jaw dropping return ride on the sky rail taking in the breathtaking views across the hinterland and out to the ocean, JJ now recalled how Charlotte had wished the others were here to enjoy this, which was to her, a magical place.

'Oh, I wish we could all be together,' she had said, 'Uncle Jim, Daddy, and I even miss Paul,' she had sighed. JJ remembered how her eyes had suddenly gone round and how she had stared at Claire.

'Don't forget Uncle Marcus,' Claire had jumped in very quickly, 'you would want him here as well, wouldn't you Charlotte?'

'Yes, of course,' Charlotte had looked at Beth apologetically, but JJ remembered how she had been puzzled by the whole scene playing out before her, 'he is so much fun, I was day-dreaming Auntie Beth, I would never leave either of you out.'

With all the secrets which were now revealing themselves, JJ could see how so many clues had been in plain sight, yet she had been too blind to see them. JJ recalled how Charlotte's cheeks had gone pink and she had lowered her head, looking at her mother for some kind of comfort through her widening eyes. It had all been there and maybe, she thought, she had just not wanted to see it, to rock the boat which sailed so steady in her life. Would it have mattered if she had known before? Probably not, she may have, being JJ, confronted both Claire and Marcus and if she had, it all may have been reconciled long before now and they could all have openly acknowledged Charlotte's parentage. Yes, JJ decided in her head, it probably would have been much easier than the way it was heading now, now when there was no one to give them answers. Marcus had another child, she could cope with the news, whereas Beth's memories were now all scarred from the revelation, back then these could all have been made fresh, no veil of secrecy and suspicion to mar each one as it was remembered. JJ wondered what he had been thinking while at the same time realising what a coward he was.

Deep breaths made her straighten up and find the resolve to face the rest of the day, she would remind them of their bond, the fun and happy times both with the men and without. They would drink too much wine and loosen their tongues, lay it all on the table and slowly piece it all back together into mem-ories they could live with. What Marcus had done, was done, and could not be changed, all they could do was accept it and move on with what they could.

As JJ moved to the door Charlotte's ten-year-old voice whis-pered in her head the words she had called when they, with heads out the windows, smiling faces and the wind in their hair had called out crazy ideas to each other as the train wound its way up to the start of their perfect day over Cairns.

'I wish I could tell you all my secrets,' Charlotte had yelled, in amongst the I love you and the, look at this or look at that, all the babble a child puts forth when they have too much to tell, and the excitement is too great to hold it all in. It made JJ pause, lose some resolve as she wondered how many more secrets like this a child could have. Maybe it was time to call in Charlotte as well.

Chapter Twenty-One

Beth

Dear JJ and Claire,

I collected the photos from the trip, what fun we had. I've sorted them and sent copies, I wanted to pick the best ones first, Charlotte is of course, in most, except the ones she took. They are actually quite good Claire, maybe I can get her a camera for her birthday, she seems to have an eye for it. It is nice to have some of the three of us, it has been a while since we had someone else with us to take one. Marcus was delayed and so I continued home on my own and it was lucky in the end as he was called to Perth and then down to Hobart. I think I'll join him there next time, if he asks, Tassie is always so pretty, and it is nice to have a break from the heat of an Adelaide summer at times. As we discussed I am still feeling at a loss as to how to fill my time, I am tempted to take some time to myself yet immersing myself in work may be what I have to do. My period arrived when I got back too, and a part of me was glad Marcus was away as the final tears fell. They probably won't be the last, but I am sure it will get easier in time. I may be the singular woman in the world who looks forward to menopause as it will take away this monthly reminder of what could have been or the possibility of it at least.

I've started walking each day, running after Charlotte made me aware of how unfit I've become as I've mourned each cycle and used food as happiness. It is all part of looking after me and I have enrolled in a computer skills class to test my brain as these wretched gadgets start to take over all we do. I've taken your advice too Claire and put a to do list on the fridge, it still surprises how it motivates me, one look and my mind gnaws at itself until it checks off every box.

Go for walk.

20 minutes meditation (not sure this is working for me as all I seem to do is plan lunch!)

Herbal tea (honestly it lasted a day and I'm back on full strength cappuccino)

Light healthy snack (Chocolate is dairy, isn't it?)

Work two hours.

Lunch

Work

Light gardening

Relax and dinner (maybe a sneaky wine ... every second day)

What do you think?. Even if I am my usual self and break the rules it does give me routine while Marcus is gone. I had never realised how much time it took, the doctor visits, the clinic time, the scans and needles, has certainly left gaping holes of time. If I don't fill it in I will swallow it up with work and I can see how it, in the end would drag me down or take over and become the most important. I do need to face this decision full on and accept it.

In spite of what I have said, I am certainly in demand on the writing front, Marcus said to take whatever suits me as his schedule is ramping up and when I have all this free time he will be away more. I know I could go with him more, but I'd rather be here than closeted in a hotel somewhere, it's not as much fun sightseeing on your own. After work he wants to sleep, and I know it annoys him if I want to go out or make plans which don't suit his mood. I am enjoying the gardening though, and you will see the benefits when you come, I never knew how therapeutic it was, or rewarding, I can blank my mind more with my fingers in the soil than when I sit cross-legged and try to make peace with my world. I planted some sunflowers, and I can't wait for their happy faces to brighten my day. I can see myself aging in ways I never expected, another birthday looms ladies and I feel content for it to come and be over with and move towards middle age. I think together we will stay young at heart and making these life changes now, will benefit us when we get to the age of spending all our time together when Marcus retires. I am taking it slow JJ, allowing the weight of expectation I have lived with each cycle fade away, it still hangs on my shoulders like a blanket, but not heavy and dragging as it was before. Time and doses of Paul and Charlotte will help me value what I do have.

As I write to you both I feel so grateful for all the support, (melancholy seems to come with age too, I think it is soften-ing my edges) I think Marcus throwing himself into work is his coping mechanism so I think I will plan a little surprise for him so we can reconnect and move forward, see the benefits of our decision, the ability to do, and go when and where we please, we both earn enough to never have to worry and we can spend it all if we decide to. I see our responsibility now is to enjoy this life we have been given and to share some of it as well, yes, to share is something I would like to do. If you have any ideas my friends let me know.

I've dallied and put off the news I have to write. I have not told Marcus, and it is in the garden in which I have found my solace in this. My brother has passed away. It all came back you know, the guilt has never faded, if his pram had not rolled, would it all have been different? Would he have been like Will, supportive and kind, or would my childish resentment of him still have lingered into our teens and beyond. I remember how he used to cry endlessly, and nothing would console him, it wore me down, yet after the accident they were always at me, reminding me how irresponsible I was, careless and thoughtless. I was nine years old, but my mother never let me forget, every day, every present he received because he was special, and I was a terrible little girl. I am sorry about Tom, I was a force to be reckoned with, full of anger and resentment or retreating so far into myself hoping the hurt could not reach. All Tom was taught, by example, was how good he was and how bad I was, and I can see now how neither he, nor I, were allowed to get to know each other and in the end, didn't want to. They used his disabilities against me and yet never really knew if the accident was really the cause. I think Mum used it to cover some kind of guilt she had and having a new husband and stable home was worth more for her than losing a daughter. How do parents put one child above another, it was something I was determined never to do if we had become parents.

See how much I have been reflecting? Years of therapy have not helped as much as this garden, here I can bury my past and help those buried thoughts grow into a better future. I can't change them, I have to live with them, I don't have to carry them anymore. After Mum died, once I moved, it was never the same, I always thought my stepfather was glad to be rid of the arguments and for once have a bit of peace and quiet, he tried but Tom was his son and mum was his wife, I was an extra battle he did not have to take on. Tom was happy to have less competition, as even the arguments took attention away from him, I was glad to try to show the world what a brave strong person I was in spite of them. I don't know if I ever told you, I went back once to see them, it was not long after I met Marcus, and I was so in love and thought how nice it would be to have a true family, a happy one. Tom sneered at me when I came in the gate, he was standing where the pram had been and said, what do you want? He looked like Mum which surprised me and was growing into a man. I came to see you, I remember telling him, and he said, well he's not your father and I don't want you here. I left and later, in the middle of the night the tears had flowed again for the child who had wanted to be loved and the mother who made other choices. He died in a road accident, and it took them a bit to find me, so the funeral is done and there is nothing to attend. It was my stepfather who finally called, he remarried and lives in Queensland, I got the feeling he and Tom had drifted apart, weren't as close, he had other kids which would have put Tom in the same position as me, a much older sibling and even though Tom had challenges, his attitude would have been well in place by the time they came along. If my mother had allowed me to love him, involved me and not pushed me aside, it could all have been so different. How lucky I am to have you both to confide in. I've taken a deep breath so I can continue:

I've never told Marcus I had a brother, he never asked, well once for the wedding he said did I have family I wanted to come or should we sneak away and elope. I told him my mother had died and said no more, so I suppose he presumed she was single mother, I don't know, as each year passed and as I pushed my memories aside, it became harder to confess as I have had no feelings for Tom to make him important in my life. Phew! It's done, I'm fine, I sort of feel a nothingness type of sad, like it is something I heard on the news which happened to someone else. I'm not sure now if I will fill Marcus in, as you know how he dismisses the unimportant and now I can't see the point. As I dig my fingers in the rich composted soil, it consoles me in a way which satisfies my decision.

Goodness, look at this, I've written more than I ever have before I think. All this time I have now, you might get all my confessions, ha-ha! Thank you again my lovelies, the trip was great, and I hope you like the photos and I also hope we see each other again before the sunflowers raise their head. XX Beth

In the end Beth had shuffled out to the garden, someone had made an attempt at the weeds which, she had learned, multiplied in the blink of an eye or a moment of neglect. The lawn had patches of brown as if splashed with paint in an abstract design and dead flower heads hung, too stubborn to fall as new buds pushed their way from beneath searching for the sun. Beth's bare feet on the grass gave her a steadiness, an inner strength she had discovered gardening gave her. She had been cruel in there, drawn it out and placed her words in a way to deliberately hurt Claire. She knew Claire's first thought, as well as she knew Claire, she didn't have to tell. What they didn't know was, they didn't. Beth too, had seen the likeness, noted how Marcus softened around Charlotte, even when her bright little personality had mesmerised them all, with Marcus there was always a special smile, a slightly longer applause and an extra cuddle. Beth now thought back to when he returned, each business trip had left him softer somehow, more content, satisfied she had thought, with a task now done. What fun they would have, he would take her out to fancy places and to sultry nightclubs where he would hold her close, and whisper sweet nothings in her ear. She would look the part, diamond earrings would sparkle and make her face shine and her body would melt into his and she would admire how they could fit so well. Dead petals crumpled at her touch as she relived the days they made love and never left the house, the days they dressed up and took on the town, the days when his agitation grew, and she knew he needed to go back to work and fulfill the need it created in him. His words always told her he wanted to stay, and now she could see how much he had wanted to leave. Beth was his fun wife, the one with no responsibilities, and once the decision was made to move forward without children, she was always available. Even her penfriends gave him breaks she did not want him to attend, free time to lie his way through their life. What a failure she was, how blind she had been.

'Beth.' Claire looked stunning even in a cotton button through.

'I think I always knew Claire, I probably didn't want to know. For all my truths, I have told a lot of lies. I think maybe it is time to come clean and see if we are the friends we always thought we were.'

'Of course we are Beth, I'm here now aren't I? I think you will be surprised to learn we know you better than you do yourself. What I did was wrong, and I can't go back, but I am willing to move forward in truth and see where it takes us. You are still a frightened little girl inside who thought she had killed her brother and was never forgiven for actually saving him. It was your mother who made the mistakes Beth, in spite of what happened, it was her choice on how to react, or at least her choice to forgive, look at her actions, and apologise. It is the same with Marcus, don't beat yourself up, it was his doing, and mine and this other woman, though she may be innocent and will be as surprised as you when we meet. Stop blaming yourself, please Beth.' A tear made its way down Claire's pretty cheek. 'It was not your fault, none of it. Start forgiving yourself even if they didn't.'

Beth knew she was right, her grieving would continue but it was time to look ahead. Her mother had used her children as a tool against each other, her brother's slight limp and the almost invisible scar on his face had been thrown in her face each time he didn't get his own way. His intellectual disabilities may always have been the person he was meant to be and his mother's over protectiveness had allowed him to use it against her. Claire stepped toward her, and Beth put her hand up like a stop sign.

'I'm not sure I am ready to hug it out yet Claire, let's give it a bit more time, I think I'm entitled to a few more jabs at my husband's mistress.' Claire looked miffed, but underneath Beth knew she would know they were on the path to forgiveness or at least an understanding of how to deal with the past.

Claire began to deadhead some of the flowers, their dried petals, often disintegrating at her touch, made her slender fingers look as fragile. Beth curled her own to hide the chipped polish and the dirt caught beneath her nails. No wonder Marcus had strayed, Claire was slender, willowy, like a soft dandelion swaying in the breeze, her hair, though long and straight formed a soft cloud around her face as it bounced on and off her shoulders with every movement. It was like watching a music score, Claire's hair had a rhythm all of its own. Her eyes were large making her face seem out of proportion yet at the same time taking all the attention, so the rest was not noticed at first glance. Claire's eyes screamed innocence and you could almost read her mind as they widened or lowered depending on her thoughts. How easy I always thought she was to read, Beth thought, and yet she was the one to deceive.

Claire seemed immersed in the chore and moved further down the path, Beth uncoiled her fingers and looking at them, for her, was like looking at her whole self in a mirror, the chipped polish around the edges of her nails was like the pieces of herself which had been torn away and her short stubby fingers represented the plainness she felt inside. Marcus had made her feel attractive, it was why she had loved him, he had stroked these very hands while he whispered his desire for her and pulled the wool down over her eyes. Beth's anger hovered like a drone waiting to descend and watching Claire, both soothed and irritated her. Claire seemed to float, sail without movement yet still always arrived at her destination. It was this, Beth realised, which had been her strength, as Claire worried about the unimportant, their fine details catching her focus, bigger issues were dealt with swiftly, decisions made and never revisited. Beth on the other hand had lived with regret and what ifs, and it was these which had sunk her down as she lived and blamed the past while being blinded by the present. Beth had always thought JJ was the strong one and Claire the weak, but now she could see all the strengths and wondered what her own had been.

A movement at the door made her jump, as JJ pushed through carrying three glasses and a bottle of white wine.

'We can move on to the hard stuff later and Jim suggested mud wrestling might help but I seriously don't think either of you would stand a chance against me.'

'Why would we have to fight you JJ?' Claire was smiling and again Beth looked away as even now Claire looked as young, and as innocent as when they had first met.

'Because we are the three musketeers, one in, all in. I'd be in it for the win not for any other reason, I'd let you two go at it until you have it all out of your systems and jump in to claim victory.'

Beth had to smile now too, JJ's tough image had never left her, the bullies she had endured as a child still made her fight hard to stay on top. The blemish on her face now faded by laser and usually covered with makeup, no longer an issue to make her hold back her tongue. Even though the mask had been covered and they could no longer hold it up as her mirror, the fight in JJ had never left her and was always beneath the surface ready to lash out at any injustice she saw. Beth could see how it had made JJ strong, yet also why it held people back or pushed them away from her until JJ decided it was safe to let them in. JJ poured the wine and Claire rearranged the stools around the table so they could all take in the view of the garden.

'Should we eat something with this or let the wine go straight to our heads for now,' Claire mused.

'I vote straight to our heads, but you two seem to have levelled out so maybe we should take it a bit slower after all.'

JJ raised her arm to look at her watch, 'after all it is now eleven o'clock, so we have a way to go before sunset.'

'What happens then, do we all turn into witches and fly away on our broomsticks to cast spells on the souls we can no longer kill?'

'You are so very morbid Beth, but at least it is a response we would expect from you, downcast, pissed off, yet optimistic revenge will sort out the karma.'

'Now you are not making sense JJ, and we haven't even had our first toast.' Claire raised her glass biting her bottom lip as she chose her words.

'Here's to us, to our challenges, our triumphs, our friendship and our love, which no matter what happens, will never diminish. I will always have your backs and I am so grateful.'

'Oh dear god Claire, I get the sentiment, but can we drink now!'

Beth saw the crease as Claire's forehead showed her annoyance at JJ's remark. Together they raised and clinked their glasses.

'I was trying to tell you both how much I care JJ,' Claire said after they had all taken too big a mouthful.

'I know I'm sorry Claire, I just want to get on with it, we know how you feel, and we feel the same back, you know I've never liked the gushy stuff you are so good at expressing.'

The scowl touched Claire's face again and Beth was relieved when she let it go. Today was not the day she needed for them to be bickering.

'Look, I'm hurt and I'm angry. I'm angry at you Claire and I'm angry at Marcus, but most of all I'm angry at myself. Pour more wine JJ, I feel so stupid, what an idiot I've been.' Beth hung her head.

'I'm so sorry Beth.' Claire's cool hand covered hers.

'I know.' Beth relented and placed her other hand on top of Claire's, she knew it would make Claire happy even though she was not sure as yet if her feelings matched the gesture.

'I'm not forgiving you yet, but I think I have always known. The night I came to the hospital and Johnno met me at the door, he knew, and I think now, I did too. You and Marcus were so mesmerised by her it surprised me, I covered it, and when he looked at me,' she gulped 'I forgave him in a moment, who else would want me if I made a scene and asked the question or told him to go. In the end did it matter? After a while I thought I had made a mistake, because he never said anything and nor did you, I thought I had been wrong, Johnno had been upset and put thoughts in my head. Of course he was mesmerised, this was something we had been trying for and not been able to attain, he was happy for you and probably glad he had been there to protect you from Johnno.'

'Oh Beth,' Claire's eyes had filled with tears. 'You have never felt you were worthy, he loved you, he did, he would never have left you for me and I did not want him to.'

'Too much information Claire, hold some back, I have to get this out, speak my truth, not for you but for me. There's another little girl out there who has lost her father and when I go to her, I want to feel whole, or at least as close to it as I can.' Claire nodded and let her continue.

'I pushed it all aside and as Charlotte grew, I sometimes pretended I was her mother, I became the fun aunt, the one who had boundaries but also encouraged her to step outside the square. It satisfied me, to show the mother image I had wanted and to hand her back and never have to bother with the negatives. I became selfish about her because I obviously, never wanted to admit the truth.'

'If you had, if they had admitted it, it might have all been smoothed over a long time ago and we could have all moved forward without the deception.' JJ's statement made Beth aware of where her hurt was too. It wasn't in the act, or in the child, never with the child she was the most innocent in all this, it was in the deception, the subtle redirections of conversations, the glossing over of dates or timelines. It was what they hadn't said after she was born which hurt the most.

'As I've thought about this I think it has been hardest for Charlotte, not being able to express her feelings out aloud, to always be watching what she said. How could you do it to her Claire, it seems to me you have betrayed her as well.'

Claire sighed and looked up at the sky, her shoulders shrank, and it was in this unguarded moment her age showed through as the lines deepened. They had all become old, Beth thought, time was spreading their hips and loosening their jowls. Even their arms were wrinkling, a surprise which happened overnight it seemed, not one which crept up on you allowing you to become accustomed. It was funny how clear everything had become. The sun even seemed brighter and as there was no going back, Beth knew now, she had to shuffle forward.

'Claire, I want to speak to Charlotte, does she know I know?' Claire nodded.

'I told her. I said she knows, and she cried, I think with relief, but it is up to her to tell you how she feels. I don't want to ever again try to manage what someone may feel. I didn't tell her anything more, not yet. Do you want me to call her now?'

'No. I will get to her later. For now, we have to plan what to say because it doesn't seem to have sunk in with you yet Claire.'

'Why, what did I miss?'

'We have to tell your daughter she has a sister.'

Again Beth felt like she had hurt Claire, it was not her intention, it was because she knew Claire so well, Beth knew she would have focused on the minor not realising the focus for her, should be on Charlotte and the news her daughter was about to receive. Claire's face had dropped as the realisation hit. Beth knew Claire would have run through her mind how she had felt knowing she was not the only betrayal, and how Beth would react to both the news of another woman as well as herself. Claire would also have run through every scenario of how the future may pan out. The one part she would overlook or not even see was the obvious, the fact her children now had a sibling, who may or may not want to know them.

'There's Paul as well, what does he know? How will it affect him to suddenly find out his sister is a half-sister, and she has a whole other family as well?'

Claire put her face in her hands. The ramifications of all the years of diversions and fibs were now coming closer and Beth knew, if the children turned against her, Claire would have trouble keeping her head above water. As she drained her second glass of wine, Beth's thoughts were of a very old saying, and it was as if Sir Walter Scott was beside her whispering it in her ear himself. Oh, what a tangled web we weave, when first we practice to deceive.

Chapter Twenty-Two

Claire

Dear Beth and JJ,

Oh Beth, how sad about Tom. I realise now how little we ever asked, I was always so happy to have you in my life I, at times, never delved deeply into yours. Don't get me wrong, you can tell me anything and I will never judge you, but I always concentrated more on your mum and the feelings you expressed there. None of it was your fault Beth, you were a kid, your mother never encouraged you to be a family, it is her fault, the wedge between you and Tom, because she was the one who placed it there. Oh Beth, there is so much hurt and guilt we carry with us through life we should have never held, or at least have discarded years ago. Stay strong my friend, we cannot change the past and it is wasteful to try to do so. I am, well we are, always here for you. I prayed for your baby to come, and as you know though it is not the same, my children are yours and I have loved how you spoil and share their lives. To hear them speak your name is always full of joy and again, we cannot change what we cannot change, but you have given them so much and I want you to try and focus on all the goodness you have shared. The garden sounds a perfect way to lose yourself, I urge you to tell Marcus though, between husband and wife there should be no secrets,

I know you have probably saved some from us, but don't save them from him, I don't think you two could get any closer, but he deserves to know you are hurting if not for the loss of Tom, at least for what might-have-been. Tell him Beth, it might help you more than you know.

Thanks for the photos, Charlotte has already pinched some for herself. Paul was a bit reserved when we came back so I tried to get her to stop skiting about how much she was spoilt by you both which was an impossible task. I think he got her back though by opening his gifts from you both in his room and it frustrated her to not know how much you sent. Kids! Always teasing each other or squabbling. I hope all is well with you JJ, I miss you both so much, our times together are so precious to me. It was good when Marcus was here a lot, it seemed to bridge the gap between us all a bit, now his business is concentrated more in Brisbane it might give you incentive to take some beach breaks away with him Beth. Spending time together might help heal some pain.

I liked your letter was long Beth, the last few years we have hurried over some of our emotions and as I get older it is nice to have some time to feel again and dwell on my thoughts, please share as much or as little as you like, all it does is make me love you more.

No news of interest really, the business almost runs itself as I get caught up in all the media and promotional rabble, I like it, but it is not a circle where I make friends, and some of them I have had to deal with as customers and I can tell you, behind the scenes they can be very unpleasant people. This whole social media fad seems to be growing and even though I'm in the industry of making people look good, some of them think this internet fame is all there is. The other day I asked a girl what she did for a living, and she told me she is a 'social influencer.' I don't even know what it is and if they saw her in a dressing room they would certainly not want to be influenced by the rude bitch

I know she is! I am sometimes glad my parents are not here to see how fast the world is changing, I am so happy my kids are so grounded and have support from you all. So yes Beth a camera is a good idea for Charlotte, she would like a mobile phone but I'm reluctant to go down that path just yet, snapping photos never to be looked at again because her friends do, I think it might be wise to hold back a bit on this whole computer technology with them for a while. Both of them will complain, and it will probably be to the both of you so don't let them break you down ok. Must go. Love, Love, Love. Claire

Claire remembered when Charlotte was a toddler, and she had wondered if she should go again, give her son and daughter a sibling, make them one of three as she had been. Charlotte would have loved a sister but there had been nowhere to hide, no Johnno to pin it on and she had known herself and Marcus would never be long term, though she had thought if she had broached the subject he would not have disagreed entirely. It had been a whim, a fleeting thought too full of the impossible and Claire had flicked it away, happy to have her two happy and well, and with herself and Marcus being the only ones to know the secret. Claire had decided she could live with it, the complications and the thought of losing Beth and JJ had been stronger than her need or want for another child. Now there was a sibling, and the possibility had never occurred to her. How stupid and selfish, Claire admonished herself. These were her children and all she had thought about was herself and her own feelings and outcomes. It wasn't exactly true, Beth had been her main concern and now Claire was appalled she had put Beth above her own children. It was like, for Claire, someone had grabbed her blouse and ripped it open across her chest to expose her evil heart inside. There were so many times she had wanted to tell, so many times she had picked up the phone or as was their way, written a note which was torn to shreds before she could finish.

Once Charlotte had confessed, it had been a relief. One less person to protect from the truth, for Claire it had eased her burden. Charlotte had been a child of ten, so she had no questions which were too deep to answer and had taken the confirmation of her parentage as something which sat right within herself, the knowledge it was true, had been her only objective. Charlotte had not been a child to point fingers nor set allegations in place for another time, Claire's child's caring nature had directed itself straight to Beth, as her mother had. In all the years, whenever Claire had stopped to dwell on her secret, paused over a letter to JJ and Beth wondering if this was the day she could spell out the truth, to suffer the consequences when she felt she had not punished herself enough, it was in all these years Claire had barely considered how her daughter felt as she matured into a young woman, nor how her son would react if he ever found out. Claire's whole focus she realised, had been in protecting the truth from revealing itself. In truth, she had never looked at the bigger picture.

JJ was on her fourth drink and her words were becoming slightly more cutting than her sarcastic best. Claire loved JJ, admired her truths and valued her support, it was the disregard of their differences sometimes, which Claire objected to. Yes she was sometimes indecisive, but at times it had shown to be a good thing not to jump into something, which at a later date, she would regret. There had been many a time she had mulled over something and a day or two later it had been proven her indecision had prevented a catastrophe. Brides were highly strung and Claire's ability to calm them, challenge them to think over their plans and ideas, had laid true with herself as well. Measure twice, cut once her mother had told her, and for Claire it was not only with material she practised these wise words. Her mother sat with her now, Claire could feel her hand soft and warm stroking her skin, she felt an invisible arm slide across her shoulders offering comfort yet giving guidance. Face what's in front of you Claire, we all make mistakes, it's what you do after, which finishes a story.

Beth pushed back her chair,

'I need to pee, and I'll bring back some food. I want to make some decisions today, otherwise time will get away and we will be no closer to getting on with our lives.'

When Beth had disappeared out of earshot JJ leaned in, her face had softened and Claire knew she was regretting not the words, but the tone in which she sometimes delivered them.

'You two seemed to have reached a plateau, what did you say to her this morning?'

'Nothing really, sorry has worn out its welcome. I think Beth knows she has to move forward, and JJ, I think she knows she can't do it without us, both of us.'

'What about you, how do you feel, and Paul surely he knows, he and Charlotte are close in spite of their differences.'

'I don't know, I truly don't. When I confessed to Charlotte Marcus was her father, she simply accepted it, she had known in her heart, so it was no big deal and life went on as before. It was around you guys I could see she sometimes chose her words more carefully. I've been so selfish JJ, what do I do now? I should be with Charlotte, she lost her father, but I told her as if he was some distant friend, what was I thinking, how could I not see, handle this better. I'm such a fool.'

Claire knew JJ agreed with everything she had said, thoughts raged in her head now of all the choices she should have made, or could have made, and none of them would give her an answer.

'What can I say Claire, you were being yourself, you don't have a selfish bone in your body, a misguided sense of emotional direction yes, but you have always put your kids first and us. Many a time you handled Beth when I could no longer be there for her, don't start beating yourself up about what we can't change and let's focus on what we can.'

Claire agreed, it was time to move forward, face the consequences she had put off for the last twenty-five years and deal with them, come what may. Claire felt her mother slip away and whispered a goodbye.

'Your Mum here again.' JJ said it as a statement not a question. Claire nodded, how much she loved these women could never be measured, they knew her so well, and in spite of it all, they would never let her down until her dying day, even afterwards she knew in her heart they would still be best friends up in heaven.

'Right.' Beth pushed open the screen door with her foot and manoeuvred a tray of sandwiches through. 'I made some tea as well, could you get it JJ, we can sober up while we make some plans and continue drinking once we are done.'

'The options weren't great in the kitchen, maybe we should order dinner in tonight as the stuff in the fridge isn't looking too healthy.'

There she was, Claire thought, the Beth who used the practicalities of life to hide her emotions, Beth had always added the layers to help herself bury the hurt underneath. It worked sometimes on small hurts, they faded away mending themselves or becoming unimportant. The big ones Beth buried as deep as she could, and it was when these then banded together and rose to the surface all at once, her world fell apart and JJ with Claire would rush in to prop her up again, hold her steady and wait for the layers to begin again. This time Claire was determined to make Beth face the future, whatever it may be. Beth owed it to herself and Charlotte to make sure the truth remained on the surface this time and was faced full on.

The sandwiches disappeared yet Claire would never remember what filling they contained. The tea was cold in her cup before she felt she could focus on their words again. Paul and Charlotte filled her head and she wished she could snap her fingers and be with them both. Her mind recalled the moment she had told Charlotte Marcus had passed away and her decision to not tell her the rest, how he had plotted to take his own life yet cover it so Beth would not be implicated even though she had long known his plans. Beth had known the why but not the when, even so it did not make it any easier knowing it was his well thought out wish to end his life on his terms. Claire tried to recall Charlotte's reaction, had she paused, caught her breath? What had she said? Claire knew, she had said how sad she was, said I'm glad I knew him. It had twigged in Claire's brain but hadn't found its place to settle Claire now realised, it sounded cold now, unlike Charlotte, had she been in shock? All their talk had been of Beth, and Claire's plans to be there for her. Charlotte had agreed, set Claire's wandering thoughts straight so she would not divert from her task and said she would call and check on her along the way. Claire had called Paul and he too expressed sorrow in a detached way. Marcus had stayed with them when he was young, but sport, friends and careers had taken them in different directions until Marcus, for Paul, had become someone he used to know.

'So, what do we take?'

Claire tuned back in on the conversation. Wine had been opened again and, although they had used alcohol as a relaxant, today it seemed like a necessity.

'Take where?' Claire cut in.

'Brisbane, to Willow, do we take photos, should I choose something for her of Marcus', something a daughter might like from her father?'

Claire felt taken aback, it shocked her to feel offended, Charlotte was his daughter too. Claire opened her mouth to speak, and luckily she thought later, JJ cut her off.

'Don't turn this around into some kind of exciting adventure Beth. This girl for one, does not know her father has died, and two, we don't even know if she knew him well or what the situation is there. Slow down Beth, we have to do this the right way, or at least the best way we know how, for Willow and for Charlotte.

Claire felt the love, JJ had the knack of looking at things from every angle, and she had often surprised Claire and made her think outside the square she had already thought, she had thought outside of. No wonder I get confused and fuss Claire thought, I do sometimes wish I was more clearly focused like JJ.

'I think there are some points we need to tidy up here first before we go rushing off.'

'But the girl has to know,' Claire interjected, 'maybe we should wing it, go and sort out the rest later, leave it too long and she might resent Beth more, and Charlotte.'

'Do you seriously think she will want a relationship with Beth? This isn't some airy-fairy dream Claire, to her Beth will be like the devil, the person to come and destroy all her memories as Marcus has done for Beth. Once she knows she will have the same doubts and hesitations as Beth and will want to take her anger out on someone. My guess is it won't be you or me Claire.'

'So JJ what do you think, tell us your plan and we can run through the scenarios. I will let you know though, I do agree with Claire, the girl deserves to know sooner rather than later, and so does her mother.'

Claire had not even thought about her, the mother, she would be like Claire, the mistress on the side, did she know the truth? This was not as simple as she had stupidly first thought. Go there, tell Willow she had a sister, her and Charlotte meet and all live happily ever after. How thoughtless I am to not think of all the people who are involved, damn you Marcus, the web you have woven may be too big and far reaching to untangle, she thought.

'You are finally beginning to get it aren't you Claire, what this all means? This is not about you, Beth and Charlotte, there are other families involved, parents, grandparents, friends, colleagues, even the neighbours may weigh in. Mostly it should be about Charlotte and Willow, with Beth and Willow's mother coming a distant second.'

'Charlotte's my daughter.' Claire objected.

'Yes I know Claire, don't snap at me, the difference is you knew, you knew who Charlotte's father was and the situation, it was you who created it. You out of all of us have had a very long time to digest all the information, plan if it ever came to light and be ready for whatever was to happen. You may not have known how everyone would react Claire, but you have at least had time to think about it.'

JJ's voice was raised, and Claire was a bit taken aback at the truth being flung at her. It showed on her face, and she suddenly felt shallow. She should be the one who had a plan, she had always known, not about Willow but at least how hurt everyone would feel and the emotions which would be expressed when her, and Marcus' infidelity was exposed. A voice inside her head was telling her to take charge, man-up as they say, coming to the funeral she had known it was her turn, her turn to be the strong one and all she seemed to be doing was being the emotional self-centred one who in the last twenty-five years had not really thought about how the others would feel, so far Claire had to admit, all she had done was make up the excuses to try to lessen the blow of her actions.

'Don't go all sookie la-la Claire. It doesn't matter now, let's move on and get this done. As I see it, the sooner everyone knows the truth the better.' Beth slumped her shoulders and Claire could see the resignation on her face, what's done is done, bury the hurt and move on so the world will think it is all ok, it was Beth's way and even though Claire wanted her to keep her emotions on the surface and not fall back into bad habits, she also knew, to get through this, the emotions of the last few weeks may have to be stored for a while. After, when all was revealed and each knew the score, then she promised herself, she would make sure they received some help, both of them, maybe even all of them, this was not something any of them should carry the blame for to their grave. Claire had to wonder if Marcus had actually known the heartbreak he would cause, and the damage he had done.

The glasses clinked again.

'One more drink ladies. To Willow, may she take it well, know she is loved, because I for one will try to show her she is. Marcus was my friend and no matter what he has done, I want to remember the good times, and may we help her see them as well.' JJ paused, and Claire couldn't imagine what her next words would be.

'Even though her dad was a bit of a cad, he had his good points and the greatest gift he has left her, is the most wonderful sister she could ever have.' They clinked glasses and Claire felt a cosiness inside, a settling of well-known feelings from a lifetime of friendship. As much as JJ irritated her, annoyed her, and called her out, at her core, Claire knew she was loved by them both, as were her children and no matter the outcome these two women would always be there for her and have her back. It was the greatest gift she had ever been given.

Chapter Twenty-Three

JJ

FOR CLAIRE: Seriously it is a wonder we are still friends, we would all have shared your children anyway, as we would have Beth's, to be honest it sounded a bit unsympathetic Claire. This was so huge for Beth, unlike me, I made the choice, children were never on my radar, I love yours but to want something and have the chance taken away by the force of nature! Beth should be sad, and she should mourn her losses, those tiny babies were real, every one of them, an hour formed, a day old on the road to birth, however long even if it was for a moment, each one I held in my heart for Beth and Marcus for each one was hope. Sometimes it is like you glide through life with blinkers on, you have me pacing Claire. AGHHHHH! Done.

Dear both of you,

As you can see I have never held back. I feel your pain Beth so be strong. Grieve, grow flowers or tear them apart, none of it is your fault, find your road and we will always be on it with you. I think you are brave, it is as brave to keep going yet somehow I think it takes more guts to stop. Step back and see the good and yes keep writing, tell us all the pain if it helps or let it ease with tears.

On our front not much is new. I have no secrets to confess or bad thoughts in which to challenge you, our life is too easy at times and my Jim so wonderful I could bore you with him for hours. We did go and update our wills, time has certainly slipped by and so we felt the need to readjust our ideas and plans. It is quite daunting is it not, to think about when you will no longer be here, no future to plan or dream, we will just be gone. I plan to live to the fullest I must say, and I hope both of you take the time to make sure your affairs are as they should be, we both said how good it feels to know it will be as quick and tidy as hopefully our deaths will be, so people can move on and I hope, enrich their lives with whatever we had leftover. I'll be checking back with you to make sure you have done it. Enough bossing from me, hold your head high Beth and I will call soon, I still love you Claire as you know I am, as always, being outspoken me. Hug the kids and talk soon xxx JJ.

Although JJ thought they should make some clearer decisions for Beth first, she had to agree it was in her best interest, for the child to be told. Claire had been annoying as usual and JJ felt like there had been three conversations going on in her head at once as she read their thoughts and tried to align them with her own. On one issue she had put her foot down and Beth was on the phone now making the appointment before they booked their flights. Marcus's will had to be read, and JJ hoped it didn't contain any more surprises. Claire had objected, it offended her sense of sensibility she had said. JJ had almost choked holding in her words, but Beth had quickly seen her reasoning.

'Yes, I can see JJ, she might ask about money or at least her mother might, it would be smart to have the answer and the legal paperwork in place. I hadn't thought about it really, but I suppose it is better to start the ball rolling there as well.'

Beth had looked at Claire who now looked shocked and drawn. Claire for all her business savvy, was so dumb sometimes JJ wanted to choke her, not literally, but at times she had to admit she had wanted to give her a smack to wake up from the daydream private life she lived in. Claire had lived in the same street all her life and once there it was like the world around was dreamy and non-existent until she had to step out into it again with her self-confidence mask firmly in place. Deep down JJ knew Claire did care for others, it was all her worrying about right and wrong which left her in the end, worrying about the worrying. At the end of the day, Claire was Claire. JJ smacked her palm against her forehead, now she was even starting to think like Claire.

The kitchen looked like a bomb had hit and even though the alcohol was calming her, it was also firing her up and small nuances aggravated her like a rash crawling across her skin.

'Claire, we need to tidy up, how can we think straight when we are living like there is no tomorrow in an utter mess.' JJ saw Claire raise her eyebrows, JJ was the untidiest of the three, an organised chaos she called it, and she knew Jim would be discretely discarding the unnecessary while she was gone. JJ had often wondered if it was because she was adopted, if her past, a blank page filled in by her parent's own backgrounds, was the reason she filled her home with trinkets and impulse buys. It was something JJ hardly ever thought about. Will was her brother as much as if they had shared a womb, and their adoption had never been hidden or seen as something which should be held above the love which was shared in their house. JJ's parents had faced so many challenges, firstly their own inability to have children, then receiving two babies who had brought with them more challenges. Will's cancer and JJ's emotional and social problems caused by her port-wine stain, were always faced with honesty and truth. JJ's whole world had been one of encouragement, affection and support.

Claire had been similar, though her parent's financial struggles had made it hard for them to see past the daily grind to the success they had achieved, three accomplished children living the dreams their mother had pushed them towards and with the drive of their father to work hard and not complain. Both Claire and Beth had a past, a history to look back on. For Beth, her runaway mother had a runaway husband who left her with a child she was probably not mature enough to have. Beth's mother's luck had changed but her attitude of blame had not and, although scattered, Beth could if needed, trace her heritage, though she probably never would. JJ gathered stuff, knickknacks and souvenirs not quite antique worthy, and books, always books. Jim had asked who she collected them for, as often once purchased or read, her interest faded, and they were left balanced somewhere or holding a door ajar, awaiting their fate. After informing her he would be the one who would inherit as there was no one else, Charlotte and Paul would certainly not be shipping them back to Australia,

JJ allowed him to tidy whenever she was absent. As always Jim understood her need, though often not the purchases. Material bits and pieces filled a gap for her, a gap she hardly noticed, yet was enough to have her fill it with memories, even if they were only to be one generation's worth.

As JJ robustly washed the dishes she could not cram into the dishwasher, she wondered about the child, fourteen, almost a young woman, what a shock it will be to hear this news. JJ wished Marcus would appear to answer the myriad of questions.

Ahh, Marcus, what were you thinking, she thought, all the fun times we had, you were such a snob and your cheeky way of putting people in their place was always embarrassing and yet often called for. I will miss you, she silently told the heavens, I will miss what we had, you got me, for all my forthrightness, you saw the truth and still loved me for it, even admired it in a way, as we were similar at times. JJ realised her hands had stilled, the suds clinging to the back of her hands as the water cooled and her mind drifted. Most of all, she thought, I loved the way you loved Beth, not once did I see you retreat from her, though her letters told us different. You, in spite of all the ups and downs, were the lifeboat she clung to. I will miss you my friend, I will never understand your need to take your life by your own timeline and means, it is too brave a decision for me to ever make, but this, Marcus, surely you could have sorted it, or at least given me the heads up. JJ shook her head as she continued the silent conversation.

Claire was your lover, I get it, and Beth was your soulmate, there was nothing any plainer to see, and me, well, we were both mentors, weren't we, who took no notice of the advice the other gave, and until now it never mattered. Now Marcus, I wish I had listened, truly listened, at least to some of it.

Memories rattled through her head, Marcus making a joke so funny everyone would throw their heads back to release their amusement, it was in these moments JJ would catch him, suddenly quiet as the laughter hung in the air around them, looking at Beth, before flicking his gaze over each of them. She'll need you, he would mouth, and JJ too would pause, puzzled, until his smile lit the room again and the doubts flew away in whichever direction he was manoeuvring it to.

Chapter Twenty-Four

Claire

Dear Beth and JJ,

I feel overwhelmed, Charlotte brought a boy home after school and when I came home they were 'studying' in her room. They were studying, well their books were open, and they were sitting on the floor chatting, but a boy. She went really red in the face, and I was probably a bit over the top, you know sort of cross but sort of smothering and over fussing, inviting him to stay for dinner. I was going to start leaving her and Paul on their own for a night but now I'm not so sure. I had a long talk with her which she told me was both embarrassing and ... hands on hips... I already asked Auntie Beth about this stuff MUM. She has assured me he is just a friend but where did it go, I want my baby back, goodness if her father lived here he would have pulled out a shotgun I think, I certainly felt like it for a second. I have to trust her and yes thanks Beth for being there for her, I don't know why she didn't ask me about the birds and the bees, but she was with you when her period came.

I know it's selfish but, (yes JJ there is a but). it made me think about when I was young, how lovely it was when Johnno noticed me and our first kiss, it really is a special time. I've been on my own so long now and one day in the blink of an eye the kids will be gone and maybe it is time I started looking again, it would be nice to be able to share with someone, have dinner, a movie. I don't know if you have heard but there is a new way to meet people online, you put in your details and a photo and if someone likes the look of you, you can chat or meet up. I'm thinking of joining up, it might be fun and at least I might meet someone ordinary and nice, I can't be bothered going to bars and the people at these gala dinners are so interested in themselves and who they can been seen with, they are not interested in who you are as a person. Anyways I'll send you a link once I get my profile done, who knows I might end up as happy as the two of you. Fingers crossed. XX C

Email reply: JJ: Good god Claire are you mad!!!!Don't tell them where you live, they could be an axe murderer or something. Make sure you have your JJ or Beth head on if you do it, remember Claire not everyone is who or what they say they are! Love you. Geez Louise some days Claire!!!

They were all packed, their three suitcases lined up at the door waiting for the uber to arrive. Beth was still trying to squash clothes into her carry-on bag, she expressed she was fine, not nervous at all she had told Claire too loudly and with a tone which relayed the truth. Along with her frantic actions and the occasional swear word, Claire thought it better to let her be. A flustered Beth at the airport would set JJ off and Claire did not want to hear it today.

Claire's insides were in a knot, part of her wanted to call Charlotte and ask advice from her sensible, free-spirited daughter. Charlotte had embraced the news, as had Paul, though Claire worried it should be Charlotte, not Beth the fractured widow and to the girl, the other woman, who should be the one to break the news. Charlotte had long ago come to terms with her feelings for Marcus and where she placed him in her life. Claire was proud of the way Charlotte had handled the situation, it had always been Charlotte who insisted the secret would never reach Beth's ears from her lips. Charlotte's love of Beth was hard to fathom. Besides Claire and her brother, Beth was who she loved most in the world. If people had been told Claire was the surrogate with Beth's egg, they would have believed it, their closeness was apparent to everyone. In the melancholy time of the last few days, Claire had reflected on her decisions in life, on Marcus and the incredible friendship she shared with these two women. At the initial talk with Charlotte as they had stared at each other in the mirror, one a carefully made-up face, the shock slightly showing in her eyes as she had struggled to hide her emotions, the other one, similar, younger with the differences of their features hidden somewhere in the reflection. As Charlotte looked on in innocence, young yet so sure of herself and the knowledge they had shared, Claire now realised the weight she had put on her daughter, by showing her relief as they had spoken about Beth and agreeing to continuing as before. What kind of mother are you, Claire scolded herself, because of Charlotte's kindness, Claire now realised how she had placed this friendship above her children, allowed her ten-year-old to make the mature decision to ignore her parentage for the sake of another. It was weighing her down, the guilt of taking the lead from a child to suit her own needs. Would Beth have abandoned her if she had known, would she have thrown all those years away? Claire now knew she would not have, they would have worked through it, Marcus would have come clean, and Charlotte would have pulled them all back together, the same yet different as she liked to say. She had been such a fool before, so was she doing the right thing now? It was all too much and if she was to admit it, Claire wondered if it was really any of her business.

JJ was crashing and banging about, there had never been any gentleness about her. JJ appeared large, though her stature was not, she filled a space with her presence, and it was the unseen parts of her Claire had often shrunk away from.

'Claire, have you seen my glasses, I'm sure they were on the table, and I'll scream if I don't find them soon.'

The uber sounded his horn on arrival.

'In your handbag JJ, you put them there last night so you wouldn't forget.' Claire opened the door and pushed the suitcases on to the porch hoping the driver would take the hint. He was at the gate which was a good sign.

'We won't be a minute, just locking up,' Claire called to him and retreated inside to round the girls up. It was with a smile as she could now feel the frustration she had heard so many times in JJ voice, usually directed at her. 'Come on, the rides here, there are shops in Brisbane you know, if we forget something.'

Beth appeared and without a word pushed past and headed out the door. Claire found JJ in the hall and stepped back so the JJ hurricane could blow through. Locking the door, Claire slid the key into her pocket next to Charlotte's letter and breathed a sigh of relief. It was done, there was no going back now, the decision had been made, the girl, Willow, had to be told and Beth had to be allowed to peer into the other life of her husband and make peace with herself. If they were doing it the wrong way, she would not blame them, for it was Marcus who was to blame, this trip was the result of his lies and deception.

Claire had forgotten what it was like to travel with them, it was almost overwhelming. JJ bossed and thought because she was such a seasoned world traveller she knew how to do everything. It annoyed JJ she was not being pampered in the airline lounge as there was a limit of one guest allowed, they instead had to mix with the masses at the departure gate. Beth was rigid, all her fears of what was ahead turning into determination to see it through. Claire left her to her thoughts though her annoyance was growing. Claire thought they were not recognising enough she would probably be facing more today than any of them, after all Marcus was her child's father and in the future this girl would, more than likely, be in her life more than theirs. Charlotte now had a sister, and this person was totally unrelated to her son, in time the ramifications could lead to a fallout she had never seen coming, it would all weigh on the girl's response. The lines crinkled across her face as she imagined each response to the knowledge they were about to share. Charlotte had embraced it, for her the more people she had to love the better, and visa-versa. Paul was easy going, he said it made no difference and he would be happy to meet or not and then take it from there. Claire wondered if he had a hidden deep resentment she did not know about. Would the children become estranged because a third was about to step into their life? Should Claire have told them! This thought pulled her up sharply and even Beth jolted out of her trance at her movement.

'Is it time?'

'No, sorry Beth, too much raging in my head, I guess one popped out quick to make room.

'Does not make sense at all Claire, no use worrying about the future, you know what will be, will be as they say. Maybe we should have more than this shitty coffee to soothe our nerves.'

'JJ really, can you imagine if we turn up with this news and alcohol on our breath, they will think we are a bunch of loonies.' Claire straightened up and tried to look indignant, JJ really annoyed her some days as much as she loved her, in a different life Claire often wondered if they would have been friends. The thought popped back. Should she have told them? Of course she'd had to, it was lies and deceit which had brought them here, to tell more would only make it worse. Marcus had started something, there was no holding back this secret now, he had left them to finish it and finish it they would. Beth would, more than likely want to take this girl on as some kind of project to lessen her grief, Claire could not let her do it and even without knowing the girl or her family, she did not think they would let her. Beth was nothing to them, her father's wife? Not to this girl, Beth was the mistress, the one who her father returned to when he should have been with her. JJ too would try to solve it, put it right and yet, what was there to correct? The situation was not going to change and how it continued was not up to Beth, JJ or Claire herself to decide. Claire wished Charlotte was here, maybe her decision to meet the girl, allow her to grieve on her own terms had been the wrong decision. Maybe it should be Charlotte telling her their father was gone. Too many questions for Claire to cope with, her fingers now felt clammy, and she could feel her heartbeat surge in a way it made her raise her hand to her chest in a movement to calm it. JJ was staring, and Claire felt as if her mind was being read right down to her deepest thought, it really was JJ's superpower and Claire had seen mightier people crumble under her gaze. Claire braced herself as she saw JJ's mouth open and was saved by their flight being called for boarding.

Saved by the bell, she thought and rose gathering her handbag and jacket in a movement so graceful people paused to watch. Claire's air of stillness returned as she glided towards the gate, her movements, so long practised as she slipped around brides in a quiet, supportive, yet authoritarian manner, made them look effortless. Both men and women stepped back to let her pass, and Claire seemed to glide by, majestic as a queen, still unconscious of the spell her beauty cast upon others. As her public mask slipped into place, Claire acknowledged those around her as some madly googled or snapchatted to friends the face they could not quite name but knew was someone they were familiar with. Claire heard JJ humph behind her and smiled to herself, as much as JJ could criticise Claire in private, in public, the mask she wore put JJ in her place and it always gave her a sense of triumph and one-upmanship to pull it off.

The flight seemed short, too short for Claire to compose herself. Their plan would be different when they arrived, each would want to change something and as much as Claire would want to stall, JJ would want to hurry, get it over with and start to deal with whatever was ahead. JJ had ordered a whisky on the plane and looked smug when the hostess handed it to her, Claire knew JJ was still trying to figure out her place in all this. In actual fact there was no need for her to attend at all, she was not the grief-stricken wife or the ex-mistress, mother of this girl's siblings, JJ was background support and Claire wondered how she would deal with being slightly on the outer with it all.

The landing was smooth, and JJ bossed again as they collected their luggage and made their way to the exit. Claire had arranged a car and a driver, unable to sleep she had imagined each step of this journey as well as each of the scenarios she thought might play out. Sleep had come when her the decision to hire a chauffeur, a means of escape if she needed it, somehow had given her a sense of security and made her relax enough to drift off for a few hours before the sun crept above the horizon.

Every sense in Claire was highlighted, she felt empty, anxious and terrified all at the same time. There had been a smaller than expected disagreement at the hotel, Claire wanted to pause, talk over a plan, she had an image of JJ taking over in an unconscious effort to make at least some of this about her. It showed in her actions JJ was wanting to break down their door and demand some answers and Beth, silent and pale looked determined to run the show at her own pace. Claire could see the tough little nine-year-old, neglected by her mother yet determined to not show the hurt, the nine-year-old Beth hiding deep inside who she drew on, in the hard moments, to get her through. Claire also knew it was in these times when the same little girl could become overwhelmed and shut down to a depth which Claire had always feared, one day, they would never be able to draw her back from. Grit your teeth she begged, trying to send Beth a telepathic message, any display of affection or sympathy at this moment could tip Beth over so Claire was careful to try and keep her calm.

They pulled into the street. Shadows were starting to lengthen across the road and the neatly clipped lawns were almost confronting, clashing with the nervous chaos they were all feeling inside.

'Stop here.' JJ's command startled them all out of their abstraction. 'I think it's better if we don't park right in front, it would seem a bit intimidating to me.' Claire and Beth nodded. It was time. Together they had decided it was better to confront at this time of day, considerations of approaching the mother alone had been swept away as each of them worried she would dismiss them, and their chance of seeing Marcus's face in a female form, the final confirmation of his betrayal, would be missed. JJ instructed the driver to park around the corner, and they waited until he pulled away before they continued. Eleven, thirteen, house number fifteen was next, Claire took a deep breath, turning back was now not an option.

Chapter Twenty-Five

Beth

Dear Claire and JJ,

Don't listen to her Claire, I bet JJ was on the phone in minutes. You might well find the man of your dreams because even you must admit Johnno did not turn out to be the dreamy type. I hope you meet the sweetest man and yes be cautious but remember when I met Marcus, I could have dismissed him for all his flamboyancy in the crowd, at first glance no one would ever have thought he was going to be the man for me. At least this way you will know a bit about them beforehand. I had to wait for Marcus to wear me down before I looked at the man underneath the social mask he wore, even then he was someone who thought flattery would get him everywhere. I didn't get the link, but I have heard you swipe left for yes and right for no or some such madness. Have you been on any dates yet? Did you tell the kids? Ooh you go girl, use a few for sex and get that body remembering, have you even had sex since Charlotte was conceived? All I can add is take precautions, you don't need a baby at your time of life and certainly not with a casual fling. Goodness Charlotte's fifteen now it would be too much of a gap. I said this to Marcus, and he said I don't know I think you'd adapt. He baffles me sometimes, just when you think you know his answer, a different one comes out of left field. Anyway, send me photos and I heard you can do this phone trick where you get someone to call fifteen minutes into the date and you have a code word so if it isn't going well they start saying there is an emergency so you can make excuses and leave. Let me know if you need my help but remember the time difference other-wise you'll be with him for another half an hour. You are dating men right/? I mean I don't care but a lot of my colleagues have jumped the fence so to speak. Enough now from me. My garden is crazy, and I am starting to not have time for it. In the cool of the evening it soothes me, but the maintenance may wear me out. Marcus is away more than home and flits in and out of Brisbane like a fly, I told him we might as well move there but he seems to like when he is here it is a real break from work, far enough away for the day to day to not interfere. In spite of it we are settled into our own routines, and it is nice to some days, not have to worry about anyone but myself. I am writing more as well which gives me solace, nothing in particular, though fiction may be interesting to attempt, I need to find my style for it, so I am reading outside my usual genres which is making me think and write in different ways, I'm enjoying the experimenting. I was even thinking of coming over to you JJ, some Canada sun might be good for me, and I would love to catch up with Will and Jim. Marcus has a nonstop period and said if I go to Brisbane I will not see him anyway so why not treat myself? I'll try and do a stop over to you Claire I will text you the dates to make sure you can fit me in otherwise I will go with the quickest flights.

Talk soon my lovelies xx Beth.

A curtain moved and held as they passed, a curious neighbour noticing something unusual on their street. They'll find out soon enough Beth thought, it looked much like her neighbourhood, everyone minding their own business until you made it theirs, yet willing to also step in when a crisis occurred, or a shoulder was needed. The house was two-storey and a painted cement path led straight to the door. Clipped hedges lined the path and roses were neatly trimmed into a ball shape behind. The metal gate was white, and Beth was reminded of her childhood, poking her toes through the wire as she waited for the postman to hand her a letter or to give him one. It was a small memory, but it helped as she imagined Willow too had hung over this gate, her imagined long blonde hair hanging down as her body doubled over the top of it. Beth envisioned her startled look when a car approached, was it him, was it her father finally home from a trip? Beth could see it all, the happy clueless family Marcus had created here so far away from her and the life they had led. A shudder rattled up her spine, a reminder her visions were not reality. Beth knew the little girl she dreamed of, the one she envisioned loving her back straight away, two souls flung together by a man who had loved them both was a figment of her imagination, a hope one day fate would turn out in her favour, and happiness would be the reward. Deep down Beth knew the girl in her dreams was herself and all the feelings she had wished for which had never come true.

JJ's hand was firmly on the gate, Claire had stepped back, and Beth knew Claire's role in this was always going to be bigger than her own. Straightening her shoulders was the signal JJ took and she opened the gate standing back to let them pass. Beth strode forward, never one to back away when it came down to the wire, she knew, with their decision made to be here, there was only one way to go. As her foot hit the top step, a car pulled up directly outside the gate and a young girl in a netball uniform scrambled out before turning back to laugh at something said by the speaker hidden behind the half open window.

'See you tomorrow,' she said and turned to move to the gate which had just this moment clicked closed. 'Oh, hello, can I help you.' Her smile was nearly their undoing, without it her parentage would have been disguised, hidden behind her shining hair and blue eyes which were now full of questions. JJ was the first to find her voice.

'Hello to you too, we are looking for someone we don't actually know, the Thomas's?'

'I'm Willow Thomas.' Beth felt her legs buckle as the truth was confirmed. A million thoughts ran through her head, the loudest was shouting, speak to her mother first. It was Claire who voiced it.

'Hello Willow, I'm Claire and this is Beth and JJ. Is your mother home?'

Willow looked puzzled now as she tried to work out who they were. Beth saw Claire swallow hard and took back control.

'Sorry to barge in, no one's in trouble we have to speak with her, I think we know your father,' Beth faltered, 'if she is here Willow it might be better if we speak to her first.'

'First? What's wrong? How do you know my father?'

'Enough questions Willow, they will all be answered, but if you could see if your mum is willing to speak with us.' JJ's voice was kind yet firm enough for the girl to weave between them and open the door. Light from the hallway spilled out and a voice from the back echoed its way through the narrow space.

'Is that you Willow?' The voice was plain, no accent or tone expressed in the question asked.

'We have visitors, can you come here please.' The sound of a utensil being cast aside and the smell wafting around them made Beth apologise for the hour before the woman was physically seen. As her figure emerged, hands busy wiping themselves on a cloth, a look of bewilderment on her narrow face as she examined the three bodies now crowding her entrance way, Beth was struck by her uniqueness. Not pretty yet not plain, her long face put in proportion by the loose knot of reddish-brown hair at her nape, her body was slender, and Willow, Beth thought would soon be taller than her mother, though neither would ever have been called short.

'We are sorry to disturb you. My name is Beth Thomas, and I was wondering if I might speak to you privately.' Beth saw her confusing look.

'What is this about? Thomas? Are you related to Marcus?'

'Yes, in a fashion, please I have a lot to explain but I would rather talk to you in private.' The girl looked frightened now.

'We can speak in front of Willow, there are no secrets in this house.' Beth felt JJ and heard the breath she released. 'Could we sit, I'm afraid this might take a while,' or she thought, it could take a few minutes if you throw us out after my first sentence. The woman ushered them into the spacious but homely lounge room and stood holding the girl close as she gestured for them to take a seat. Beth could see Claire admiring the quality of the furnishings and frowned at her so she would snap out of Claire mode and concentrate on what was happening in the room. The walls seemed to be closing in when the woman cleared her throat before speaking.

'Look what is this about, is Marcus alright, you are beginning to frighten me, and Willow. Who are you anyway, his sister?' JJ leaned forward as if to soften the blow, but the words slipped out before she could as Beth tossed her head in an almost act of defiance and she held her hand up to JJ, this was her job, her moment, Marcus had left her this one chore and she wanted to be sure the words were her own.

'No, I'm so sorry to tell you but Marcus passed away almost six weeks ago.' She waited for a reaction, for the tears and the denials but there were none. Both paled and clung to each other with a firmer grip, the whites of their knuckles showing the pressure. The room had steadied, still closed in, but no longer applying force. Beth could not take her eyes off their faces, she had never been good at reading people, but this was more than judging character. JJ gasped behind her as the penny dropped. They knew.

'You knew.' It was a statement more than a question.

'Yes, well no, we knew it would come, he talked with us both so we could understand. His condition was deteriorating, and he said he wanted to do it alone.' Tears now streamed down Willow's face as her shoulders shook. Claire stood to assist, guiding her to a recliner she balanced on its arm and rubbed Willow's back in a circular motion as the woman crouched before her clutching both her hands and resting her head against Willow's as her own silent tears fell. Beth waited, slumping forward slightly, her knees pressed firmly together, her forearms laying along her legs with her hands clasped, the only movement her thumbs as they alternately rubbed along each other in an almost irritated fashion.

JJ slipped out of the room and Beth realised she was turning off whichever appliance was running and hopefully saving their meal from spoiling, it was unlikely anything would be consumed tonight now. Part of her wished they had a large ticking clock to interrupt the quiet tension and give them back a rhythm to their lives. Tick, tock, tick, tock, her head heard the tune and if she closed her eyes she could see a pendulum swing. Beth had more she had to tell, and obviously now, more she had to hear. It felt frustrating and Beth felt mad, not angry, just really, really, annoyed. It felt strange, as if he was in another room and when he entered she could have a go at him, tell him how he had blocked her grief, given her a task to stop her in her tracks and do his bidding, she wanted to go back, back to her home and wallow in her own grief, not share it with others, this was her time, he had taken his and now he was taking hers. It was selfish, this girl had lost her father and Beth's silly dream she would be the one to comfort and console was exactly what it was, a dream. Willow had her own mother and friends, probably other family as well, to her, Beth would merely be the person who told her about her father's death. Beth's heart hurt, she had thought he had left her someone to cling to, but she could see now it would not be the case.

Willow's sobs had slowed, and Claire returned to her place on the lounge. JJ offered to make tea, which was declined, and Beth realised all eyes were back on her.

'I'm sorry, I didn't catch your name.'

'Robyn. My name is Robyn, and you are, sorry was it Beth?'

'Yes I'm Beth and this is Claire and JJ. We are truly sorry to intrude but I was the one Marcus asked to let you know and once we knew about Willow, we knew she had to be told.'

'We?' Robyn motioned her hand at the three of them and then lay it out as a question to be answered.

Beth felt nervous now, Willow was staring at her with big, red-rimmed eyes and Beth could see the questions and accusations forming in her head.

'Are you my Aunt?'

Beth took a deep breath and both JJ and Claire slid a hand toward her in support. She shuffled forward on the lounge wanting to keep eye contact as the news was received.

'No Willow I'm not.' A look, like disappointment, flashed across the girl's face. 'I'm not your aunt, I have the same name as your father because,' she faltered, 'because I'm his wife.'

Beth heard the gasp from Robyn as she watched Willow's mouth drop open. Obviously this was something they didn't know.

Chapter Twenty-Six

Willow

Dear Willow,

A quick note to let you know I can't make it to your games, work has swallowed me up and it might be some time until I see you in person again. Don't worry if you don't hear and keep being your bubbly self. I promise to spoil you with ice-cream next time we meet though the years have flown, and it is probably some gadget or jewellery you would now prefer. Say hi to all.

Love Marcus

PS: yes I know I could have texted, but I like this old-fashioned way, did I ever tell you I know someone who has had a penfriend for over fifty years? Maybe one day you two can meet.

The three older ladies were staring at her, she felt Robyn's hand tighten on hers as the wave of shock rolled over them both. His wife? Marcus, what have you done now she thought. Willow turned to look at Robyn's face, she had drawn her eyebrows inwards both puzzled and frowning at the same time, and Willow searched for an answer as for what she should do. Robyn seemed to nod slightly, and Willow decided she should find out more before spilling the beans.

'I know this might be a shock to you, and I um, I realise you might be a bit angry at us barging in here, but you needed to know, and we thought it was best to do it in person.' It was the middle one who spoke. Willow could see how her friends, or were they sisters, were so protective of her. It was confusing, had she known? What a shock it must have been if she hadn't, to find out your husband had a child you didn't know about and for him to ask you to relay the news. It was cruel and yet coming from Marcus, Willow thought, it was barely a surprise.

Willow was sad, Marcus had been her father, her biological one and yes, he had tried but the role was played on his terms and Willow from a young age had understood the situation. These women were curious and so was she, the pretty one puzzled her, she had seen her face before, alone and also with Marcus. Willow had googled him once and a photo had come up with him at some gala function with his arm around a stunning woman, Willow studied her face and was sure this was the same person, slightly older but still as beautiful. Was she another wife? There were so many questions and yet Willow knew once they were told there would be so many answers. Robyn cleared her throat and Willow jumped in, wanting her own answers, and also wanting to know how much they knew so she could ease them in gently. The middle one, Beth she had said, looked fragile and sometimes Robyn was one to speak first and think later.

'Are you sisters?' They all looked at each other as if they were unsure of the reply.

'No, we feel like we are but no, we are actually pen pals and life-long friends. Maybe we should start at the beginning.' The tall one with the slight blemish on one side of her face paused as if asking silently for the others to agree she should continue and as they nodded Willow thought she could see their invisible link. It was uncanny to watch almost like the twin thing she had read about where twins knew and felt what the other was feeling without it being expressed verbally.

'Are you ok for us to continue? Would you like a pause to have your dinner which we have interrupted?' Robyn shook her head and Willow squeezed her hand.

'I think we have a lot to talk about with you as well so start and we can take a break if it all becomes too much for now.'

JJ continued. 'As I said we are pen pals and have been corresponding with each other since we were nine years old. We have shared a lot over the years and have become very close as we have lived through our ups and downs, our marriages and children, everything really. We meet up when we can and at times this included our husbands, they themselves were friendly with each other, but we are not a group of friends if you know what I mean, it is Claire, Beth and I who are a family.' JJ cleared her throat and Willow could see her love for the others. 'When your father died,'

'You can call him Marcus,' Willow interjected, 'I do.' They looked surprised but didn't add any layers of questions, somehow knowing the answers would come.

'Marcus then. When Marcus passed away we of course came to support Beth, and he was to me, a very good friend who I am so sad is no longer here. He left Beth a note telling her of your name and address and asked her to let you know about his passing. It was the first time she had any inkling you even existed.' Willow leaned forward on impulse to take Beth's hand who was looking at the floor now and it was clear the hurt and shock he had caused. Willow tucked away her own feelings, Marcus had been a myriad of emotions to her, a distant part time dad yet more like an uncle she hardly knew, a friend at times and a partner in crime when her parents had said no when she was little, and treats were on offer. On Beth's face she could clearly see the betrayal and together with her own experience of him, she knew these women were telling the truth. JJ continued.

'I'm not sure if I should say it now,' she looked at Beth who nodded her approval. 'Marcus has left you something in his will, we have a letter from the solicitor for you, but I think we might leave those details until later.' Again, she paused, for Willow's agreement this time. Although JJ was a commanding figure, Willow could already see the kindness hidden beneath. The pretty one Claire stared at the floor the whole time and Willow felt she was somehow afraid of what was to come.

'Beth and Marcus had been married for thirty-five years when,' Robyn gasped loudly, her eyes wide with the shock of the length of Marcus's deceit. 'when he passed away.' They all were silent as if each needed a moment to remember the man and not the awkwardness of the situation.

'What a shock for you,' Robyn said, 'but it is for us too, we knew he had been married in the past, but he never offered up any information. Once though' she looked thoughtful, 'he said my wife is irreplaceable and I remember thinking he had mixed up his verbs and meant was.'

Willow did not want to get into their side of it yet, it was all a bit too much at once though she could see by Beth's face there were a million questions hovering below the surface. Willow squeezed her mother's hand.

'Can we take a break now, would you like some tea or wine maybe,' she looked at Robyn quizzically trying to prompt her into her usual role of hostess. The others murmured apologies, maybe they should go, come back once the news had been digested more, go and find something to eat for themselves. Willow nudged Robyn again.

'What do you think, we could order in pizza and hear it all or ...' Willow felt torn and overwhelmed but knew there was more, Claire was hiding something, and Willow was worried it would be too much while at the same time wanted to get it over with. To keep going back to more pain might be harder than taking it all on at once.

'Are you ok?'

'Yes I'm good, but can we have a moment, just you and me, I feel a bit ... to be honest, I'm not actually sure how I feel.'

The ladies fussed and Willow led the way as they exited the room and hurried down the hall to her own room. It felt weird and Willow somehow felt guilty her tears were not flowing and the expected grief did not feel as painful as she believed it should be after losing a parent. Robyn rubbed her arm.

'How do you feel, truly?'

'It's weird isn't it, how brave she is to come here, she could have left it, no one would have blamed her for being selfish and looking after herself, she has lost her husband, the love of her life but it is typical isn't it, Marcus leaving it to someone else to do the hard yards and tie up loose ends.' Robyn sat back on the bed not even trying to deny the facts Willow stated were true. Marcus was a rogue, a lovable one who had given her life but a selfish one who wanted the good bits and turned his back when real life became tough. 'What do I tell them? They seem nice and she obviously loved him. Thirty-five years they were together, and he didn't think to be honest and tell her he had a daughter in there somewhere? Wow I'm spinning out a bit.'

'Calm down, do you want them to go, I'll tell them it's a bit too much tonight and we can arrange to meet tomorrow or on the weekend.'

"No, let's get their side over with tonight, somehow I think the quiet one Claire has something to say and I'd rather hear it now. We can fill them in on us tomorrow.' Willow stopped and looked stunned as the thought occurred. 'They think you were his mistress! Well, they would, wouldn't they? Omg she thinks he was having an affair, and it seems he has set it up to look like it too. I'm not sure what will be worse, what she thinks now or what we have to tell her. Either way it will look like she did not know the man she was married to.' Willow threw her hands up to her face. 'I didn't even ask how he died.' The sobs returned, unfortunately more for her own self-worth than for her father.

Robyn wrapped Willow in her arms. 'Come on,' she said, 'let's get this over with, we'll hear them out and ask them to take a break until tomorrow. In one way I'm glad Jed and Iris are not here so we can sort through what they have to tell us without the others throwing a spanner in the works. 'I'll order pizza and get some wine, you can't have it but somehow I think I am going to need it.

Chapter Twenty-Seven

JJ

Dear Claire and Beth,

Is it me or did I lose a decade here. I feel like I stepped back to the future and am wondering how I got here. Jim mentions dementia far too often, his Aussie sense of humour will long outlive him I am sure. Again, too much time has passed since I saw your faces. Beth, how is Marcus? I'm taking no news is good news, but he is skilled at looking terrific in spite of it all. He has lived through a lot and there is no turning back, but his choices should be looked at with a clear mind. Oh, your husband, a stronger man I have never known but determined, phew! Hang in there when he retires Beth, what a whirlwind it will be. I know it should have been long ago, I see your points Beth, but he has always loved it, even the travel, to actually travel to look at sights are not his joy unless there is a paper to read or a contract to be signed. If he is happy Beth, maybe you should be grateful and leave him be. A caged Marcus is not something I would want to confront.

So how many dates are we up to now Claire, must be thousands, and are you getting any? Believe me and I've said it before, you have been a waste to mankind with that body and those looks, I hope you pause on one soon who might fill your needs so to speak. The ones you described in your last letter should most certainly have been swiped whichever way, geez do they not think when they walk in you will recognise they have airbrushed their photos? The old one was clearly a better artist than a teller of the truth, maybe he should have written maestro on his bio!

Charlotte as you know came to visit, remember our gap year, it was called annual leave in those days and lasted four weeks not a year! Yes I'm grumpy and I don't know why, caught between wanting to retire and wondering what I will do, if I do. Is it too early? Work is tiresome, and with my parent's inheritance we invested, Jim questioned me on if it was worth it. He is able to move his work around so if we wanted to duck away for a weekend we could pick up and go. I think I just have to find my secret passion.

Not much else from here, Charlotte spoke about the job in the US so hang onto your hat Claire she seemed keen. At least I could fly to her and spoil her on a more regular basis without having to sit a whole day on a plane. Paul called as well, how sweet he is and how blessed we have been to share the joys of them both. I hope my melancholy mood lifts soon and your replies are filled with news to uplift me.

Much love my sweets x JJ.

Claire was fussing which as usual irritated JJ further, her stomach was rumbling and a whole lot of her wanted the task to be completed. Willow and Robyn's reactions had been both surprising and puzzling and actually, downright confusing. Willow called him Marcus. They had all presumed from his letter to Beth they would have been close, and each, in their own way had made up a life story for Willow which had settled their psyche and allowed them to move forward with their grief and their expectations for the future. Instead, a million more questions had been raised. The pushy JJ wanted to urge it out of her faster and lay the many sides of Marcus before them so they could begin the process of working out the truth and discovering the man behind the ever-growing amount of masks. JJ had to hand it to Robyn, she had raised a daughter who knew her manners but also demonstrated a connectedness to them which was displayed in her tone, control and mannerisms. Willow's empathy with Beth had already demonstrated to JJ she was not an immature teenager, but a young woman who for some reason, was already wise beyond her years.

Beth looked worn out and JJ longed to draw her away, in part to shield her and in part to talk it out, deal with it now so their Beth could truly return to them, still in a shattered form from Marcus's passing but Beth just the same. Quickly they had decided to agree with Willow on how to proceed, she was young, and the focus today should be on her. Robyn seemed to be allowing her daughter to make her own decisions and JJ knew they all admired her strength and support. JJ had noticed Beth stealing glances, probably as Beth's self-worth hovered in the lowest sector, she would be assessing Marcus's choice in Robyn. Marcus had known Claire, and JJ did not think any man could have refused if the door there had been left ajar. Marcus had also known Claire for her softness and vulnerabilities, she would have been an easy target. Robyn was not unattractive, but she certainly had never been in Claire's league. Robyn also had a hardness, like a force shield hovering beneath the surface and JJ could feel she was well practised in pulling it out as a woman to protect herself, and also as a mother to protect her cub. JJ heard the bedroom door open and turned expectantly as Willow and her mother returned.

Chapter Twenty-Eight

Claire

Dear JJ and Beth,

What can I say, well yes JJ, I have been taking your advice and I must say am feeling very liberated. With Charlotte gone and Paul settled with his life I did take a deep breath and get serious about taking some time for me, but JJ on my terms. I must say this dating whirlwind has nearly worn me out and I was going to give it away when the other day a charming face came across the screen, and I decided to give it one more chance. Oh my goodness he is simply delicious and so handsome and well mannered. We have had three dates and I was a bit guarded at first (no Beth I haven't told him where I live) and yes JJ I googled him and could not find anything except the truth of where he had worked and Charlotte has told me to check on social media but I'm only on there so I can track her while she is away, the world is moving too fast and it seems now we have to communicate through a computer more and more, Paul said one day soon I will be able to call him and will be able to see his face on the screen. It is a bit Dick Tracey or Maxwell Smart-ish for me! I told him if I have to lift my shoe to my ear he can write me letters, as I won't be doing it. I really think they are missing out, look at all we have shared over the years and the absolute joy I feel each time there is a letter in the mailbox, call us old fashioned but I love how each time I hold it to my chest and take my time to savour it as I anticipate the replies to my silly concerns and to hear your news. I think sometimes I get more joy before I open it than at any other time. Remember in our emergencies when a telegram would come, or you would pick up the phone and the overseas operator would ask you to take the call. Those times the panic would rise, and we knew without speaking the need was there. Now, it seems everything is urgent, or can't wait, it is all getting too fast for me. I do feel proud though, what great people Charlotte and Paul have turned out to be, even if I do say so myself. They are so close and have honestly taught me more than I have ever taught them. I have never regretted all I did to get Charlotte, and is it age or this horrible menopause which is making me nostalgic?? Either way I am so glad they have each other.

XXX Claire

PS: JJ, maybe it is the change of life with you too?

Claire slid forward in her seat, she knew it was now her time to confess to Willow and enlighten her on her siblings. She was not ashamed, not anymore, Beth had forgiven her and after Beth and Charlotte had talked for hours on the phone, Claire knew a lot of the hurt had been healed or at least sealed over enough for Beth to move forward. Paul and Charlotte had enriched all their lives and over the years Claire had known deep down it was the children who would do the healing if Beth ever found out. In saying this though, Claire had also thought they had gotten away with it and as much as she wanted to grieve for the friend she had lost, she was angry, so angry it was at this time he had chosen to reveal some of his secrets, after he had run away not only to avoid any consequences but also to take the answers to all the questions with him. It was taking all her strength to keep her temper under control so she would not lash out at the innocent. JJ had visibly backed off on a few occasions which allowed Claire to take a deep breath and control her anger.

Willow and Robyn settled themselves again on the comfortable lounge.

'Do you all like pizza? Robyn's going to order some as we think maybe, you have a bit more to tell us. Um, we, um.' Robyn took Willow's hand.

'We have to talk about us, we need to tell you, but I think after you have finished,' Robyn paused to glance at Willow, 'we might leave our side until tomorrow, it has been a big night and I think we all will need some space before we continue.'

Claire saw Beth and JJ nod their agreement and Robyn left the room to make the call for food. JJ also stepped aside to call their driver and tell him to go to get some dinner and return in an hour and a half which irritated Claire as it was her turn now, and maybe she would require more time. It was typical of JJ though to take control and at least, Claire thought, it showed she was feeling more settled and returning to her usual self. The JJ of the last few weeks had been just as difficult to deal with as her indecision, and detachment, had been hard to watch and left a giant hole Claire had struggled to fill. Over the years they had all found their roles and Claire longed for them each to claw back to fill theirs as she could feel the pressure and was unsure of how much longer she could support them all. As selfish as she felt at her thoughts, Claire was also firing up so the words heard next, would be her own, with no interruption. As everyone fussed trying to fill the time before the food arrived, Robyn poured wine and they each left the room to use the bathroom.

Claire lingered on her way back, glancing into rooms, comparing Robyn to herself in a way she knew she shouldn't. This should be about Beth, yet the emotions Claire felt made her want to shout, he was mine too as she somehow felt lost in the drama of it all. Claire paused at a photo on the wall, four smiling faces around a wet dog who was clearly trying to shake free and droplets of water as he shook were captured, sparkling across the scene as if the dog too was truly enjoying the situation. It was a photo of pure joy, a precious scene taken in a moment which could never be replaced. Claire smiled, she had photos of her kids the same, unposed, the laughter captured on their precious faces. Claire wondered who they were, the other people, maybe an aunt or cousins, friends out for the day, the doorbell rang, and she moved ahead, storing her thoughts for later as to where they were and what would have played out at the end of the scene. The smell of the pizza filled the room and Robyn had put out plates and serviettes so they could all help themselves from the boxes and continue with their discussion.

Claire took a bite, it was delicious but hard to swallow, she gulped at the wine to help and received a glare from JJ. Placing her plate carefully on the edge of the overfilled coffee table Claire patted her mouth gently with the serviette and cleared her throat. Willow looked straight at her, and Claire knew she was curious as to her role in all of this.

'I might tell you about my side in all of this if I may.' Claire ignored the JJ look again and continued. 'As JJ said we have all been pen pals and friends for a very long time. Before you hear what I have to say I want you to know these women mean the world to me and you might find this hard to understand when I am finished.' Claire chanced a look at Beth, but her face was blank. It was a tiny punishment from Beth who was going to make Claire do this bit on her own.

'Almost twenty-five years ago, I had an affair with Marcus.' Claire waited as Robyn tried to contain her thoughts and Willow stilled, continuing to stare as if she knew this was not the full tale. 'I fell pregnant with my daughter Charlotte. Willow,' Claire reached for her hand, but Willow drew back as her words sank in. 'Charlotte is your sister.'

Claire panicked as the silence grew like a cloud enveloping each of them. Beth and JJ remained stonily silent, watching the reactions as they flashed across faces. Surprise, a tiny hint of delight and wonderment from Willow, confusion and a sympathy for Beth followed by a shock to be sitting here, all in the same room yet not with the instigator of the whole situation. Claire began to babble to fill in some gaps quickly.

'I have a son too, but he has a different father, not a good one but technically not related to you at all. I suppose Paul is your half-brother, no, stepbrother maybe, anyway he is Charlotte's brother. You will love her, everyone does, you even have some features the same. I can see splinters of Marcus in you.'

'Claire!' JJ pulled her up, 'let them have a moment to think will you, without the babble.' Claire was miffed but sank back, exhausted now her hand in this had been shown and waited for the onslaught. Willow's eyes were huge, and Robyn had snuggled in closer to comfort her.

'Wow a sister, where is she, does she know about me.'

'Yes she does. She is quite excited, but we decided to wait and give you some time. Both Paul and Charlotte would like to meet you, Marcus was a father figure to both of them, and they called him Uncle Marcus not dad. Charlotte found out when she was ten and Paul and I have never really discussed it, but the children have worked out how they feel between themselves and as strange as it seems, we talk now as if they had always known. Beth and JJ found out recently, but I think it is a story for another night. We can video call them if you want to.'

'No, but I will, I might, some other time. It is a shock though, Marcus really was a piece of work wasn't he.' Willow sounded angry.

Claire felt sad, she had not meant to ruin the girls dreams of her father and yet there was something she couldn't put her finger on which told her Marcus's behaviour was not as big a surprise as they had suspected.

'It took two of us, not something I am proud of, and the emotions there are between Beth and I and nothing to do with anyone else. Please know you have us all and Charlotte to support you, after your mum of course, and we will answer any questions honestly. How you want to continue the relationships after is up to you, but with it being so few weeks since Marcus left, I hope you will not judge us too quickly and take the time to get to know us before deciding what to do. For us, you are a tiny piece of him we can rejoice in.'

'He didn't leave Claire, he died,' JJ blunt as ever interrupted. 'Marcus was a cad, a lovable one and the man who adored my friend like no other, yet still a cad as we are finding out. I think maybe it is time we left to give Robyn and Willow time to come to terms with the news.' Robyn seemed to be agreeing even though they could see Claire had more to say. 'It's for the best Claire, leave Charlotte's number and Willow, when you are ready please call one of us and we will be available at whatever time suits you.' JJ had organised and bossed as usual. Claire flushed as she bit her tongue, there was so much she wanted to explain, how wrong she had been to betray her friend and yet the result had been so right, none of them would be the same person without Charlotte in their lives. Claire wanted to tell Willow, it may turn out to be the same for her, she so badly wanted her to know, and explain.

JJ had helped Beth up, she looked old, even frail would be the term to use. To see the proof of Marcus's betrayal was proving too much and no one could ever be fully prepared for something like this. It would be hard to watch this vibrant beautiful young creature and know, to your own husband, she had been someone to hide away, to lie about and to leave to you as a burden to bear of his deceitfulness. Claire could see it all and the mother in her, the friend in her, wanted to right it so everyone in her world would be happy again. JJ loomed into her personal space.

'Come on Claire, there will be time for you to finish your tale, but for tonight, for them, it is enough. Come on, you know it is the right time to leave. Hate me outside not here.' Claire knew her thoughts had been read and felt without words, it was how they were, and she knew JJ was right. Robyn was gracious though encouraging for them to depart. Willow sat nodding her acknowledgement as they all said goodbye and they let her be. JJ scribbled their numbers and Robyn indicated for them to allow some time and promised to call or text when she felt Willow was willing to talk with them again. Claire hesitated as Willow called to her mum, Claire indicated she would shut the door and as she did slowly she glanced back and saw Robyn and heard Willow clearly.

'They don't know Mum, they don't know I have two.'

Two, two what Claire thought, oh my god she thought, two fathers. No wonder she had not looked surprised.

Chapter Twenty-Nine

Beth

Dear JJ,

Thanks for your reply. I was so scared you would blame me, and we would never talk again. This will be the last time I do it just between us as I feel guilty too, about not confessing to Claire. My life is so crap and I can see now I will have to man-up as they say and live with what I've done. Whatever happens in this house from now on is the choice of others and I can't change my life goals for them. Death is a finality you cannot come back from, or change, though I think she will haunt me for the rest of my life, even in death I think she will make it her mission to never forgive me for being born nor for what I did, and I will never forgive myself either for taking Tom's mother away from him, I can see now how much he needed her. I am trying to lock it away in my head and the nightmares are becoming less frequent, the less busy I am the more they intrude. I promise you I will try to be a good person and help anyone I see in need in an effort to make up for the terrible human being I am. Thankyou JJ for your friendship, support and love, I will never again let you down, I promise. XX Beth

'I said I would never let someone manipulate my life ever again. I can see now I was being manipulated and didn't even know it. What a fool I have been, and what a fool they must think I am.'

'Hush Beth, they were in shock, and I thought they were very sympathetic to your position. The girl had to be told and if not Marcus, I think you were the right one to tell them. Never forget how much he loved you,' Claire knelt now in front of her and took her hands. 'Marcus adored you, I have never seen anyone care as much for another person, he put you on a pedestal and even Jim, as much as I love him, didn't go so far for JJ. Marcus never wanted to share you with anyone it was always clear, except we were good friends, I often felt he resented me and JJ as well. It was clear he struggled when we were all together in spite of all he was hiding. When you were in the room Beth he could never take his eyes off you. Remember him Beth, remember the good.' Beth had to agree, half of her brain seemed to be working logically and the other half was the one which continued to throw in the spanners and the self-doubt, Beth was struggling to remember the Marcus who had been truly her own.

'It was like they knew, even though they didn't.' JJ plonked herself on the plush motel lounge. 'I somehow feel there are more secrets to come. I must say I was impressed with Willow, she is certainly mature beyond her years.'

'Why did he do this, why didn't he tell me? I'm questioning everything about our life together, every moment he must have been calculating the right words to say so as to not slip up and let his secrets out. How did you do it Claire, how do people deceive so easily.' Beth knew it was cruel and saw the tears spring to Claire's eyes. In spite of all her promises to be kind, the venom Marcus had stirred in her continued to leak out, Claire was the easy target and, although she was trying, Beth could not seem to allow Claire to escape with no punishment.

Every self-doubt she ever had was returning and no years of therapy or good deed from her life seemed to be enough to redeem her, Beth's mother's voice was loose in her head and was fighting against being locked away in the corner of Beth's brain again where she had hidden these last thirty years. Beth had even wondered, in moments, if Marcus had been right, if she could ask him if peace had been found in the place he was now, maybe she would join him. These moments passed as she looked at those who were supporting her, JJ probably understood more than Claire, Claire had always seemed to live on an even keel, her downs were merely ripples, compared to some, in which they had caught her each time and her inner courage had pulled her through. JJ's downs were different and the masks she had used to hide her face became words which she used, sometimes harshly, to protect herself. Words were her strength, along with Jim, who saw through JJ's dictionary coat and loved the still sometimes insecure girl, hiding inside. It was his strength JJ leaned on when her own failed her. Beth thought she had found this with Marcus, he had adored her, in public and in private. The many memories of his support and tenderness had often overwhelmed her. Beth could see now how she had held back, not told him her truths, yet to be honest, Marcus had never wanted to listen. Life for them was to be fun and at a pace set by Marcus, his hurry through life was to prove to his body he could do it all, career, wife, social extrovert, loved by all for his personality so he would never hear a note of sympathy in their voices. It had surprised Beth someone would love her so much, would want to share her thoughts and triumphs with a joy not for themselves but for her, unconditional love had been foreign to her, and Beth now knew it had blinded her too. Now all she could ponder is how much of it had been true as all the thoughts and fears she had never spoken gathered to destroy the little of herself she had left inside. JJ looked pensive, Marcus and JJ had been close, and Beth knew at times they had talked about her, had JJ told him her secrets?

Marcus had never been curious about her past, life to him was for today and he had carried her through on his never-ending wave, some days when he was away, delayed, too busy to help her keep high on the crest of it with him, the self-doubt had returned ,and it was in these times the girls had saved her, a letter would arrive and push her through the moments she could no longer bear. When Marcus would return, full of apologies and bearing expensive gifts all would be forgiven, and the roller-coaster would begin again. Marcus had suffered enough, his body betraying his zest for life, or maybe it had been encouraging it to get the most out of life while he had the time. Beth would hide away her feelings of doubt, loss and her deep grief for the little lives she had never been able to meet, to keep him up and, she must admit, to keep him. Her biggest fear had been of losing him to someone more vibrant, more beautiful and certainly more interesting than Beth had ever thought herself to be. They had each other he had said, and it was all they needed, she was his rock and so Beth hid her lows to please him and make him smile. JJ was speaking and as Beth's head dreams began to merge she wondered if it was herself and not JJ at all, who had worn the biggest mask.

'Are you with us Beth? Hello, I was saying, Robyn actually said very little, I can't seem to work it out, I thought she would have been horrified to learn about you, plus Claire's little bombshell. You would think there would have been some anger or denial even. As a mother you would have thought she would ask more questions or want to talk to us alone, it almost seemed like Willow was the adult as Robyn let her take the lead almost every time.'

'Claire, could you make some tea, I think I have reached my alcohol peak for today, thank goodness you ordered the driver, the couple of wines we had there went straight to my head.'

Beth tried to deflect to give herself time to make peace with her thoughts.

'Did you hear me Beth? I said what did you think of Robyn?' JJ did not give up and Beth snapped back.

'I thought she was prettier than me but not as pretty as Claire, I thought she had a style Marcus might find attractive and I wondered as I have always done, what it was about me he fell in love with. Was I a fool all these years, someone plain and stupid he could hide behind while he lived out a whole other plan which didn't include me? Did he deliberately seek out Claire or was it an accident, a moment which went too far and from which they both gained a thrill.'

'I didn't Beth...'

'You did Claire, if not from the sex then at least from the secrecy. After Claire were there more, is Willow the only one we know about, and if she is, why not fess up the whole truth about the affair. If I hadn't seen him with my own eyes, would I really believe he was dead, or is it all a hoax and he is living another life somewhere else now with someone else who will be blinded by his lies. THAT is what I was thinking JJ, not about Robyn or Willow or you and Claire, I was thinking about me and how much more there is which I am not sure I want to hear!' The anger was like a fire which had crackled at the start and was now a raging inferno of the anger, hate and guilt she felt was the legacy Marcus had left her. Beth realised she had jumped up and with shoulders tense and fists clenched, was pacing the small room in an effort to not damage anything, or to be honest, anyone. One word filled her head. Why?

Chapter Thirty

Claire

Dear JJ,

Thanks for letting me know. Beth has always been insecure and blamed herself. Since the day the pram rolled off the porch it seems she has never forgiven herself or been allowed to. It's ironic it was the same day she posted the first letter, I don't know if she would have survived without us. I feel so sad we never knew for so long how desperately unhappy she was. This may completely crush her, and I am trying to get leave to go to Adelaide (and dad's permission which is harder) for a few days, though she would probably hate me for it as I'm not sure it is the circumstances under which we all thought we would meet. I think it is fine we wrote to her individually as well as our normal one, her mum died, and I could not imagine the pain. I need you both so much in my life and hopefully between us we can hold her up without her knowing, you are the strong one and I know I may frustrate you at times, but we must both do this for Beth. I promise I will never tell, if there is one thing I am good at it is keeping a secret. I know you think I'm a bit airy fairy JJ, but I will never let you or Beth down, I love my family so much but you two have given me so much strength and encouragement and the support to tread my own path, I triple promise to always be here for you both. I'm crossing all my fingers and toes we can finally meet each other soon.

Much love Claire xxx.

PS: I know you will but destroy this letter and I will burn yours to me, so we never have to worry about Beth seeing the contents and again this secret is safe with me.

Claire was letting it all slide tonight, to hang on to the emotion Beth was displaying would be harmful and deep-down Claire knew Beth was merely venting, and for all Marcus had done, Claire was the only one here on whom she could lay the blame in person.

Robyn had puzzled Claire as well, while she had stayed quiet as JJ and Beth spoke knowing her turn would come, her anxiety rose as to whether Willow would be accepting of a sibling. Part of Claire wanted her to be happy and for the three of them to become a happy and supportive family as her own brother and sister had been for her. Part of her wondered if it would be better if they never met, after all, her kids were happy with their lives, and this could bring up old feelings or eventually resentment for Paul who had always been the one who, Claire felt, was a bit left out. No more hiding Claire she admonished herself, you hid behind lies for too long and it is a tinge of luck and a lot of love which has almost cleared the hurt away, don't pass it on to the next generation, let destiny run its course in truth, your part has been played, now it is up to others to make their choices.

'Why don't we get some sleep and talk about it all tomorrow. I keep remembering small bits and tomorrow I might make a list, so I don't forget in the moment. Did you see the photo in the hall? Who do you think they were?'

'There you go Claire, saying we are done with questions for tonight and asking two more.' JJ shook her head and it irritated Claire, as it had when JJ had made her finish up and not let her complete all she had to say to Willow, tonight her head urged her to let it go.

'Sorry, yes JJ you are right, I'll make some cocoa and we can try to sleep. Who knows, it may be days before she decides to let us visit again, we will have plenty of time to talk tomorrow.'

Beth was still rigid with anger as Claire boiled the kettle in the tiny kitchenette and thought about the night. Of them all, it would be herself and Charlotte who would be more than likely involved with Willow from now on, there would be no reason for her to continue a relationship with either Beth or JJ. They had no connection now, Marcus's semen the only shared connection between them all, except JJ of course. Claire gasped audibly at her thought, what is wrong with you she thought, thinking about Marcus like he was some kind of donor of body fluids, Claire had to admit she had shocked herself.

'What are you surprising yourself with now Claire?' JJ had sidled in while Claire was lost in her thoughts. 'Shh, nothing, well not what I want Beth to hear while she is upset.'

'She's in the bathroom so come on, spill the Claire beans.'

Claire pressed her lips together to show her distaste at JJ's remark. 'Well, it popped in my head, you know random ..'

'You, random? I'm appalled.' JJ laughed softly but rubbed her arm in forgiveness. Claire wondered if they would ever stop teasing her for being such a flibbertigibbet.

'Shh JJ, what if they want nothing to do with Beth? How will she feel, could we bring her back from it. These last weeks it seems forming her imaginary relationship with this girl is what has kept her going. What if they don't call back and we have to all fade away into the abyss? It could happen and then where will we be, Beth can't live on being angry at Marcus for the rest of her life. You know this will sink her for the last time, it will release all the anxiety from her mother and everything since, there is only so much a person can bury JJ, before it explodes for the last time. I'm so worried.' Claire covered her face with her hands and leaned in to gain support from JJ.

'Now I have to tell you to shush.' JJ lowered her voice to just above a whisper. 'You know we must never talk about her death, I know Beth knows we shared a bit now, but those letters were always a secret, Claire, don't let the cat out of the bag now.'

'What cat?' Beth's voice was stonily cold. 'Have you more secrets to share Claire or is it you this time JJ? Why don't you both unravel it all now and be done with it. Make my whole life a complete lie.' Beth's hands were on her hips, her legs slightly spread. Claire thought a gun belt would almost complete her stance.

'Beth no, I'm worried is all, maybe we should pack up to go home, get you sorted and take a holiday or fly back with JJ, what do you say? We have done what Marcus asked you to do, so let's move on, forget about the others, it is for them to sort out now and time for us all to forgive and remember the man we knew. It is how he was with us Beth, with you, which should be the focus. All of this,' Claire waived her hand at the window to indicate the world outside, 'this has nothing more to do with any of us.'

'She is your daughter's sister, my husband's daughter, do you think I want all this Claire, are you seriously too stupid to see how you have all ruined my life? I wish I had never met you, any of you, so why don't you pack your bags and leave, go back to your little family, half of which you stole from me and oh, you could hook up with this new one, I know you want to Claire it is written all over you, how you should be the star in all of this. Well why don't you step off your runway for once and see how the other half lives. JJ and I have spent our whole lives propping you up Claire, oh poor Claire can't cope with two kids and a brilliant career, oh no poor Claire who thinks it's ok to sleep with her friend's husband, have his child and think it is ok to lie about it for more than twenty years. Get out Claire, I think my stomach is too full to take another moment with you.' Beth turned and stormed out, slamming the door so hard the room shook, and Claire thought the other residents would think there was an earthquake.

'Now you've done it.' JJ raised her hands in two stop signs stepping back as if she had not been to blame in any of it.

Claire felt the fury rising, how dare they, how dare they pretend she had never been there for them, it was clear now they really had been laughing behind her back, well she was not going to take it anymore, she was done, why should I put my life on hold anymore she thought. I have a lovely man who wants to spoil me and take me out for dinner, I have my two beautiful children and I have a career I couldn't be prouder of. I will go, and they will see, see I can live without them, I can survive on my own and they will be sorry, two lonely old women with nothing else to show for their lives.

Claire tipped her drink in the sink, rinsed the cup and placed it upside down to drain. Stepping around JJ and without another word she gathered her belongings and snapped her bag shut. A final glance and glare at JJ and Claire left the room, closing the door in a much more dignified manner than Beth had. Straightening her shoulders, she fought back the tears as she wondered where in the hell she would now spend the night. Don't turn back Claire she chided herself, this time don't give in.

The manager was helpful in finding Claire another room on the second floor. She held her head high until the door closed behind her and was determined to stay strong. In a similar kitchenette she boiled the water and poured herself a hopefully soothing earl grey tea. The aroma from it drifted across her nostrils which were still flared in anger. This was the worst fight they had ever had, and Claire had remained silent as words said in anger could somehow never quite be forgiven or forgotten, they often came from the deep place where those unspoken words were hidden and as they stewed there together, false truths were often the result. Claire did not want to dwell on the hurt she felt, surely all these years of friendship would not be thrown away now. Claire desperately wanted to ring Charlotte but as it was the middle of the night and Charlotte would want every detail, especially about Willow, Claire hesitated knowing it would be better to wait until she had more details to tell her. Sighing deeply, she showered hoping the water would wash the last few weeks away and she could have them all over again.

The letters filled her mind, to Claire every one of them had peeled back a layer of themselves, now she wondered how many of them had been band-aids to cover up something they had been trying to hide. Claire felt hurt, she had never thought herself better than anyone, the society she'd had to parade in had never been her circle. Work was work and the promotional side the hardest part. Beth knew it, Claire thought, all the times I stressed about some gala or show and they would calm me, talk me through so once I was there I could waltz my way in as if it was my daily life, and so others never saw the nervous kitten hiding inside. The times Beth and JJ had cheered from the sidelines as she took a bow and knew they were the ones who understood there was a shy worried Claire hiding beneath the surface. Claire knew she could not live without them, she would give them time, let Beth make the first move when she was ready. Don't take it personally, Claire tried to mimic JJ as she scolded herself, you promised JJ you would not let her down and this mess has turned into so much more, stay focused on why you came.

Sliding into the cool sheets Claire felt her hidden strengths returning, pick your battles JJ often said and Claire knew this was not one of them, tomorrow was a new day and hopefully Willow and Robyn would allow them to slot the last pieces of Marcus into place so they could all start to move forward, if not together, than in an amicable way everyone was comfortable with. It was the best Claire could hope for and as the strain of the day drained away, her muscles relaxed, and sleep eased the endless questions in her mind.

Chapter Thirty-One

Willow

Dear Willow,

My name is Charlotte, and as you would now know I am your half-sister. It must be such a shock and it was for me too. I have an older brother Paul, who is also my greatest friend. I don't know how much you have been told so I will say it like it is. My mum was married to Paul's father, they split up and she had an affair with Marcus who is both your dad and mine. We are a family of halves, but I hope for you, as it is with us it will not matter. I understand you may want some privacy, but I do urge you to talk with Beth, Marcus was a complex man and to be honest I never thought of him as being my dad and only ever called him uncle. It is all a bit mixed up, but I wanted you to know both Paul and I are happy to meet or even correspond until you figure out how you feel about it all. I always dreamed of having a sister and don't want to pressure you in any way, but I am the sort of person to jump in first and worry about the rest later. Take care and please know these three women have your best interests at heart and they are the people I trust most in my life. I have added my email address and will leave it to you to contact or not. My very best wishes to you Willow, take it slow it is a lot to absorb on top of the grief you must be feeling. Love Charlotte.

Willow had found the note tucked under her bedroom door. Claire must have left it when she went to the bathroom, not rude enough to sticky beak in the rooms but her name on the door was an absolute giveaway. The letter made her feel settled in an odd way, there was definitely a lot to take in and it was nice to have Charlotte's letter of support. Willow too had always wanted a sister, but this was not the way she had ever imagined she would get one. Robyn had allowed her to sift through the thoughts in her head at random, she had never been one to take over, though occasionally interjected by suggesting a different train of thought for Willow to consider. Willow had watched each of them, the puzzlement on their faces when she called him Marcus had been clear, it was more complicated than any of them could imagine, and Willow was unsure where to start.

Marcus for her had always been a background figure, he blew in at times and showered them all with gifts and it had not taken Willow long to realise this was about him and not about anyone else. Marcus was fun, funny and a whole lot of all about me. The older she became the wider the gap between his visits. Robyn and Iris had urged her to get to know him better but his favouritism of her, actually made her push away. Iris and Jed were her family too, and as Marcus's rejection of them became more and more obvious, Willow had often wondered if it was because Iris had the knack of seeing right through him. When Willow had been old enough to google, it was Iris she had gone to and shown the photo of him and Claire. Like Robyn, Iris had been direct with her own thoughts whilst leaving room for Willow to make up her own mind. They had marvelled at Claire's beauty, and both decided she would probably be in for a fall when Marcus moved on to his next conquest. Willow had considered if they really were a couple, it was something about the way Marcus had stood slightly back allowing her to shine which had puzzled them, maybe this woman was important to him. Iris had discussed with her how much it actually mattered and by showing the others, would it make any difference to their lives? Willow had considered this and eventually wiped the history from the search and never bothered again. Marcus had a role but his influence on her day-to-day life would never change, his opinions were not her concern. When he appeared they welcomed him, accepted the joy he spread, not for them they had realised, but to fill some gap within himself and when they closed the door behind him, the whirlwind slower and apologetic, full of promises he would be back soon, hugging her yet only waving a hand to the others as if dismissing them as he moved away. They would sigh, shrug their shoulders and easily slide back into their lives, often not giving him another thought.

Willow had lived it and was happy with her feelings, she was sad, it was sad for anyone to leave this life and thirty-five years would be like a tornado to come down from. Willow felt sorrow for Beth, to find out in a letter was cruel, yet from the way JJ had spoken none of them either, seemed entirely surprised. Willow wondered how they would react when she told them, it was hard for people who knew them to digest, though her relationship with Jed had been accepted. Willow was proud of how she had been brought up, and she could see how lies, betrayal and hiding the truth were all playing out the repercussions for those who had chosen their path, though in this instance Marcus was not here to see the ripple effect of his actions. Willow wanted to call Iris, she knew Robyn would be filling her in and it was getting late. Tomorrow they could speak, and Willow crossed her fingers hoping they could come home soon and face this together.

Flattening out the letter she opened her computer and quickly typed in Charlotte's address.

Dear Charlotte, Thanks for your letter. I know it is late, but I wanted you to know I was grateful for it. One day we will have a lot to discuss. When I am ready I will contact you again, I will speak to Beth, to all of them, and once it all settles down I might know more about how I feel. It is all fairly raw tonight. Thanks again Willow.

Willow pressed send before she could change her mind.

Chapter Thirty-Two

JJ and Marcus

Dear JJ,

What can I say, you really are the one I like the most, I miss your big laugh. I have taken to writing lately, my end is coming sooner than most, as is my decision. I'm sure it will amuse you to know I have been reminiscing and feeling a sense of melancholy I suppose as to my choices in the past. As you know I have loved Beth as I have loved no other, (the theatrical side of me is about to show). To see her unhappy was always something I could not bear, and I think I have made her happier than she ever thought her life could be. I did see the depths, as we have shared in conversations before, but it was always my job not to dwell there and those trips to Paris or Rome pushed them out of her mind and it filled me with satisfaction to share those incredible moments with her. I have been selfish I know, wanting her all to myself but I will not apologise for the person I am, I certainly never wanted outside distractions with her. I wanted to tell you now, as I may never write again, how much I have valued this pen-friend relationship, it actually suited my life more than you will know. Beth having the both of you filled the side of her I did not need or want to see and left her time to me. I think when I look back, together we have made her whole. As selfish as I have been for her full attention, so have you and Claire, though from a different angle.

I write with one last favour if you will. I trust you to do as I request, and I know you will always be there for my Beth without me having to ask. I suppose it is what prompted me to ask you this way, in a letter, as you have done with her all these years. Claire has had her own part to play, and I somehow feel you will know what this is by now and if not it is sure to come out in time.

As you can see there is another envelope in the back here. I want you to keep this and after I'm gone I want you to keep it until you know it is the day it should be opened, you will know, and it may be weeks or even months before you are ready. All I ask is for you to let all the chips fall and when they have spun on the table and wobbled unsteadily, allow them to lay for a bit to absorb the silence before you open it. You will know when the time is right and your decision after reading it will be your own, I hope you can see she would never have coped, Beth's lifelong quest to prove herself would have eaten her away and I would have lost her, as she could have lost herself. My decision to leave the unknown to lie and let her cope with the here and now took away my fears of the life in her head not going to plan. I am sorry to talk in riddles, and I know you will decide what is right because as I move closer to leaving her now, it is haunting me if my decision was the right one. As I say, when all the pieces are in place you will hold the trump card to play.

I feel tears now as I say this final goodbye, I hope eventually you will forgive me, I have been a selfish husband, not a good friend and some may say a self-centred you know what, and they would all have been correct, but I have enjoyed every moment and as you know it is not in my nature to consider either the future or the past with too much depth. Thank you JJ you have enriched my life, saved me from boredom at times and most of all, been all I couldn't be for my Beth. Look after her, she will need you more than ever. See you in the hereafter and what a wicked time we will have.

X Marcus.

JJ waited until Beth returned, she did not ask where Claire was. JJ let her settle in her own time. Showered and ready for sleep herself, JJ sat patiently until Beth's need was known. Beth at this level would be too hard to reason with and though some of the words she had said were true, most of it was past anger and the need to release it. In the end Beth knew their letters, like blood, were thicker than water. Claire could say sorry all she liked but it was never going to undo everything which had happened, there was no going back, so they all must move forward. The years of joy with Charlotte and Paul overshadowed any wrongdoing and it was this JJ strongly suspected, had been the reason which had stopped Claire from confessing earlier, each year had added a level of forgiveness she had hoped Beth would not be able to break down.

'I was a bit harsh.' The statement was an acceptance and apology rolled into one.

'True, though she probably deserved it, or at least part of it.'

'It's hard to be innocent and yet feel so guilty.'

'You were always innocent Beth, right from the beginning, it's about time you started to forgive yourself.'

'Never going to happen, and you know it, I think the day I was born, my memory cupboard of disappointing someone was opened, and I have been piling stuff in there ever since. It has been a struggle at times to keep it closed. It has been you and Claire who have helped me push it, sometimes with all our might and with our backs against the door.' JJ smiled and remembered. 'I feel weak JJ and I'm not sure if I can push it closed again.'

'Who have you disappointed? Your mother died, it happens, your brother was his own personality, you tried, he had choices too, as has everyone else in your life. Marcus killed himself, he and Claire had a secret affair which even I didn't pick, nor the fact he had a child with someone else as well, again not your fault, you have done what he asked you to do by telling Willow and Robyn, you have been the best friend any of us could have had and that includes Marcus. You loved the man and gave up everything to make him happy. Forgive me for being stupid here Beth but who have you disappointed because as an intelligent woman, I certainly cannot see how the answer is you.'

'It is a long list though isn't it.'

'Yes it is Beth, but none of them lead to you. You have spent your life taking on other people's problems, even when you stopped working what did you do, you went out and helped others, encouraged other writers, supported Claire and me and the kids. Step back for once Beth and see all the takers in your life. The reason you are in the centre is because you are the giver. When we were nine years old you knew you would need some help, and you reached out, but we needed you too, every day since we have needed you and have taken from you and as much as I have tried to give back you always gave more because it is how you survive, how you breathe and now it is time to give to yourself Beth. Look in the mirror as it stands before you, not the distorted carnival one you seem so fond of. You are a good person and the bravest person I know. What we did tonight was way out of my comfort zone and you did it Beth, you did it for him, with both dignity and grace.' JJ's tone had heightened along a steady upward slope as the words formed and spilled out into the room. It had to be said, Beth had to be saved. JJ thought of the letter stashed in the bottom of her bag, she had been tempted, thinking forewarned would be forearmed but her knowledge of Marcus held her back, the chips were still spinning, and she trusted he had a reason for waiting for them to fall. Until she had all the facts his last bombshell would stay hidden, it may even, once she knew, never be revealed. It was becoming an extra burden to her about which no one else knew.

Beth rubbed her eyes and with relief JJ saw genuine tiredness there.

'Time for sleep, tomorrow we will worry about tomorrow and who knows whatever tale they have to tell may be far better than we expect. In my opinion it certainly couldn't get much worse. Come on into bed, we will have to face Claire at some ungodly time I expect, so our day is sure to start with tears.' JJ settled Beth in her room and made her way to her own. The bed felt hard, and she stared at the ceiling trying to pretend she was back home, Jim was within reach and there was peace in the world. Picking up her phone she calculated the time difference and decided against calling, tomorrow may bring some closure or at least she hoped so.

Chapter Thirty-Three

Willow

Willow's computer pinged and she lay for a minute wondering if by staying in bed she could stop the rollercoaster ride it felt like she would be on today. Marcus had been her first thought, the puzzle of why he would deceive his wife, why not tell her, it would have been so much simpler. This way made Willow feel dirty as if her existence had been something he had been ashamed of. Two days ago, all I could think of was turning fifteen, and now it feels like I am rushing towards thirty she thought. Now he was gone and once it all was revealed, he could do no more, at least his passing would end some hurts and anything from now on would be how each of them decided to move forward. The flashing on the bottom of her screen made her rise, the message was brief:

Take care and take your time. xx C

A sister, it would be nice, strange and she was much older, but still nice. Robyn was rustling around in the kitchen, deliberately, Willow thought, to make enough noise to wake her so they could discuss the day. Willow already knew Iris and Jed would be on their way and though it was always her habit to protect him, he in the end would not care, the soul of him held no malice and his outlook on life had taught Willow so much more than she could ever say. For once she straightened the bed, today her life needed order and routine to set the pace for conquering one small step at a time. Willow knew today would bring Beth some relief, her husband had lied, but he had not cheated, at least not with Robyn in a physical way. Although Willow had lost her father, all the sympathy she felt was for Beth, and even her friends who had lived a lifetime far longer than her own, and believed they knew the person they had loved. Willow was not sure she could imagine how she would have reacted and if she, as Beth had done, would have been able to complete his last wishes with the same level of dignity. Her tummy rumbled, the pizza had not been enough to absorb all the energy of emotion from last night.

'Morning, how are you feeling?'

'All good,' without turning from the fridge Willow knew Robyn was paused, expecting more. 'I'm fine truly, when will they get home?'

'An hour or so.' The warmth in her voice was enough for Willow to know Robyn was smiling. 'We talked till late, Iris was quite upset. I explained we would wait for her and told her I thought we were still in shock, but we had managed to control our feelings in front of them because it was clear Beth was close to the edge.'

'I thought she was brave, and their connection to each other was extraordinary. You know Marcus told me once about someone he knew who'd had a penfriend for fifty years, I remembered last night and pulled out the letter. He said maybe I would like to meet her one day, he meant Beth, his own wife, and then he does this, writes her a letter to tell her I exist. I can't understand why, it is crazy, why didn't he tell her, she seems a kind and reasonable woman, was he ashamed of me? What about Jed, was this his plan to have it as the final swing at us both?'

'No, no, honey, don't ever put any kind of blame on yourself for this.' Robyn moved in to put her arm around her daughter. 'Marcus was a selfish man, we all knew it, even he knew it, whatever his reasoning we may never find out, so let's pull together and move forward. Do you want them to come back today, or is it too soon?'

'Give me some time with Jed and today, yes I think they need to know, it has dragged on long enough, I want in some way to ease her burden, for it all to be out in the open.'

'This is a lot for you Willow,' Robyn said drawing forward some stools so they could sit. 'We have never lied to you, and I think sometimes our honesty about your conception and our lifestyle has made you grow up faster than others your age, we never wanted it to be a burden later on if you found out from someone else, but last night we worried we had been too up-front, too forthright with our own opinions on life. Take your time honey, even for mature adults someone's deception like this would be hard to handle so please reach out when it does feel like it is too much.' Robyn rubbed her hand. 'It was fine for us to be crazy radical free thinkers, but it does not have to be a burden for you, and don't worry, Jed will be fine, you know he will. As long as he has us is all he cares about. We have never treated him any differently as you know, but it is times like these we may have to hide some tiny truths as his personality will not be able to comprehend or understand exactly what is occurring here.'

'Did Iris tell him?'

'In a manner he could comprehend, he knows Marcus's friends are going to be here and Marcus is gone, don't try to protect him, let him absorb what he can. and the rest will be what we have to live with. Jed won't care, because his brain is a bit different to ours we must let him sort this out himself in his own time. Let him know you are fine and don't baby him, then he will be ok too.' Robyn's hand added pressure. Willow held back her tears, it was hard, her brother was the sweetest person in the whole world and his smile lit up any room. As a little girl she had protected him from stupid kids who did not understand, they had soon left him alone as there were so many other ways they could tease her and get a greater reaction to fulfil their selfish desires. It had been hard to have two mothers in a school full of straight parents, an absent father and as some termed it, disabled brother. Jed's syndrome was not who he was, and it was probably when people thought it defined him which made Willow the angriest, it made him different not special. It was almost a defensive maturity she had. Willow's upbringing gave her strength to stand up and be brave as she knew Iris and Robyn had strived to do to be true to themselves. Attitudes were maturing, and the older Willow became the easier it was becoming to be accepted for who you were and not judged as often by your race, nationality or sexuality. Willow's own nurturing nature extended a natural kindness and especially to those who were categorised by others. In spite of it all, there was one secret she never told anyone.

The door burst open, and Jed's bag echoed as it hit the tiles and he ran to find her.

'I missed you,' she said, and they hugged each other tight.

'Mama said you would be sad, don't be sad Willow, cause I'm back now and we have new friends coming.' Willow smiled, Jed was never going to let her feel down, each day for him was a challenge and every day he showed them all no mountain was too high if you took small steps. Jed's zest for life often brought more happy tears than sad ones. Willow swallowed hard, if only Marcus had been more accepting and open minded, she realised now he had wanted a perfect world, his perfect world, with everything slotted in the place he thought it should be and Jed, well, Jed was his own world, and one over which Marcus had no control. The mood had lifted in moments and as Iris hugged her tight as well, the peace of being with those she loved and who loved her, returned.

Today was a big day, and it was time to get started. Robyn arranged for the ladies to come at one pm giving Willow time with both Jed and Iris. Jed had been easy, eager to tell her about his camp with, as they called it, his friends with similar abilities. Iris had volunteered to be the assistant parent and Jed had loved having her there. Overflowing with all the news of the activities and games and his new skill of cooking pancakes, had lifted Willow's spirit. In amongst it all he had paused, his mind sorting thoughts in his head to try to place them in a context all of his own.

'Are you sad Wills? Uncle Marcus never tried to play with me so I don't feel sad he has gone far away, Mama said he won't visit anymore with treats, but she said sometimes she would buy chocolate for me, and we can sit and remember him. I think I will be happy just to eat the chocolate.' Jed had smiled at the thought and Willow envied him a little. Jed's world was full of love and the ever-expanding rings of ramifications of people's actions would never touch him. For him face value was as deep as it went and all else did not exist.

'You know these people who are coming are friends with Marcus don't you?' Jed nodded. 'They are old like him, and they are very sad so we must try to be very kind and patient with them. Once you meet them, if you like, you can have a special lend of my computer for a while and I will ask Mama to call Lachlan's mum to see if he can play too.' Jed looked excited. 'I'm sure after the camp he will need some relax time today as well.' Jed was nodding excessively now. Willow thought about the times she forgot his inabilities, when they would bump in the hall and how her head now barely reached his ear, his lanky limbs and grown-up clothes hiding the ever-present child inside. Sometimes she had wished it was different, wished Jed had been able to play normal games with her and be in the same class at school, able to talk to her about friends and teachers, assignments and the future. It wasn't often, he was the person he was meant to be, and Willow was so grateful her parents brought them up to look at the positives in life and never the negatives. Leaving Jed to amuse himself, Willow took some time to try and focus on all the positives of the mess Marcus had clearly left behind.

Iris had let her talk, it was their way, each one of them allowed to express themselves while advice was given as a consideration, not the answer. In these teenage years especially, Willow could see how they were allowing her freedom of choice, with guidance, in all subjects. Willow had never felt afraid to express what was in her heart and it was only with Marcus she had learned sometimes it was wise to keep some thoughts to herself. Iris reassured her anything she said would be ok, these women deserved the truth as they knew it, and herself and Robyn would always be present if it became too much or more had to be explained. Willow knew their whole lives Iris and Robyn had been trying to explain to people how they felt, when all along they should have been accepted for who they were, for Willow's generation they wanted truth and compassion to be the goal. Young as she was Willow could see sometimes a layer of kindness had to soften some of the blows, Robyn and to a lesser extent Iris still had a tough shield they held up to the world as a barrier against the inequality they had fought against for so long, and even as the times changed it could not fully be pushed aside. The doorbell broke her thoughts, and it was almost with a sense of relief Willow made her way to the lounge room.

Chapter Thirty-Four

Beth

Dear JJ and Claire,

Each year the clock ticks over and I wonder where the time went. My days are quite filled, Marcus has no more trips to Brisbane, and they were the last to wind down. He seems at last happy to be here and each day I see the struggles increase. I have decreased my tutor classes and 'aunty' roles for now as I feel my time with him may be closer than I can bear to think about. He tells me he is happy, but his grumpiness shows he is not, I can see the fight draining out of him and I think he has finally sat back to look at his achievements and somehow, been let down by them all. I know you will not judge me when I say I feel a bit suffocated by it all. We know what is ahead and he will not let it come to a natural one, he already feels each tiny loss of movement as a hurdle he can no longer jump over. His body is finally winning and though we have talked about it I still try to show him every day how much better my life is with him, in any form, than it would be without him. It is so hard, I go to the bathroom to shed my tears as they seem to inflame him, not soften him. The doctor tried to talk about his mental health, but I can't betray him, it is his life and all I can do is keep trying to show him how much it will take from mine if I lose him. I feel selfish at times and though I know he has lived his life with no restrictions from me, I can't help but wonder if I could have done more, gone with him on those business trips, put off some of my own. I am jealous now of the time I have wasted on the superficial when I could have spent time with him. He is the love of my life, and as I write now the tears fall, how will I live without him, should I stop him, tell someone what he wants to do, he would hate me, and I wonder if I could live with the guilt. Is one person responsible for another? Does he have the right? Or do I? I knew he would go before me, the aging timeline has always predicted older people should die first, the difference in our ages was a given. I respect him and his choice, but now as it looms close I want to yell at him, tell him to stop, am I not enough, he tells me I am, but if this happens it will prove I was not. Some days I am scared to leave the house, and yet I must, there is life out there and it is in his plan, the plan with no date known to me, the plan which will bring him peace and bring none to me. It will come soon I'm afraid, and I have to warn you, it is when your burden will begin. I think often now of the bus, the stupid bus which hit my mother. In my head I can see it clearer than I can see her, and I wonder if it will hurtle towards me at the same pace, some days I look for it and wonder if I will have the guts to step out, some days it is what I want and after he goes, I fear the temptation may be too strong. I love you my friends and am so grateful to you both, my life has been richer because of you, and I apologise now for the time ahead, I will need all your strength to fulfill his wishes.

Love and kisses, Beth xxx

Beth put on a bright dress to make her feel optimistic about the day ahead. The mirror was not her friend at the moment and the young at heart image she had always portrayed now felt like it was in an aged care home. The wrinkles on her face seemed to have bred overnight and her hair could certainly do with a little TLC. Beth had soothed it over with Claire, though Claire had put her stubborn foot down for once making Beth dig deep to swing her around. The day felt lighter, time heals all they said but she knew, from experience, the expression was untrue. Time slid by, and as other emotions crowded to the front, the old stacked up, building until it could no longer take the pressure before bursting to wash over all ahead of it to weigh you down again. Time it seemed was equal to how high the stack became, then played no other part.

In the car they had been quiet, the words today would all come from their destination. Marcus's world about to be revealed and his dirty little secrets unveiled. Beth was fine with it, her venting of anger at Claire had cleared some air and the tiny Beth inside who had always tried to hold her head above water was swimming frantically, though with a lifeboat of support beside her. The Marcus she knew and the Marcus who was about to be revealed were the same man and somehow Beth knew, as she had about Claire, seen the clues he had laid out which she had not ever desired to put together.

The glass inlays in the front door for a moment reflected the women standing before it. Beth saw three young faces looking on, each with a future which was being reflected as the past. The door opened and Robyn welcomed them with a genuine smile.

'Come in, oh it is a keen breeze today, though for you it has probably cooled it down a little.' Another woman stood at the entrance to the lounge, she stood back as they shuffled through, murmuring a greeting as she examined each of them. Beth felt the weight of her eyes the longest. As soon as they were seated a tall lanky boy rushed in, his smile filled the room and each of them, after, commented how it had broken the ice and made them feel like family.

'I'm Jed,' he announced, and as the other woman followed him in he shook all their hands and took a moment to look each of them in the eye as if reading their thoughts. It was clear he had some challenges and yet his welcome and manners made them seem insignificant. 'I like chocolate,' he said.

'I'm so glad' Beth said, 'because I have a whole box in my bag we could share.' Jed looked excited and the other woman spoke.

'Let's all introduce ourselves first Jed and after you might take them to the kitchen to put in a bowl so we can share.' Taking the box he nodded and stood back as Willow entered, stroking his arm as she passed before coming to each of them to say hello.

'This is our Mama Iris,' Beth felt surprised Robyn had not told them last night she was not the one they should be speaking too. It hurt a bit, but she pushed it aside.

'Jed's going to stay a while and after he is going to play so we can talk.'

'Willow's letting me use her computer so I can play a game with my friend.'

'That's right with Lachlan, he was on camp with Jed this last week. Robyn is making some tea and I'd like to wait for her if you don't mind.'

Beth's list of questions was growing, this well-spoken young lady was commanding the room with a grace which defied her age. Beth's tension was coiled around her, it felt like a rope pulled taut though every second it was still pulling tighter as she waited for their Marcus to be revealed.

Robyn entered with a tray of tea and goodies to share, and they swapped stilted small talk until Jed was satisfied and clearly showing they were not the entertainment he desired.

He had amused them and been friendly but clearly now the treat of a computer was calling. Iris settled him and seated herself on the arm of Robyn's chair when she returned. The look they shared was enough for Beth to know their opening sentence.

'Sorry, I know you are anxious to hear what we have to say, Jed's understanding of life is different to ours and it is better if he is happily amused, so he won't cause a distraction.' They all nodded, and Beth knew the others were now as curious as her. 'So, Willow has asked me to speak first.' She paused and Beth wondered if she thought they would flood her too soon with questions.

'Robyn and I are partners, and parents of both Willow and Jed.' Again a delay as she let the information sink in. Claire's mouth was open and Beth wanted to reach out and snap it shut. 'I first met Marcus about twenty years ago at a conference. We hit it off, as friends.' Beth felt the sympathy in her gaze. 'Marcus was both charming, and funny. It became a habit for him to stay here when he was in town, and we enjoyed his company. Of course, over time, we expressed our desire to have children, and at the time, as a same sex couple it was more difficult than now, there were still a lot of walls to be broken through and we did not know if we had the energy to do it.' Iris took a breath and Robyn squeezed her hand urging her to continue. Beth thought you could have heard a pin drop the others were so quiet.

'Marcus told us his wife had passed away and they had not been fortunate enough to have children. It was one of the few times we saw, what we thought was a deeper side of him. We never asked too much and could see it was a delicate subject for him and over time we thought he might tell us more, he never did. As far as we knew he lived in Sydney and had business interests in Adelaide and Perth. I changed jobs so my work never actually crossed over into his world again and when we moved here it was only our friendship which was ever discussed. He was certainly about living for the here and now.' JJ agreed and Beth could see some memories flick across her face. 'Beth.' The intense gaze made Beth brace for the punchline. 'I never slept with your husband, Robyn and I are partners in every sense of the word, and I would never have cheated on her, even for a child, and to be honest it was never offered. Marcus agreed to help us out with the IVF process and without going into everything we went through medically, it came down to the fact we would have to go about it in a different way to others. Robyn and I have different fertility problems and in Australia the law was not going to bend for a surrogate and especially not for a gay couple. Marcus told me he had been through the process before.' Beth nodded not wanting to interrupt with her own painful journey down the fertility path. 'We also for us, had the dilemma, no dilemma is the wrong word,' she looked to Robyn for support.

'It will do.'

'We were both able to carry a pregnancy to term, it was the before bits which were complicated and to cut it short we ended up going overseas. Our donor eggs were fertilised with Marcus's sperm and this, luckily, resulted in two viable embryos, so we had one implanted in each of us, crossed our fingers and prayed for a miracle. Both of them stuck and we were overwhelmed by it all' All three of them gasped as they digested the news.

Robyn took over.

'We couldn't believe it, so even though Jed and Willow are not conventional twins, we treat them as such, and they certainly act as if they are at times. I gave birth to Willow a few days before Iris gave birth to Jed, so their birthdays are different though their parentage is the same.'

'Marcus...?'

'Marcus was over the moon, they are his biological children and before they were born we'd had intense discussions to lay out rules, the birth certificates, legal complications both here and over there, you can imagine it was a time of great anxiety and anticipation. When it worked we were probably the most surprised.'

'Legally we were surrogates who kept the baby and as the birth mothers we were able to be listed as the parent. Marcus wanted it to say father unknown and yet after going through it all with us, we were happy the children would know who he was if ever they needed to know. We even argued about it until he conceded, even though he thought it would be less complicated without it, he did our heads in at times.'

'Did he interfere?' JJ was curious.

'Yes and no. When we found out Jed's condition he changed. Willow then after, was clearly his favourite and Iris and Marcus struggled to, well, they struggled to reach a plateau if you know what I mean. He would flit in and out of our lives and I think even the children knew who he loved the most and it caused division between him and Willow as well. From a young age she was protective of Jed even though we never asked her to be. They have their own code between them, and we are very proud of them both.' The silence hung as, like Beth, the others now wondered how relevant their questions were.

Willow cleared her throat. 'It must be a shock, especially to you Beth. Marcus was my father, my biological one, but these are my parents. When I was little I started calling them by their christian names, I was confused when kids asked me which one was my real mother and other taunts they wouldn't understand the answer to, so I changed. Jed calls Iris Mama and always has. Personally, I don't care, Jed and I have the two most caring parents and they have raised us to recognise what's important and not dwell on what is not.' Beth had to admire these women who had done a remarkable job.

'Marcus used to visit but, I'm sorry, ... he was never my father, he would bring treats and spoil me, but he practically ignored my brother and the only reason for it was he did not like Jed was not perfect, his perfect. Our mothers' show us every day we are perfect because of who we are not because of what others think we should be, Marcus was never going to learn the lesson.' Beth felt like applauding, this was a very special family and Marcus would never know the admiration she now felt for these women and this girl, his daughter.

Beth could see it, Marcus had loved everything to go his way, if it wasn't fun it was not to be on the list. She wondered why he hadn't told her, she could have supported this, at least now, knowing them she thought she would have. By the time Willow was conceived she had ended her own journey and they had moved on to the next phase of their lives. If Marcus had told her he had wanted children, she might have persisted even as the ticking of her body clock slowed. I'm happy just with you he had said, and so she had moved forward, valued what they could have, and do by not having children, spoil Charlotte and Paul more, overindulge in luxuries they may otherwise have never been able to afford if their time was sparse. To Beth, Marcus had never seemed to care one way or the other, a baby to him had not been high on the list and yet here he had gone to far-flung arrangements to help Robyn and Iris conceive theirs. Bile rose in her throat, and she rose unsteadily to go to the bathroom. Willow stepped forward to help her and Beth shrunk back to move past. Leaning back on to the bathroom door the tears welled, and her chest felt like a hard lump of clay, had she known him at all, how could he hide so much? Questions and accusations raged, had he encouraged her to fail, why had he pushed so far for them, when had he been overseas without her knowledge? What if they had tried one more time, how could he love one child more than another. The obvious answer to all was, he was Marcus. Marcus her lovable infectious, moody, arrogant selfish love who had filled her life with as many joys as he could and taken away whatever caused her pain. Selfish, well she had been too, arrogant, not so much, though proud of what they had which was a far cry from where she had come from. Moody, it went without saying and his infectious joy had pushed aside many of the dark moments which plagued her. You didn't see because you didn't want to Beth, and you could never have been a mother as good as these two, it was meant to be. Maybe it is because you thought you, and Marcus, were on the same journey, which was the problem, when you in the end were merely one of the stations at which he stopped. It was like JJ and Claire were in her head, each weighing up a way to pull her back on track, enjoy what you had and let go of the rest, Claire whispered, he was the cad you loved and who loved you, accept it and move on JJ demanded. Beth washed her face, the lump was easing, for all her emotions, the young girl in the lounge room and her brother, had a whole lifetime to live and Beth did not want to add any layer to them which would leave a scar on their future.

Back in the lounge, she acknowledged the looks and gestured for them to continue. Willow looked concerned and also relieved to get it done.

'There is not much else really, Marcus would visit or call occasionally, the older we got the less he did, there were always excuses, work or travel. He was a puzzle and believe me I am sad, though he was not such a large part of my life as to leave a huge gap. It feels mean to say it when you are all missing him so much, but I want to be as truthful as you have been with me. Part of me would like to know more about him, how he lived and how he was with each of you. The part of me who knew him didn't like some things about him, how judgemental he could be and even self-centred, he always wanted to be the centre of attention and in our home no one is, even Jed with some of his special needs. I'm sorry Beth but he was never here when I needed him, and he was never ever here for Jed, or wanted to be. I'm not sure if can ever fully forgive him for ignoring him.' Willow looked sad and Beth was glad for her honesty. Willow had seen Marcus for the man he was, probably clearer than anyone else who had known him. Beth hoped there would be times in the distant future when his face would flick across Willow's mind, or she would remember a funny remark and could smile for a second to remember the good. Willow may carry his genetics, but her heart was certainly bigger, and more open than his had ever been.

'Thankyou Willow. Thankyou Robyn and Iris, what can I say, these last weeks I have imagined the woman my husband had an affair with and also his daughter and his interactions with you all, I had come to accept it, what else could I do? Marcus gave me a job and I have completed the task. I feel now as if I am in your way, my job is done, and you have no connection to me in any way and I think we all should get out of your hair. Of course you may want to speak to Claire. Charlotte is someone we love dearly, and it may help you to talk, as she too has had an unusual relationship with Marcus.' JJ made to butt in, Beth raised her hand, her words were prepared, and she wanted to get them out. 'I want to congratulate you Robyn, and Iris, it is brave of you to tell us your story, to raise these children, it has been a delight to meet you and I wish I could have done so sooner. Why Marcus never trusted me to tell me about your situation and why he wanted to help you, whether it was for your sake or his, must remain a mystery, but the result we can all see is a blessing. It has been so wonderful to see Willow and Jed and I feel sorry in a way I was not here to support you as well and urge him to get to know you better.' Beth felt small as if her world had closed in, it was like a darkness, a cloud descending yet not thick like depression, it was her soul pulling itself back to shield her from the loss she would feel when she left, her daydreams had Willow running to her, wanting to share their moments of joy with Marcus together, reality she realised was going home to her empty house and trying to fill gaps which had never existed before.

'Oh Beth, I hope we will stay in contact, for some reason Marcus wanted us to meet and we all seem to have had a disjointed relationship with him, maybe together we can make some sense of it.' Robyn's words surprised her. Iris jumped in as well.

'Yes, all of you, please stay in touch, at the moment every-thing is jumbled and there will be times ahead I'm sure, as we all grieve his passing when Robyn and I may need you, if not to help us bring back happy memories to the kids, then to help us remember ours. Marcus gave us the greatest gift and support in the early days and every day I am grateful, I think he should be remembered, not for the mess he left behind, but for what he gave, to all of us. Don't worry, I still think he should have been more mature about it and allowed us to make our own decisions, nevertheless somehow I think it may have turned out the same, after meeting you, I would like to think so.'

Claire was crying and Beth closed her eyes and held her lips firm. Marcus sat with her now, she could feel him stronger than ever, he had wanted her here, with these people, he was passing her on, giving her a focus and more people to love her. She wanted to grab him, shake him, and hold him close. I love you she whispered, and he smiled then faded from her sight.

Chapter Thirty-Five

JJ and Marcus

JJ fingered the envelope, it had tempted her several times when she was in Australia and yet she had known it was not the time. Part of her did not want to open it at all. Everything had settled down so well, Twelve months on Beth was in a good place, taking small steps forward but with light in her heart. Willow and her family had taken it slowly with so much consideration for them all, especially Beth. Charlotte and Willow had connected and in a few short weeks were going to meet up with Paul in Brisbane for the first time. Robyn had thought some quiet time together would be better than a large family do. Jed was looking forward to having a big brother they said and already had purchased a football to kick around with Paul. JJ thought Paul would love it too.

Coming home had been like saving her soul. Jim had met her at the airport, and she had literally fallen into his arms. It had added up to months she had been away, and she could see how he had improved having so much time to rest and was glad he had not come with her.

Routine had been her healer, Jim let her retell it all over and over, Willow, Robyn, Iris and Jed became daily words to add to their family. Charlotte had flown up and spent time with

Jim while she was away, Jim had been the one Charlotte had sought out when she needed a father figure and not a playful uncle, they had always connected, and JJ couldn't wait for him to meet the other children as well. Jed would win Jim's heart quickly, she could already feel their bond during their calls. JJ had not told Jim about the letter, somehow she knew its contents should be for her to consider first. Jim would be honest about whatever secrets it held, though his opinion of Marcus had not improved even with his death. Marcus's actions would never have been Jim's.

Claire's new man seemed to be working out, she had sent a photo of them both and JJ could see how relaxed they were together. When Charlotte came back from Australia they were sure to have a lengthy chat about it all. It was her travel bag which had reminded her. Searching for a scarf she wanted to wear she had pulled it down and the letter had still been hidden in the side pocket. Marcus's handwriting had sprung a few tears. Their letters had been almost weekly when she returned, their time spent together each day being able to talk about their thoughts had left them all feeling slightly lonely and so their letters again had expressed their mood and with each one JJ had seen Beth was on a steady rise. Beth's plans to sell up and move were discussed and her destination undecided. JJ wouldn't be surprised if it was closer to Willow, already their friendship was strong and JJ could see it was not sympathy on Willow's part, but a true respect and admiration of the woman she had begun to know. Beth loved Jed too, her eyes sparkled when she spoke of him and JJ wondered if he reminded her of her brother, his simple ways were similar though his temperament was a polar opposite.

It was like fire between her fingers begging to be opened, JJ remembered the first note, *when they have spun on the table and wobbled unsteadily, allow them to lay for a bit to absorb the silence before you open it.* They had spun, wobbled precariously, and fallen as he had predicted. It was time, time for the final chapter, the world was changing, computers ruled it. Whatever the letter contained JJ was sure, with all they had been through, together they would manage, there were more of them now, more to hold Beth close so the darkness would not fall in again.

JJ slid the knife under the sealed flap. Placing the knife down she tweaked back the curtain to watch Jim as he sat back on his heels to survey the weeds he was trying to master. JJ's heart filled, it was time to fulfill her friend's last request and move forward, time was pushing faster, and JJ was determined not to waste another minute of her future.

There seemed to be two parts, one looked official, its typed header bold and clear. Marcus's writing scrawled across the back, *read this first before I explain*. JJ placed the thinner lined paper down, she would do as he asked, play out Marcus's last game with his rules. Deep down she knew, they would be copies of birth certificates of others, Charlotte, Willow and Jed could not be the only ones, he had set up a pattern and JJ, as she had pondered, realised he would have thought to take it slow, allow Beth to get used to one child and let the others follow as a matter of course causing a mere ripple instead of the wave which had crashed before them. JJ sighed and sat down as she unfolded the documents and rubbed her hand over them to iron out some creases.

Creation Fertility Clinic. JJ scanned the contents, it was the details of the embryos and their subsequent transfer overseas. Why had he given them to her, wouldn't it be better for Iris and Robyn to file these details, why keep them at all? JJ flicked through the pages again,, the first four were from Adelaide, the next Sydney, and then overseas. The last copies were in both languages. It was typical though she was still confused as to why Marcus had created a drama just for this. JJ rustled back through the pages, was this some mistake, was there something she was missing? The pennies rattled in her head, Marcus she thought, what have you done? The first penny dropped, her mouth fell open and JJ raised one hand to cover it to stop the scream.

Chapter Thirty-Six

JJ

My dearest JJ,

I can see you now, as you work it out, shocked and angry, wishing I was there to slap my face and curse the ground I walked on. I told you I was selfish, and it wasn't until now, now I'm at the end, I realised how selfish I have been. I just did it, it is all I can say, I wanted her for myself, and it is the only explanation I had. When I met Iris we clicked as colleagues and as friends. The more immersed I became in their lives the more I saw how, if I'd had children, I would want them to be raised by free thinking people like her. Beth could not have done it, admit it JJ, one mistake and she would have crumbled, blamed herself and her self-worth would never have returned. Beth would have given them her all and it would have crushed her, and she would have no room for me as she fell.

People I think, were often bewildered why Beth was my one, Claire was prettier, you were smarter, who is to know, maybe it is what I will find out when I get to the other side, but I loved her more than life itself and yes I am taking my life away from her, but I would never have coped without her. For all her insecurities and self-hate she was my rock, my Beth, and for all my jokes and high jinks, when we locked eyes across a room the world fell away and there was no one else. You laugh now, I see you, but what about Claire, why did I go there? I don't know, it happened, it was pleasant, and I did enjoy the children, until they started to grow, it became awkward and Claire to be honest was needy. I love her, don't get me wrong, but she was a sideline in this life to be enjoyed. What a cad I am! Though at least honest. This may be one letter you should destroy, these words are for you, and I mean no harm, it has been what it has been and now cannot be changed.

Now you are calmer: the documents show the truth, I lied. The children are mine, mine and Beth's. I feel sick writing it now, I think this is something on top of everything, she could never forgive me for. After Beth stopped the IVF she thought no more about the logistics, nor did Iris and Robyn, they all trusted me to take care of the paperwork, only heard what they wanted to hear and left the rest to me. I suppose I was getting older, softer, the clinic contacted me to say we still had two embryos stored and how did we wish to proceed. I had met Iris and Robyn by then, each with their own issues, fighting a world of discrimination which every other woman had a right to. It seemed so simple. They needed some embryos, and I had some I didn't want. What can I say, the mortality in me kicked in. Beth did not know about them, and it would have killed her to destroy them, somehow my head told me we could live on into the future, together in a different form, these two little dots were the future, and we would still be together.

Sounds crazy now I know. As I planned for my demise Claire's god has taunted me to believe and I think this was my act of defiance, I was shaking my fist to tell him I can live on, for generations now, after all the torment he has thrown at me, punished me with, a part of me would still continue on this earth into eternity. I was not blind, stupid maybe, but no one would be harmed JJ, they, if the eggs survived, would have good parents, be raised in a nice home and go on to live good lives. Arrogant of me I know, I played God and I won. The only stopping block was Beth, should I tell her, or was there another way. I have always been lucky JJ, the internet was still in its early stages and documents were slow transferring to digital. I called the clinic back, told them of my loss, my wife had passed, and I was moving overseas, I'd like to keep them, I understood their viability may be diminishing, the lies poured out JJ, it was almost too easy, yes I knew it would be costly but once the special courier had them it was like clockwork.

Iris and Robyn were grateful and made the decision to implant one each, the language barrier helped and soon it was done. I assured them the egg donor wanted to remain anonymous she was a friend, intelligent, healthy, with similar colourings and a giving nature, she would never interfere or want to know, it was better this way, and simpler for the paperwork to proceed. It was my sperm, and it was, though I even faked a day at the clinic to donate, it was soon done. I can't tell you how easy it panned out. When they were placed in their mothers, and the pregnancies ran smooth, the system took over. They were registered to their birth mothers when they were born and as the father, I was available, visible and it all flowed through the channels with ease. I'd done it!

To be honest I have never felt any guilt, until now and to tell you the honest, honest, truth, and to you I mostly have, it made me feel powerful and strong in a way I had never felt before. I was playing superheroes and I had conquered them all.

They are good women, Willow is a delight. Jed I have found harder to deal with, his antics confuse me, and patience was never a virtue. I have far more enjoyed being an 'uncle' than I ever would have as a father. Give me the spoiling and the laughter and you can keep the tantrums and the tears. What else can I say – it is who I am.

I have held this to myself and argued if I should tell. Mostly I have asked myself, who would it benefit? My future is decided, and I know the burden I place on you by passing it on, maybe it is age or maybe it is the moments when Beth doesn't know I am looking and I see her sadness, the loneliness which will come which has swayed me. Should I have given her these children earlier, in her own womb or even still in theirs? Has my selfishness been too extreme?

To be honest it is Jed who might finally show her peace, she never spoke about her brother to me and quite frankly I didn't want to know, he was unimportant to me, could his condition have been genetic, something passed on as a quirk of nature undetected in days gone by? Will she see now maybe it was never her fault, he was always going to be different to most, as Jed is, whether the pram fell or not, as you always said she was nine and didn't push it, yet because of her parents she carried it within herself from then on. Along with her mother, we have all seen this was her hidden burden.

My time is fading, and I leave you to decide, I know you will consider every angle and when it is right to tell, whereas the whole world would know by now if I had told Claire, her indecision would have made her blurt it out in the totally wrong time and place though it has been her loyalty to Beth which has kept her quiet all these years about Charlotte. Lie if you must and most definitely blame me for any delays while you plan it out, I deserve the scathing remarks and criticism. I can only hope all the goodness in the people I have surrounded myself with, will shine through and may they, in the end, remember the Marcus who underneath it all, loved each of them in his own way. I will leave you now for the final time, play it as you see fit, I shall die as the biggest coward whose only excuse is he loved a woman too much and for this I am not ashamed. Oh how tangled the web becomes. Goodbye JJ and thank you for completing what I could not.

Marcus.

JJ was unsure how long she sat, her trembling hands rattled the sheets and curled them in her hands. A movement outside aroused her, and she watched as Jim chatted to a neighbour and the world continued to turn. JJ felt no feelings, the emptiness into which she reached searching for anger and hatred, disgust and loathing was ungiving, a void so deep all emotions had disappeared. JJ's life flashed before her, all the letters, all the moments, she thought of Willow and Jed, Beth's brother she had never known and Marcus, his wicked smile, cutting tongue and generous persona which had hidden a man as troubled and tormented as his wife. It seemed surreal, birds still flew, a push mower murmured in the distance and a child's laughter rang out in play. JJ was frozen, frozen in a moment where she wanted to turn back and her mind showed her the steps, the pages refolding, her hands rubbing them over putting the creases back in as the pages slid into the envelope and the knife sawed backwards resealing the information inside. JJ wanted to go back, she didn't want to know, this was not a favour, it was a punishment. Marcus thought he had played god and now he had left her the most hideous inheritance. It wasn't fair, she didn't want it and yet now she knew it could never be returned. The pages were still clutched firmly in her hand, she could see all their faces and begged them all to tell her what to do. The void was full now and stuffing the pages into the desk JJ ran to the bathroom and vomited violently into the toilet.

Chapter Thirty-Seven

Claire

Dear JJ and Beth,

I hope this really does find you well Beth, to be honest I was tempted to come. I discussed it with Paul who said to leave it for now, Auntie Beth will let you know, she will never adjust if you are under her feet. He is so smart, every day I thank the lord for these two. Charlotte has a new boyfriend and I fear it might be quite serious, you may be the one to meet him first JJ and somehow I think, like my brother and sister, she may never come home. I'm happy for her, I miss her, but it is what I raised them to be, independent and confident to chase their dreams, it is certainly what I know my mother taught me and I am grateful for the life I have had. Maybe it is age, more and more I seem to look back instead of forward, we are at the top of the food chain, and I have promised myself to make the most of each moment. Marcus did inspire me, I think back now and remember how he made us laugh and filled so many moments with joy, I intend to do the same though I will leave it to the lord to decide my fate.

Willow and Charlotte have video called and it all seems to be working out. I have been calling Robyn every few weeks (is it too much?) Robyn seems to welcome the chats and says Willow is coping well and they all feel, like I do as if, for all his faults,

Marcus has given us all a gift and I can see it continuing. Jed has jumped on occasionally and he is so funny, we are like aunties or grandparents to him already and I feel sad Marcus chose to miss out on this. For you Beth I must say they have the greatest respect, Robyn told me Willow had expressed how she instantly felt connected to you and is eager to spend more time with you and of course JJ and I when she can. In spite of it all, I think some of your little daydreams may come true and you will find a family at last who love you as much as we do. I think selling the house is great, I always have a spare room as you know if you need time to decide where to go. I think we all know it will be north, the weather would suit you and a fresh start, with the right attitude can only turn out to be good. Paul will like it if he has one of us closer as well, his wedding is not far off and I pray at least one of them will make me a grandmother before too long, I have even made a few stylish baby outfits in secret. Shh! Chin up Beth, I will see you soon, and let me know how you progress, and I will come to help you pack.

JJ Is all well? Your letter was short, and it concerned me, are you busy or is something amiss? It sounds as if Jim has taken a turn for the better, how lucky we are to live in this time, new medical advances seem to be announced every day and it is so wonderful to know someone who is actually receiving the benefits. I still marvel when I can talk to you, Charlotte or Paul and can see your faces, I remember years ago Paul told me it was possible, and it seemed so futuristic I never dreamed I would be doing it in my own home. What next, will we be flying around like the Jetsons or teleporting to Canada and back in seconds and doing away with the tiresome flights? I suppose it is the one gadget we would like, to be able to walk through a door and be with you and Jim in an instant. Maybe it will not be in our lifetime though.

The postman caught me out the front today, he said I was probably the only person he knew now who received letters with handwriting on the front. I told him about all the years we have written, and I think he was quite amazed. It is a dying art and one day it will only be the zip noise on a computer which will tell us we have mail. After he left I looked up and down the street, it looks the same as when my parents were here, oh yes the cars are more modern and some house colours have changed, but basically it is still the same. I tried to imagine it without the variety of letterboxes at each front gate and it made me sad to think one day they will be no more. Such is life as they say. I'm glad you liked the photo, Matt is a kind and gentle man, we fit well together and last week we had lunch with his family, I'm happy with how it is, he in his home, me in mine, I have lived too long on my own to share my space I think, and he is happy to do the same. I spend some nights at his and he here at mine and it works. Moving in would be complicated so why not live the best of both worlds? See JJ you have finally liberated me!

Keep on keeping on Beth, we will talk soon and as another anniversary slips by, take the time to remember what he has left you, in the end it has been the most special gift of all, more people to love our gorgeous Beth. Marcus would be proud of how you have come through the mess he left, and it is because of who you are, you have been able to rise above it and move forward.

Love you both. XX Claire.

Claire beamed. The bride looked stunning, it wasn't only her new mother-in-law was an award-winning designer and had created the most stunning dress, Sarah glowed, and Paul had never, Claire thought, looked so handsome. As people smiled and congratulated the happy couple JJ sidled up and whispered in her ear, 'thank god your ex didn't show, so it is absolutely perfect.' Claire smiled, it was true though, nothing could put a smear on today. They were all here, Charlotte and her partner Oliver, a shiny new engagement ring sparkling on her finger, Beth, JJ and Jim of course. Willow, Jed with Iris and Robyn now very much a part of the family. Paul had asked Jed to be one of his groomsmen and Jed's excitement had entertained the crowd in the most loving and special way, totally unrelated by blood these two, bonded by sharing the same sisters, had grown closer than any of them could have ever imagined. Beth looked happy, her move to the Gold Coast had been wise, Paul and Sarah were close by, and Willow and Jed loved knowing someone who lived right on the beach. It had all worked out and today seemed to be a celebration to leave behind all the pain and upsets of the last few years.

JJ was the worry, every time they spoke she seemed not quite herself, Marcus's passing had paid a heavy toll on them all and for JJ being away from Jim for so long had been a sacrifice she would never have refused but Claire could see she was still struggling to get her energy back. Both herself and Beth had been able to move forward, the spark of having Jed and Willow in their lives, Paul's wedding and the close friendships they were forming with both Iris and Robyn had allowed them to look to the future and fill their days. Claire also had Matt to support her as no other man ever had, both spiritually and emotionally.

Together they had been to hell and back, and at times Claire had wondered if they would pull through. The chain of letters had held tight and the bond they had always shared had grown even stronger in spite of her deceit being revealed. After to-day Claire would seek JJ out, get to the bottom of it, maybe she was feeling a bit left out being so far away. Claire pushed her thoughts aside as she heard the photographer call for the mother of the groom.

Speeches done, bouquet thrown, a tiny tear slipped down Claire's face as her son held her close to say goodbye. You did good he whispered, and she knew she had. The children were happy, good people who had welcomed their new siblings, and their mothers, with maturity and respect. Their gentleness and caring towards JJ and Beth, their solid bond with Jim had shown Claire how much more a family could be, related or not. She had so much to be grateful for and as Charlotte's ring sparkled and Sarah and Paul turned for their last goodbye, Claire gave herself an invisible pat on the back and sent a tiny thank you towards the heavens.

Marcus would have loved today, the dressing up, the speeches, even the cake. Claire knew he would be proud to see them all so strong and so together, he had left his Beth in safe hands. Claire thought it may even bring a tear to his eye.

As the crowd dispersed and people approached to say goodbye, Claire kept one eye on JJ, her quietness was almost like a neon sign flashing something was wrong, though nothing they seemed to do or say had been able to pull her back. Claire wondered if the future was weighing on her, JJ without Jim was like Beth without Marcus, though more so. Jim was a solid rock on which she had leaned on from the beginning, looking in the mirror to see time had ticked over, having friends pass at an age you now thought was too soon, could take its toll. Of course JJ's forthrightness still popped out at times, but it was her times of contemplation which seemed to have extended themselves and made her somewhat wary about her words. It worried Claire more and more and today she had observed her, standing back, checking on each of them, laying her eyes on certain ones for moments more than a glance. Maybe it was because it was the first time they had all been able to be together properly, Claire had seen Willow and Jed several times and Beth was now a constant in their lives. Maybe it was the ease in which they all had melded which was the problem. JJ had not had the chance to get to know them as well, a touch of jealousy perhaps.

Moving back to say final goodbyes to Sarah's parents and the few stragglers reluctant to let go of a perfect night, Claire grabbed JJ's hand and pulled her along. Beth was outside and they stood for a moment watching her through the shiny glass doors. Willow seemed to be teasing her for something and Jed put a protective arm around Beth pretending to fight off his sister as she did. All of them were laughing, and Claire hoped the photographer would capture this last moment which would be the perfect snapshot to finish the night.

'She looks so happy, I'm proud of all of them. I think the children get as much, if not more from knowing Beth than she does from them.' JJ seemed mesmerised by the scene and Claire wondered if she had heard her. 'It's funny sometimes I see more of Beth in them than Marcus, impossible and silly, but they all seem to fit. I think it gives them a little of their father too, Beth making up for what Marcus could never be.' Claire turned now to fully look at JJ. 'Is everything ok JJ, you don't seem yourself and I've been worried.' JJ nodded but Claire saw the glistening in her eyes before she turned away.

'All good, a bit of jet lag still I suspect, you would think I would be used to it by now.' Claire could tell she was trying to throw her off. Maybe tonight was not the time but she would make time before they flew home to have a good heart to heart.

'It was a beautiful night Claire, and Paul, in his speech, when he talked about the three of us and began it like a letter, geez, I thought Beth and I would never recover, I don't think I have ever cried so many happy tears.' Claire gave her a hug.

'I know, it was so special, I will get a copy and send it to you, he is certainly the best son I could ever have wished for, and you both were always so important to him. It's funny isn't it, Johnno and Marcus, the lousiest of fathers, ended up being the ones to give us the greatest gifts of all.' JJ didn't disagree and glancing back to the scene outside took a long moment as if weighing up in her mind what she was going to say next. For JJ, Claire knew what ever was holding her back, must be serious. 'You are not sick are you JJ?' JJ looked startled and actually stammered.

'No, what? No why would you think I am? I'm just so happy to be here today, it has been more emotional than I had expected. They are so grown up, I think it has hit me today how fast these years have gone by.' JJ squeezed her arm. 'I would tell you if I was ill. I'm fine Claire, truly, all good.' With a weak smile JJ turned away and mumbled an excuse of going to find Jim. Perhaps she was looking too hard, it was an emotional day, and Claire had been able to take the time to reflect on other days, during the preparations surrounded by all of them. JJ would be fine, Claire reassured herself, she always was.

Matt approached and again Claire thought it warmed her heart to see it was not only her family but also her dearest friends he treated with the utmost respect as he paused and spoke to JJ. Claire glanced back to Beth as Willow swung her hair and it gathered around her face as if in slow motion, and a picture of Beth at the same age, loving her life, looking to the future, flashed through her mind.

Chapter Thirty-Eight

JJ

Dear JJ and Claire,

Here is the photo Jim took at the airport, I think it is lovely of all of us. I can't wait to see all the wedding photos and thanks Claire for emailing those first ones. Let me know when you are ordering some as I think I'll get a few to put around the unit, it will be so good to have at least one of all of us together.

I wanted to thank both of you, my life feels so special now. Sarah and Paul are so good to me, and Iris and Robyn have become good friends. Moving here was the right decision, the weather is more temperate, my view is to die for, as you know, and the beach has given me a sense of solace I could never reach before, even in my garden (I don't miss the work either.) I could never have made it here without you, every step of my life has you both in the background, even when we weren't physically together. You have made me whole, balanced, when often my world was teetering on an angle. Your encouragement and support every year but especially these last few have meant the world to me. Looking at this photo actually made me cry, we made it! I often wish I could go back and thank the teacher who urged me to take out a name and pretended to look the other way when I took two, this could all have turned out so differently. I am mellowing, as I told you, and the wedding, seeing all of us together is a memory I will treasure. Marcus would have loved it. Don't worry I am fine, he made his choice. I still miss him terribly and I spend a moment each day recalling the special times we had. He loved me and I loved him. The rest, how it all fell into place, was more luck than I ever deserved, he gave this to me, and I am nothing if not grateful. I feel now I am truly looking towards my future, it is different to how I imagined and to be truthful I think it better than I ever could have. Your support continues to carry me through every day, and I am here for the both of you always and forever.

I must go, now Charlotte and Oliver have set the date I can already feel the excitement building because we get to do it all over again. How blessed we are. Bye for now.

Love Beth xxx

JJ studied the photo, they were all smiling and the moment as they turned to look at Jim had been both happy and sad. Claire had been flying back to Sydney and herself and Jim were about to board the first leg of their long flight home. It had been the best week, the wedding had felt like the finale of Marcus's legacy, and they could all finally move forward. In spite of his lies and coverups each one of them had reached deep to find the joy and pulled it to the surface. JJ thought, in all his arrogance he would be sitting up there now looking down and saying, I knew it would be ok, see JJ, it all turned out fine. A tear rolled a jagged path down her cheek. He had someone to sit with now and she would be happy, sad to leave them, but he was always her all. Beth's body had been found on the floor of her unit, her heart they said, though JJ could still not accept the why. It was not her time, surely not yet, she had been so happy, they all were, it almost felt cruel. It was quick though Claire had said, and she was the happiest she had ever been so surely it was a perfect time. A part of JJ agreed, she had never thought about it, losing one of them had never entered her head, friends forever was meant to be longer than this and the thought of losing them was something JJ had never thought she would have to bear.

The letter had arrived an hour after the call. Paul, barely able to tell her what his mother could not, struggled to lessen the blow. Jim had been there, and the world had stopped, the emotion so huge she could not release it. They had sat silent, stunned, waiting for the flood to begin and it was the call of the postman which had jolted them from their reverie. Jim had rubbed her back then risen to move towards the door, there seemed a need to reach out to make sure the world still revolved around them, make sense of their disbelief, do something, see something or hear anything normal. JJ had watched as he opened the door and disappeared from view, the sun shone outside, and the light now streamed in stretching into dark corners to lighten the room. Jim had returned and closed the door gently, he had moved slowly as if in a fog. JJ's eyes had felt heavy as if they were dragging down her face and she watched as he leaned back against the door and closed his eyes. Jim she had murmured as she realised he was about to break, saw the tears begin to fall. Jim, her voice had faded away as he raised his hand, and the familiar shaped envelope came into view. It had hit her then, hard and fast, the train which had been screaming towards her smashed into her body and she had both welcomed the pain and wished for more.

....

'You ok?' JJ nodded though her heart was breaking. 'I've put the last of the bags in the car and rechecked the flights are on time. We can head off as soon as you're ready.' JJ took his hand.

'I'm good, just give me a minute. Once we leave it makes it all too real, I know it is, but this is one time I don't want to go.' Jim moved his hands up to hold her upper arms and tried to make her lift her eyes so she could see into his.

'I know how you feel but we have to go, we have to do this, not only for us, but for them and especially for Beth.' Again JJ acknowledged what he said was true with a movement of her head.

'I know, I'll be there in a minute, I want to do one more thing and then I'll come, wait in the car I won't be long.' Jim looked puzzled but did as she asked. JJ moved to the desk and stretched out her fingers to reach the letter she had pushed to the back. JJ held them both, the familiar handwriting of Marcus and Beth smeared by both travel and time. Opening the one from Marcus she fingered the pages for a moment before tearing them in two. Ripping them again JJ dropped them in the bin and then drew out the liner pulling it into a firm knot.

'They don't need to know Marcus, I leave it now for you to tell her if you must, though I urge you to just love her as you did, it is all she ever wanted. As you said, and it is this which has haunted me, who would it benefit?' JJ's voice echoed in the room, and she lowered her eyes from where she had been searching for the heavens above.

'Goodbye Marcus, look after her.' JJ swung around towards the door and locked it securely after her. Dropping the bag into the trashcan, with a faint smile JJ moved towards the car and the man she loved. The photo and Beth's letter were still clutched in her other hand, she would deliver this one to Claire by hand, and for the first time, without her own reply tucked inside. Jim took her hand once she was settled, JJ bowed her head as the tears fell and Jim reversed out on to the leafy street behind.

Chapter Thirty-Nine

JJ

Dear JJ,

I have never betrayed the code before, but I really need some advice and somehow I don't want to hear all of Claire's alternatives. I'm feeling really trapped. I have to look after so much now, Jason is trying to pretend he has it all under control but as much as mum and I quarrelled she really did take care of everything practical. Tom is no help but I'm feeling really torn as he wouldn't understand if I left but he doesn't really want me here and sounds more like Mum everyday with his criticism and sniping remarks. I think he knows it was my fault, I did it JJ, it was me.

There's a whole world out there waiting for me, and I feel like it is slipping away and I'm sinking into a deep mud hole. No matter how much I struggle it won't let me free. You know I want to be a freelance writer and I've been offered a scholarship and I want to take it, I want it so badly, but I will be letting them down, as I always do, fleeing from responsibility. I'm drowning and I don't know where to turn. I want to ask you something, I want to ask you to break the code, to not tell Claire. I can't bear her to know.

I know what I'm asking, and it's wrong but I choose you because you are strong, and I think you will understand. If you want to walk away I will stop the letters and you can be friends with Claire. I need to tell someone. I tried writing it down and burying it in the yard, but it haunts me not having a reply, something to set my mind at ease or send me down the correct path, so please, if it's the last thing you do for me, can you write back to me. Here goes ... and I hope I have the courage to post this ...if you are reading it, you will know.

I did it. I killed her, I killed my mother. It was all my doing, and this is not the first time I have destroyed someone else's life, I did it to Tom and now I've done worse to her and taken her away from him. If I abandon them now, it would be exactly what my mother would expect of me, but don't I deserve a life too? She never let me forget it. Oh JJ, I hate her but what do I do? I keep hearing her voice in my head about what a failure I am, my face looks calm, but I am dying inside. Mum was being nasty, mouthing off, she was supposed to drop me off but made me stay in the car until Tom was in school and she demanded to know if I was sleeping around as she was disgusted at what I was wearing and said tramps dressed like me! It came out of the blue and she was screaming so loud, this is the worst bit, she accused me of sleeping with Jason??? Like why would I? Somehow she got the idea in her head and was trying to find a way to blame me for all her own insecurities. Turns out, according to her, I was everything she had ever said about me and more, a disgusting little tramp she called me, that's when I had to run away, she wouldn't listen and she was yelling, I don't know why she thought it, how did she get the idea, as if I would JJ, and when I turned back, well, I wanted to hurt her and I wanted for her to finally stop blaming me for her own life decisions and I, I did, I wanted her dead. I ran back because she was still yelling when she got out of the car and I pushed her and told her to leave me alone, I told her I hated her. I was angry, why couldn't she love me JJ, what did I do wrong?

I ran then, I didn't look back, I was crying so hard and people were staring. I hid in a park until it started to get dark and when I finally went home, there were all these people there and they were nice to me, and they told me she was dead. I couldn't stand it JJ because I knew it wasn't an accident and they told me about the bus and Tom, Tom was crying and he glared at me, he hates me too.. I miss her but I hate her. It's not right is it, to say it, but my whole life she never forgave me for being born, I ruined her life, and she made sure I knew it. Please don't tell Claire, you two are all I have. I couldn't hold it in anymore, but I don't want everyone to know what a terrible person I am. I'll try to change and make it up to her, I'll look after Tom if he will let me and Jason ... why would she say those things, I never did any-thing wrong ... I want this scholarship and how can I do both, no wonder she hated me I am so selfish, what do I do JJ? If I stay I am so afraid I will turn out resentful like her, but if I leave, I will be proof she was right. How will I ever live with the guilt, I feel so bad, I'm so unworthy no wonder she hated me. Some days I wish it had been me under the bus.

I'll go now before the tears blur the ink, I'm sorry to burden you but if you have any advice please, please tell me what I should do because I don't think I can bear it another day. Should I tell, how would it help? I didn't mean it JJ I wanted to hurt her feelings as much as she hurt me, but I never wanted her dead, not really dead. Please help me. I love you xx

JJ thought about the letter. It was the one Beth had to write to keep her going, a moment she'd had to share to hold her sanity and try to manoeuvre her future, it was the letter a lost little girl had written as she blamed herself for a moment which had never been her fault. The time between Beth pushing her mother and her mother striding out in front of the bus had been minutes apart and yet to Beth, the lack of love she felt from the person she wanted it from the most, had been blurred and blinded by a teenager in crisis, to combine in her head as being one and the same. JJ thought about the time since, all the moments when she had seen Beth tuck it away and push through her self-doubt, it had not been strength, it had been endurance. The letters had been a solace to them all, a link which until this time had remained unbroken, she had thought about them all, some she only had to touch to know their contents, others she had re-read, to make herself smile.

Letting out a deep sigh, JJ rose and walked to the front of the chapel. Charlotte, Paul, Sarah and Matt surrounded Claire, huddled together in grief, they each looked tense, as if anxious she would not be able to get through it and they may have to stand up and assist her, their eyes sent silent support. Willow, Iris, Jed and Robyn together, a supportive family and in the end, a gift from Marcus which had helped Beth to forgive both herself, and him. JJ looked out at the congregation and wondered if Beth had ever realised how much support she had and the number of lives she had touched, just by being her. Finally, her eyes locked with Jim's, he nodded, and she knew it was time. Clearing her throat, she began.

'Hello everyone, my name is JJ and Beth was my very good friend. Also, as many of you know, I am one of her pen-pals. This not something you hear of much these days but over fifty years ago I received a letter in the post, as did Claire, and it was here our friendship with Beth began. Today I thought it was appropriate to say my goodbyes to her, just as we started, in a letter and I hope you will bear with me as I read it to you now.

Dear Beth,

Over fifty years ago I received a letter in the post. I can't begin to tell you how excited I was and have been every time since. Your letter began, my name is Beth, and I am 9 years old. From that moment we were friends and half a world away from me, Claire was receiving the same. You came up with the idea our letters should circulate and so it began, you wrote to Claire, and she wrote to me and I in turn wrote back to you. Each year on your birthday we reversed the circle and went the other way. Today I have a box with me,' JJ indicated the long box on the casket. *'I will place this one in its rightful place at the back behind the others.*

Whenever an envelope became too full to post, you would place the last one in a new envelope, so we could always keep up with the last conversation and tuck your reply behind it before sending it on its way. This was your brilliant idea, and you were definitely good at ideas.' JJ noted people smiling as they too recalled their own memories of Beth.

'Through our tweens, our teens and into adulthood we shared the highs and lows of our lives. At times, in my youth, the letters from you and Claire were what pulled me through as I battled bullies and rudeness from people you would never meet, you were both always there to support me and reassure me. I hope I was the same for you.' JJ paused to take a deep breath to enable herself to continue. *'When we finally met, it was as natural as if I had seen you every day of my entire life. Through marriages, illnesses, careers and children we came together with written words which always felt like hugs as big as the ocean which separated us and were always full of love. I don't know how we will live without you. Claire and I will continue to write or pass notes even when we are together, it is part of our lives, a habit you gave to us, and we never want to lose. Today I feel so sad, and*

yet grateful for so much. Grateful it was my name you pulled out of the box all those years ago, grateful for all you shared, grateful for you allowing Claire and I to see how sometimes you were paddling so fast beneath the surface yet looked to the world as if all skies were clear. You made it ok for us, not to be ok and allowed us to share those feelings. I will miss you my friend. I will miss our chats, I will miss our discussions, I will miss your smile at the airport and your scolding when my mouth speaks before my head thinks. I know at times I will still imagine you are here, on this side of the world, keeping busy and quietly supporting those around you, but it is when the postman no longer stops, and the mailbox is empty, my heart will break again.

Although you were doubtful about heaven, I hope you are there, and if angel stamps are available I know Claire and I will be hearing from you soon.' JJ sent a silent prayer it would be a possibility.

'I will fold this letter now and put it with the others. We are sending them all with you and I can tell you, this was the hardest decision we had to make about today. They were always yours and only ever something we borrowed. Claire will pop hers in too and together we decided it was the right thing to do. I hope you get to read over them again, to see the joy you brought to us all and finally discover the blemishes in your life were never yours but were placed there by other people.

Goodbye Beth. May Marcus be there to hold your hand and again, I hope there is one big mailbox in the sky.

All my love, JJ.'

Claire came forward and together they tucked their letters into place. Stepping back they held each other as the curtains closed around her coffin and they whispered their final goodbyes.

Still holding Claire, JJ moved back to the microphone and paused to watch as many blew their nose and tried to dry their eyes. It allowed her a minute to try to gather herself for her final words. Swallowing hard to clear the lump in her throat she said:

'Our greatest sadness now, is we may never receive a reply. Thankyou my friend.'

Chapter Forty

Epilogue

Dear Willow,

Can you believe it has been ten years. It is still funny when I tell people my sister is also my pen pal. I've been to see JJ and she has settled into the care home really well. I know her and Mum have loved we still continue to write and include them in the circle. As usual I have popped my general letter in behind, it has all my day-to-day news and I know you will remove this one from the fold. It is quite a legacy isn't it? I do still sometimes wish they had kept them all and not sent them with Beth, they were all quite extraordinary women and the older I get, the more I realise how important those simple letters were to each of them. I still miss her and am so glad you were able to meet her and get to know the wonderful person she was. It is hard to think ahead and believe one day it will be only us writing, and I wondered if we could get the kids interested in continuing this old-fashioned way of communication, probably not, though they still love the story of them and tell their friends. By the time your little one grows writing with a pen may be a thing of the past, time will tell I suppose. Thanks again for checking in on Mum, she is getting so frail and each visit I fear may be my last. I will see you soon, love to all. XX Charlotte.

Dear Reader,

I hope you have enjoyed the story of JJ, Beth and Claire. The writing of a letter can bring joy to not only the one holding the pen but also to the receiver. These days it is an almost forgotten art and yet a handwritten letter carries so much more than just words. As in the story, it can carry hugs, tears and laughter because as you read it, you know the sender held the same pages, folded them with care and wrote your name on the envelope, these actions alone carry far more emotion than the send arrow on a computer ever will. I urge you to pick up a pen today, grab even a snap of paper and send a few words to someone you know who's life would be uplifted by hearing from you.